THE FOURTH SHOT

THE FOURTH SHOT

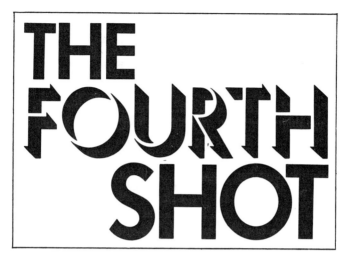

by L. Christian Balling

AN ATLANTIC MONTHLY PRESS BOOK
LITTLE, BROWN AND COMPANY   BOSTON/TORONTO

FIRST EDITION

Library of Congress Cataloging in Publication Data

Balling, L. Christian.
The fourth shot.

"An Atlantic Monthly Press book."
I. Title.
PS3552.A468F6   1982   813'.54   82-12670
ISBN 0-316-07968-5

ATLANTIC-LITTLE, BROWN BOOKS
ARE PUBLISHED BY
LITTLE, BROWN AND COMPANY
IN ASSOCIATION WITH
THE ATLANTIC MONTHLY PRESS

BP

Designed by Dale Cotton

Published simultaneously in Canada
by Little, Brown & Company (Canada) Limited

PRINTED IN THE UNITED STATES OF AMERICA

For Livia, Christy and Daria.

THE FOURTH SHOT

. . . . ONE . . . .

The .45 automatic in the old man's raincoat pocket bumped heavily against his thigh as he made his way along New York's Lexington Avenue. Though he was not yet seventy, he walked with the slow, awkward gait of a man half crippled with age. Bustling, sweating New Yorkers hurried past him in both directions, determined not to be slowed down by the suffocating heat that enveloped the city. The midafternoon sun was still high in the sky, and thousands of air conditioners poured additional heat into Manhattan's concrete canyons, pushing the temperature toward the one hundred mark.

The old man pulled a crumpled, sodden handkerchief from his pocket and wiped away some of the sweat streaming over his gaunt, hawk-nosed face. The raincoat he wore over his shapeless black suit made the heat worse, but it was necessary to conceal the pistol. He gave no thought to his discomfort; it was just something to be endured, and the old man had endured much in his lifetime.

Ahead of him the sidewalk was blocked by a construction project, and he was forced to quicken his pace as he was swept along by the stream of pedestrians being funneled into a narrow protective passageway beneath the scaffolding. The deafening chatter of a jackhammer drowned out the blaring of automobile horns that blended alternately in harmony and dissonance to help create the city's constant background noise.

A bleached-blond youth in tight pants and a diaphanous pink shirt brushed against him and flitted past, and the old man's lips twitched in an expression of distaste. Pink was the right color for fairies, he thought. The Nazis had even made it official. In Dachau, the homosexuals had worn pink badges on their prison uniforms. The old man had spurned their company, partly, perhaps, out of jealousy, for the prisoners with the pink patch had survived longer than those with the patch the old man had worn — the yellow Star of David.

At the corner of Lexington and 44th, he had to wait for the light to change. He tilted back his head and, squinting against the sun's glare, looked up at the towering Chrysler Building two blocks away. Sweat trickled into his bleary eyes, but he continued to stare upward in the direction of his quarry. *He's up there now, cool and comfortable, but tonight it will be his turn to sweat.* The light turned green, and the old man set his protesting legs in motion. The gun in his pocket thumped rhythmically against him as he crossed the street.

Erich Ritter sat in his office on the sixtieth floor of the Chrysler Building, insulated from the heat and noise in the streets below, but he was neither cool nor comfortable. His palms were slick with perspiration as he listened tensely to his employer's angry voice relayed by telephone from Bogotá, Colombia. With his free hand he shook a cigarette loose from the pack on his desk, inserted it between his lips and flicked his lighter. He drew the smoke deep into his lungs, trying to suppress the queasy feeling in his stomach where a late lunch still lay cold and undigested. The voice on the other end of the line rose another notch, and Ritter's lips compressed in anger.

"No, Mr. Garcia, I didn't expect Tenneco to drop three points," he said sharply, tension bringing out a light German accent. "But I bought that stock for the company with long-term appreciation in mind."

Ritter tightened his grip on the receiver as he listened to Garcia's abusive response. Unconsciously he straightened up in his leather chair.

"Look, Mr. Garcia, let's clear the air. If you no longer have confidence in my judgment, you can fire me."

For three long seconds there was silence on the other end of the line, and Ritter felt a trickle of nervous sweat run down over his ribs. But when Garcia finally spoke, his voice was calmer and grudgingly conciliatory, and Ritter felt a flush of relief. Garcia went on for a few minutes and then ended their conversation. Ritter hung up and leaned back in his chair with a deep sigh.

He felt drained, and gradually his relief gave way to depression. For a while he stared blankly out the window at the haze-shrouded skyline. The most distant buildings were indistinct, their outlines merging with a gray, horizonless background. Like the skyline, his life had lost definition. His hopes and ambitions had slipped out of focus. His plush office, part of the trappings of executive power and privilege, seemed to mock him silently. At that moment he would have traded it all for a secure, tension-free existence.

Ritter was manager of Garcia Exports, a firm that conducted a brisk triangular trade between Europe, the United States and South America. He was good at his job, and in the six years since he had joined the company he had expanded its operations. But Garcia, the Colombian millionaire who had founded the company, was unpredictable and irascible, and Ritter knew that Garcia would fire him one day. Yet he hung on, increasingly weary of his job, but afraid of losing it.

The image of Ritter's late wife smiled up at him from a photograph on his desk. Silently his lips formed her name: Jane. He recalled her excitement the day Garcia had selected him to run the company. Neither of them had foreseen the nervous strain to which it would subject him — any more than they had foreseen the rampaging cancer that had killed her only ten months later. Ritter blinked and looked away from the picture; even after five years, it still evoked the ache of loss.

Abruptly he shook himself free of his melancholy, crushed out his cigarette and stabbed the intercom.

"I have some letters to dictate, Marianne," he said.

"I'll be right in, Mr. Ritter."

A moment later, Ritter's bilingual secretary, Marianne Becker, knocked and entered the office. She was a trim, twenty-five-year-old woman, as intelligent as she was attractive. She pointedly wrinkled her nose at the stale tobacco smell in the closed, air-conditioned office and said, "You're smoking far too much, Mr. Ritter."

"I should quit smoking, and you should get married," he said with a smile.

"Mmm," she responded noncommittally and sat down in a chair beside his desk. She flipped open her steno-pad.

"I want you to take a letter to Dr. Karl Mueller at Farbwerke Riem," Ritter said, automatically lighting another cigarette as he focused his thoughts. He began to dictate in German.

"Your order of yellow phosphorus will be shipped from New York on August twenty-fifth by the Bendler Shipping Company. Regulations require that the one hundred oil-filled drums be stowed on deck, and, in the event of a severe storm at sea, the captain of the vessel may elect to jettison the cargo. The insurance premium for this shipment will be unusually high. . . ."

Ritter's mind had slipped back into the comfortable groove of business, and he smoothly dictated a series of letters in English and German. The South American correspondence would have to wait until his Spanish-speaking secretary recovered from her bout with a severe summer cold.

As he dictated, Marianne stole occasional glances at him. She knew what Garcia's phone calls were like, and she was pleased to see the signs of strain in Ritter's face gradually disappear, for she liked her boss. Garcia, she thought contemptuously, would not have the nerve to shout at him face to face.

Ritter was a physically imposing man, over six feet tall, with broad, muscular shoulders. His rough-hewn Nordic features could have been sculpted from clay with a few quick strokes of an artist's knife: a long, straight nose, high forehead, and a wide, straight mouth with little curvature to the lips. Age had begun to thin his ash blond hair and thicken his waist, but he still looked younger than his forty-six years. He was the kind of man whom women gave a second glance.

Yet Ritter seemed unaware of this, and with women, particularly, Marianne had noticed, he could be painfully shy. He was an easy man to work for, quick to smile or laugh and slow to anger. In the years she had known him, she had seen Ritter angry only once — with a man who had tried to cross him — and then his normally quiet voice had thundered and his green eyes had blazed. Men did not try to push him around.

Ritter, she had decided long ago, should never have become a businessman. He was competent and he worked hard at his job, but somehow the business world did not suit him. He should have been a sea captain or an adventurer.　　　.

In the street sixty floors below Ritter's office, the old man pushed one of the revolving doors to the Chrysler Building and passed from a world of heat and noise into the cool hush of the building's stately lobby. He paused inside the entrance to savor the cool air and to allow his eyes to adjust to the dim lighting. People's footsteps echoed softly off the marble-covered walls and were swallowed up, as in a cavern. Pink marble columns rose to a cathedral ceiling high overhead, the mural covering its surface barely visible in the gloom.

The old man mopped his face with his soiled handkerchief and defiantly stared back at a black building guard who was watching him suspiciously. "*Schwarze,*" the old man muttered sourly. He didn't need to be reminded that he looked disheveled. He was disheveled, he was old, and he was tired — but he wasn't senile. That's what they had thought when they had pensioned him off. Poor old Sol, they had thought, getting a bit dotty in his old age. *To hell with them.* He had carried on alone. Alone, he was also free — free to do what justice demanded. Slowly, carefully, he had begun to exact retribution.

He walked toward the express elevators, stifling a groan. Just a few seconds of standing had stiffened up his joints. One elevator stood ready, its richly paneled door open to receive him. He stepped inside and pushed the button for the sixtieth floor.

Bauer had underestimated him, too. The old man smiled wickedly in recollection. Bauer had looked so surprised when he had killed him. The old man heard a voice and realized that he was talking to himself. He stopped and instantly refocused his thoughts. His work was not yet done.

"That's it then," Ritter said with satisfaction as he finished his last letter. "We'll close down the office early today to beat the rush. It's too damned hot to fight the crowds."

"Shall I keep the reception desk open?" Marianne asked.

"No. Tell Barbara she can go, too."

"Helen Borg is our receptionist. Barbara quit two weeks ago," Marianne reminded him.

"Yes, of course," Ritter said, slightly embarrassed.

His secretary turned and walked gracefully to the door, not unaware that he was watching her.

"Marianne . . ."

"Yes?" she said, turning back toward him. She was looking at him levelly, a slight smile on her lips, and he was sure she could read his thoughts.

"Nothing," he said lamely. "I'll see you tomorrow."

"Good night, Mr. Ritter," she said and left the office. Someday, she hoped, he might finally take the plunge and ask her out.

Another office on the sixtieth floor had closed early, and Ritter found a group of men and women waiting in the corridor by the elevators. Two elevator doors opened at once and the group divided itself between them. Ritter didn't notice the rumpled old man who appeared from around a corner in the corridor and followed him into the elevator.

The door closed, and the old man felt his ears pop with the increasing air pressure as the elevator raced toward the lobby. He looked closely at Ritter, who was to his left and slightly in front of him, to make sure that this was the man in the photograph he had taken from Bauer's apartment.

Chance had led him to Bauer — chance and weeks of exhausting legwork, backtracking a rumor that he had been seen in New York. Bauer had not died well; the fool had thought to save himself by betraying a "more important" man. The old man had let him talk, and he had added a new name to his list: Erich Ritter.

The old man was carrying the picture of Ritter in his jacket pocket, but he didn't need to look at it; he had memorized the image. There was no doubt; this was the man he was after.

In the lobby, Ritter started for the Lexington Avenue exit and then changed his mind. He turned and descended a short flight of stairs to an arcade beneath the Chrysler Building, hoping that the underground route to the subway would be cooler than the street. The old man followed him through the arcade, ignoring the elegant displays of expensive clothes and jewelry in the windows set into the black, polished stone walls. His eyes never left Ritter's back. Ritter had fallen into the brisk stride of the habitual commuter, and the old man knew it would be difficult to keep up with him. Already he was panting from exertion.

The arcade was relatively cool, but as Ritter entered the grimy passage to the subway, hot, fetid air, laced with the odor of urine, hit him like a slap in the face. Instantly sweat broke out on his face and neck, and soot began to settle on his damp skin. Ahead of him he heard the rattle of turnstyles and the steadily swelling rumble of distant subway trains.

Ritter came to the turnstyles, dropped a token in the slot and passed through into a wide underground transfer area crisscrossed by streams of hurrying, overheated commuters. It was not yet the rush hour, but the crowds were building rapidly. The sour smell of sweating bodies mingled with the odors of steam exhausts and of hot, oily food from fast-food counters.

Ritter didn't hear the thin ringing of coins spilling onto the concrete floor behind him as the old man hastily fumbled for a token buried in a handful of change. The sound was lost in the subway background noise. Ritter headed for the passage that led to the Times Square Shuttle, quickening his pace to match the flow of the crowd.

The old man was falling behind. He was wheezing, and sweat ran in rivulets over his face, which had turned an ominous gray. People coming from the opposite direction noticed him and shook their heads. A man had to be crazy to wear a raincoat on top of a suit in the midst of a heat wave. The gun in the old man's pocket seemed to gain weight with each passing minute, dragging down his right shoulder. He felt the warning pain in his chest and cursed between clenched teeth. He knew he should heed the warning, but if he slowed down he might lose Ritter.

As Ritter neared the Shuttle platform, a horde of passengers from a train that had just pulled in burst into the passage and surged by him. Perfect timing, he thought to himself. He looked at his watch and saw that he might just make the 4:50 out of Penn Station. The sooner he got home, the sooner he could have the shower and beer that were looming large in his imagination.

The train waited with its doors open, and it was filling rapidly. Ritter entered and took up a position near a door, gripping a white enameled stanchion for support as passengers swarmed in behind him. He tried to ignore the obscene heat of the bodies pressing in on him from all sides. The doors closed, and the train started forward with a lurch. Ritter was thrown against an old man beside him. One look at the sweat-slimed, gray face told him that the old man was ill.

"Are you all right, sir?" he asked, but his voice was drowned out by a rattling roar as the train hurtled into the tunnel.

He raised his voice and tried again, but the old man did not respond. Pointedly ignoring Ritter, he stared straight ahead, his chest rising and falling in a ragged rhythm. Ritter frowned and opened his mouth to speak again, but then he shrugged and gave up. Sick or not, the old man wanted to be left alone. The lights in the car went out, plunging them into darkness, and when they came on again, Ritter saw that the old man had moved away.

The brief Shuttle ride ended almost as soon as it began, and Ritter was ejected from the car by the human herd stampeding onto the platform. He was swept along by the crowd into another underground transfer area similar to the one he had passed through at the Grand Central end of the Shuttle, only here the crowds were thicker. He headed for the Seventh Avenue IRT.

The old man struggled after him. The pain in his chest had intensified and was spreading into his left arm. He knew what it meant, and he knew he should stop and rest. *Why not give up for now? I can follow him to his home tomorrow.* The old man broke stride, slowed and stopped, swaying and gasping for breath as the crowds swirled around him. He lost sight of Ritter, but the direction Ritter had taken indicated he was heading for the IRT and Penn Station. *No! Tomorrow might be too late for me.* The old man staggered forward and pressed on.

The Seventh Avenue downtown platform was nearly empty, and Ritter cursed in annoyance. He had just missed a train, and now he might not make the 4:50, after all. It was a petty annoyance, but he felt frustrated just the same. He chafed as the minutes slipped by and the platform slowly filled with commuters as hot, tired and ill-tempered as he. Ritter thought he caught the hint of a rumble from the uptown tunnel, and he stepped to the edge of the platform to look up the track to where it disappeared into the tunnel's black mouth. The rumble grew louder.

The old man watched Ritter through a film of tears as a band of excruciating pain tightened over his heart, and he felt the clutch of fear — not fear of death, but of failure. Death was too familiar to him to be frightening. He gasped as the band squeezed tighter, and he knew that he had run out of time. He slipped a shaking hand into his raincoat pocket and gripped the butt of his pistol. He couldn't make it look like an accident, as he had with the others, but that made no difference now.

He started to draw the pistol, but then he, too, heard the rumble of the approaching train. A bullet was too easy a death for such a man, he thought suddenly, and Ritter was unwittingly offering him a more satisfying vengeance. The old man took a faltering step toward Ritter and then another, one hand on his gun, the other clutching his pain-racked chest. The train was very close now; he could feel its vibration through the soles of his feet.

Ritter saw a patch of reflected light from the train's headlights appear on the white-tiled station wall near the tunnel mouth. A moment later the train burst from the tunnel, pushing a mass of hot, sooty air before it, and roared down the track toward him. He started to step back from the platform's edge.

A climactic vise of pain closed on the old man's tortured heart as he hurled himself forward, his arms extended toward Ritter's exposed back. The old man's hands struck Ritter below the right shoulder blade, driving him back toward the edge.

A man with slower reflexes and less coordination would have pitched headlong into the path of the oncoming train, but Ritter reacted swiftly and surely, his body responding to the danger even before his mind registered fear. Pivoting on one foot, he allowed the impact to spin him to his left, at the same time dropping into a crouch to lower his center of gravity. He fell onto his hands and knees on the very edge of the platform as the train blasted by.

A woman's shrill scream was matched by the squealing shriek of the train's brakes, both giving voice to the silent screaming of Ritter's nervous system as the shock hit him. A man pulled him back from the edge and helped him to his feet.

"My God, mister, that was close! The old geezer must have been reaching out for help just as he collapsed."

Ritter nodded dumbly. Moments before, he had been sweating from the heat, but now his hands were ice cold. He turned and looked down at the crumpled body on the platform, around which a crowd was gathering, and saw that it was the old man he had noticed on the Shuttle. A gum wrapper that had been swirled into the air by the train's passage had stuck to spittle drying on the dead man's lips. The man's eyes stared sightlessly at Ritter's feet, and Ritter felt a wave of sadness sweep over him. Why had the old man waited until it was too late to reach out for help?

Passengers had begun to board the waiting train, the crowd eddying and flowing around the old man's body. A man, apparently a doctor, emerged from the crowd and knelt on one knee beside the body. He examined the eyes, checked for a pulse and shook his head. Ritter turned away and allowed himself to be swept into the train by the crowd.

Thirty feet away a pair of cold, gray eyes watched Ritter disappear into the train. They watched as the doors closed and the train started forward. Then they turned away and searched out a bank of pay phones at the far end of the platform.

A phone rang in an expensive high-rise apartment on Manhattan's East Side. After three rings it was answered.

"Ritter was very nearly killed a few minutes ago," said the caller without preamble.

"What! How?"

"An accident. He was standing on the edge of a subway platform, and a train was coming. An old man behind him collapsed and knocked him off balance."

"Is he all right?"

"Yes. The incident was quite instructive, actually. He still has excellent reflexes."

"If nothing happened to him, why did you call?"

The caller's eyes narrowed, but otherwise they remained flat and expressionless. "This is the second accident in as many weeks. First your man, Bauer, slips, hits his head and drowns in his own bathtub, and now this. Doesn't it strike you as strange?"

"Coincidence. What else could it be? Forget Bauer; he was a liability anyway. One day, someone with a long memory might have recognized him. It's Ritter I'm going to need. You said his reflexes are still good. I take it, then, that you have no further objections to his activation."

"I've learned as much as I can by observing him, but it is your responsibility. Can you be sure of him after all these years?"

"No one has failed us yet."

"And if he is the exception?"

"Then, my dear Kadinsky, you will eliminate him with your usual dispatch. I assume that is the reason you were sent over here — as a precaution against just such an eventuality."

"When will you send him the signal?"

"When I am ready. He has waited almost twenty years; he can wait a bit longer."

, , , , TWO , , , ,

The signal came by telegram.

On a sleepy Saturday afternoon in the first week of September, a scrawny young Western Union messenger sauntered up to the door of Ritter's suburban Long Island home and rang the bell. As he waited, scratching at the acne on the back of his neck, he casually assessed the house, trying to gauge the size of the tip he might receive from the owner. The messenger liked delivering to Garden City addresses, but this one was not as promising as he had hoped. The brick Cape was expensive, but still modest by the wealthy suburb's standards. He noticed the tracks of the Long Island Railroad across the street, screened by a thick hedge, and dropped his assessment another notch.

"Hey, mister!" called a shrill voice behind him. "Mr. Ritter's not home."

The messenger turned and saw a freckle-faced ten-year-old girl on a bicycle at the curb.

"Mr. Ritter is over at our house," the girl yelled, pointing down the block. "Number twenty-seven."

"Thanks," the messenger said and waved.

The girl waved back, pushed off from the curb and rode away. The messenger shrugged and took an attempted-delivery notice from his pocket. He was tired and thirsty, and he was more interested in having a cold beer than in pursuing his dwindling chances of a tip; but then he saw that the girl had stopped halfway down the block and was watching him. He was still young enough to be ashamed of an open display of laziness, even if the witness was only ten years old, so he pocketed the notice and reluctantly started walking toward number 27.

Erich Ritter leaned back in a lawn chair and stretched contentedly, enjoying the warmth of the sun. Across from him sat his neighbor, Tom Brixton, who was hunched over a chessboard set up on a low aluminum table between them. Brixton gnawed on a worn briar pipe and worried over his next move. In the background, Brixton's wife, Lorraine, worried over the hamburgers he was neglecting on their outdoor grill. The scent of charcoal smoke melded pleasantly with the smell of cut grass from the freshly mowed lawn.

"You know," Ritter said lazily, "I'm still stiff from cutting my lawn. I think I'll hire some kid to do it for me."

"Baloney," Brixton said. "You love it. It's the Kraut in you — a compulsion for neatness and order. Besides, you need the exercise."

Ritter regarded Brixton's still-powerful but distinctly overfed body and shook his head. "It doesn't seem to have helped you much."

Brixton grunted and continued to ponder the chessboard. He was a Wall Street lawyer, but he looked like a dockworker. His swarthy, broken-nosed face belied his patrician education and razor-sharp mind.

"Are you going to move, or what?" Ritter said.

Brixton looked up and grinned. "It's no use trying to rush me, but you try it every time I'm about to blast you off the board." With that, Brixton reached out and moved his queen's bishop, and his grin turned piratical.

"Damn," Ritter growled. "I didn't see that one. I just didn't see it!"

"Hey, you two," Lorraine Brixton called. "The burgers are ready."

Ritter sighed, tipped over his king and stood up.

"Cheer up, Erich," Brixton said, still grinning, "the burgers will be great. I always do them just right."

They walked across the lawn to a wooden picnic table on a patio at the rear of the house.

"Dish out the potato salad, will you, hon," Lorraine said as she transferred the hamburgers from the grill to a large platter. She was a pretty, lively girl, as fair as Brixton was dark, with blond hair in a ponytail, freckles and a turned-up nose.

"First things first," Brixton said, reaching into a cooler for the beer. He opened three bottles in quick succession, the tops coming off with a hissing pop, and handed one to Ritter. "You had a narrow escape, my friend," he said with a wink.

"How so?" Ritter asked.

"Lorraine invited the Reeds over — with their recently divorced daughter — but they couldn't come. I'm afraid my wife is still trying to marry you off."

"I am *not*," Lorraine said, coming over to the table. Her cheeks colored, and she gave her husband a withering look. "I just thought Erich and Marjorie might hit it off."

Ritter smiled. "Don't listen to him, Lorraine. I would have liked to meet her."

Brixton began to dish out the potato salad as his wife distributed the hamburgers. "Where are the kids?" he asked her.

"Off running around somewhere with their stomachs full of peanut butter and jelly."

"Then who's going to eat all this?"

Lorraine reached across the table and patted Brixton's ample stomach. "You'll manage," she said. Then she cocked her head and listened. "Did you hear the doorbell? There it goes again. You guys dig in, and I'll see who it is."

She turned and hurried into the house.

"Probably one of her girlfriends with some gossip hot off the presses," Brixton said, biting into his hamburger. He shook his head. "You wouldn't have liked her."

"Who?"

"Marjorie Reed. Hell of a good body, but she talks too much. Has fixed opinions on everything. But your reprieve is only temporary; Lorraine won't give up. Unmarried men make wives nervous; they're an affront to the natural order of things."

"I don't mind," Ritter said easily.

"It's none of my business, but is there any particular reason why you haven't remarried?"

Ritter shrugged. "Well, for one thing, I don't meet that many single women."

"And for another, you're too damned shy with them. Hell, man, don't you realize you'd be a catch for any woman?"

"Erich, a telegram for you!"

The screen door banged as Lorraine came running out, waving a yellow envelope. She thrust it into Ritter's hands.

"What the devil could this be?" Ritter muttered, annoyed at being disturbed on a Saturday by what he assumed to be business. "How did the messenger know I was here?"

"Karen," Lorraine said. "He said a girl on a bicycle told him you were at our house. Aren't you going to open it?"

Ritter nodded and slipped his index finger under the flap of the envelope. He tore it open, unfolded the telegram — and froze. There was no greeting, nor was there a signature; the message contained but a single word: WEREWOLF.

For a moment Ritter couldn't breathe, he couldn't even blink, as he stared in shocked disbelief at that single word. Above him the sun still shone brightly in a cloudless sky, but inside him the world had suddenly gone dark, as swiftly as the snuffing out of a candle flame.

"What's the matter, Erich, bad news?"

Brixton's voice seemed to come from far away, the sound distorted and barely audible above the sudden roaring in Ritter's ears, and Ritter realized that he was close to fainting. He forced open his fingers and let the telegram flutter to the ground, so that he could bend down to pick it up, lowering his head.

"No, it's nothing," he heard himself say.

At that moment, the Brixtons' nine-year-old son, Tommy, came pounding around the corner of the house and raced up to the table to snatch a handful of potato chips, creating for Ritter a desperately needed diversion.

"Watch your manners, young man!" Lorraine said severely.

"Sorry, Mom. Hey, Mr. Ritter, take a look at my new BB gun."

Ritter slipped the telegram into his pocket and put on a smile he hoped looked natural. He wanted to get away, but there was no legitimate excuse he could think of.

"That's a beauty," he said, accepting the BB gun. "Are you a good shot?"

"Not as good as Dad, but he was in the war," the boy said proudly. "Can you shoot, Mr. Ritter?"

Ritter shook his head. "I'm afraid not, Tommy."

"But weren't you in the Nazi army?"

"Tommy!" Lorraine cried. "Mr. Ritter lived in South America during the war. Besides, it was the German army. Not all Germans were Nazis."

"It didn't make much difference when they were shooting at you," Brixton said wryly. "Okay, son, you've had your potato chips. Take off."

Ritter handed back the BB gun, and the boy scampered away.

"I just hope he never has to go off to war," Lorraine said.

"Amen to that," Ritter said quietly.

"Well, if Kennedy doesn't stop mucking around in Indochina, we'll get sucked in there one of these days," Brixton grumbled. "Eisenhower was right when he warned us against a land war in Asia."

"Kennedy is too smart to let it go that far," Ritter said, amazed that he could speak normally with his insides churning.

"Smart? Did you say he's smart?" Brixton exclaimed. "I could think of a lot of things to call Kennedy, but smart is not one of them. Come on, Erich, you haven't touched your hamburger. Eat up, man."

Ritter sat in his living room, staring at the television image of E. G. Marshall lecturing a client in an episode of *The Defenders*, but he wasn't watching or listening. The TV set was on for background noise to hold back the silence in the house. On the coffee table beside Ritter's chair were the remains of a half-eaten TV dinner. His stomach was empty, but he wasn't hungry; his throat was dry, but he had no desire for water.

Ritter looked at his watch; it was just after nine in the evening, and he had been sitting in the same chair, waiting, for two hours — waiting for the phone call he was sure would come. He looked around him, trying to keep a toehold on reality. The Colonial furniture his wife had bought when they had moved to Garden City was still as she had arranged it. Her own oil paintings hung on the walls, still-lifes and woodland scenes she had painted while at their summer cabin in Connecticut. Everything was comfortably familiar and yet strangely unreal, as if he had dreamed the last seventeen years of his life. It was the reality of a more distant past that reached out to claim him now.

When at last the phone did ring, Ritter jumped. He took a deep breath, got up from his chair and went into the kitchen, where the wall phone shrilled insistently. He wiped his damp palms on his trousers and lifted the receiver.

"Ritter," he said.

"Mr. Erich Ritter?" asked a man's voice.

"Yes."

"I assume you received the signal."

The voice was as dry as a desert wind.

"Yes."

"I can guess what you must be thinking," said the man, and now Ritter detected a European accent. "You must have given up hope of ever seeing this day."

"Instructions," Ritter said, intentionally clipping his voice lest it betray him.

"Very good, Ritter. No pointless questions. Very professional."

"Well?" Ritter said sharply.

"Be on the Coney Island boardwalk by the Parachute Jump tomorrow at two P.M. Don't be late."

There was a click, and the line went dead. Ritter swallowed in a vain attempt to relieve the dryness in his throat and slowly replaced the receiver. On a shelf below the phone was a telephone directory. He picked it up and opened it. On the inside cover, included in a list of emergency numbers, was the number for the FBI. He replaced the book, lifted the receiver again, and started to dial; but he didn't finish. He had tried the Bureau once, long ago, and they had refused to listen. Why should they listen to him now? It wasn't worth the risk — at least not until he had something concrete to back up his story. For now, he had no choice but to follow Werewolf's instructions.

The voice on the phone had been unfamiliar. Either Ritter had never met the man, or he had forgotten him. But Ritter knew what he would be like: intelligent, efficient — and twisted inside. Ritter caught himself scratching absently at a small scar on the underside of his upper right arm. The man who had called undoubtedly had the same telltale scar on his arm, where a tattoo had been surgically removed. The tattoo had marked the wearer's blood type; it had also identified him as a member of Hitler's SS.

. . . . THREE . . . .

The huge steel tower of the Parachute Jump loomed over Coney Island's amusement parks, dwarfing the roller coasters and Ferris wheels. It was visible from miles away, silhouetted against a backdrop of billowing gray clouds pushing in from the sea. Near the tower's base, Ritter stood leaning against the rail of the wide boardwalk that separated the amusement area from the beach. The freshening sea breeze ruffled his hair and tugged at the light cloth of his windbreaker. He lit a cigarette and looked at his watch; it was almost 2:00 P.M.

He turned, putting his back to the rail, and gazed bleakly out to sea. In the distance, a tugboat hauling a barge inched across the blurred horizon. Gulls wheeled over the empty beach, their shrill, mournful cries rising above the calliope music, the insistent calls of barkers over their loudspeakers, and the thin screams of roller-coaster riders.

A nightmare Ritter had thought long over was beginning again, and he was trapped within it; but the initial shock had worn off, leaving him cold and empty inside. His wife was dead, and he was alone in the world. No longer young, he had little to lose, and there was some consolation in that. The hold his would-be masters once might have had on him was gone.

Excited shouts from overhead caused Ritter to look up over his shoulder at a boy being taken up for his first parachute ride. At first, the boy called out gaily to his parents on the ground below, but at fifty feet the boy's grin faded and he stopped waving. Grimly he held on with both hands as his wooden chair, swaying beneath the oversized parachute, rose ever higher. Going up was the nerve-racking part, slowly rising higher and higher toward the spidery network of girders surmounting the tower. At a dizzying height the ascent ended with a heart-stopping jerk as the parachute hit the top and was released. By contrast, the descent was a relief, as the parachute, guided by steel cables, floated smoothly to earth.

It was just the reverse with the real thing, Ritter reflected. Going up was the easy part; it was coming down that took the nerve. Ritter's first jump had terrified him. He had frozen in the jump door until a well-placed kick from his sergeant had catapulted him out into space, the aircraft's slipstream whipping away his inarticulate cry of terror. He had forgotten all he'd been taught, and instead of spreading his arms and legs to stabilize his fall, he had curled into a fetal position, somersaulting head over heels as his body plummeted earthward. The parachute had come out between his legs, and he had been lucky it had opened at all.

They didn't always open. One day during training, his company had tested a new camouflage chute. The folds of the dye-impregnated silk had stuck together, and eighteen men had Roman-candled into the ground before the jump could be stopped. Ritter had learned to jump, but he had never lost his fear of it.

"Mr. Ritter," said a voice close beside him. It was the voice he'd heard on the telephone.

Ritter turned and faced a man in his early sixties wearing a hand-tailored gray suit and expensive Italian-made shoes of soft leather. The man looked like a Prussian, Ritter thought, with his close-cropped hair, high cheekbones and large rounded nose. Drooping eyelids hooded his pale blue eyes, making them difficult to read. When he wasn't speaking, the man's expression was one of perpetual disdain.

"Dietrich," the man said, extending his hand. "Welcome back to the battle."

"*Is* there still a battle going on? I hadn't noticed," Ritter said, accepting Dietrich's hand.

"Yes," Dietrich replied, stretching the final consonant into a drawn-out hiss. Abruptly he switched from English into German. "I can understand why you might have assumed that Werewolf was dead, but I assure you it is not."

Dietrich turned and started walking along the boardwalk, and Ritter fell into step beside him. As they passed a succession of clam bars, ice-cream stands and fast-food counters lining the boardwalk, the cloying odors of buttered popcorn, stale beer and steamed clams, snatched by gusts of wind from the concession stands, assaulted Ritter's nostrils. The sky had turned dark and threatening, and the crowds began to drain from the boardwalk and amusement parks, streaming back across Stillwell Avenue toward the subway, and the vendors along the boardwalk looked up at the gathering storm in frustration. They could ill afford the loss of even one Sunday; Coney Island's once-proud amusement area was going downhill. Everywhere, amid the glitter, were signs of neglect and decay.

"For many years, Werewolf lay dormant," Dietrich said. "Several of our key men were killed in the final collapse of the Reich, and important records were lost. It took time and enormous effort to reestablish our control apparatus. Only then could we begin to activate our agents. We proceeded very slowly and carefully, contacting our men and women only as they were specifically needed. In the past five years our operations have greatly increased in number and in scope, and yet no government even suspects Werewolf's existence. You are among the last to be activated, and the Werewolf you are rejoining has grown strong."

Isolated drops of rain began to splatter onto the boardwalk.

"Then you have a specific assignment for me," Ritter said, turning up the collar of his windbreaker.

"Yes. An assignment that demands the use of your — special talents. But the timing of this operation is, of necessity, uncertain, and I cannot discuss it with you yet."

"You don't trust me?"

Dietrich halted in midstride and fixed Ritter with a cold stare. "If we didn't trust you, my dear Ritter, you would be dead."

At that moment, a little blond girl running out ahead of her mother crashed into Dietrich's legs from behind. She looked up at Dietrich with wide, startled eyes.

"That's all right, little girl," he said, stooping to retrieve the Kewpie doll she had dropped. He handed the doll to the girl, patted her head and gave her a saccharine smile. A shiver passed over Ritter's spine. Men like Dietrich had produced similar smiles as they had passed out candy to children on their way to the gas chambers.

The heavy raindrops were becoming more numerous, and Dietrich glanced upward in annoyance.

"Then why did you haul me out here?" Ritter said. "If you don't get to the point of this meeting, the rain is going to ruin that fancy suit of yours."

Dietrich's eyes flashed angrily, but he began to speak more rapidly. "We do have a task for you now. Next Saturday afternoon, a man named Max Braun will arrive at Idlewild Airport on Lufthansa Flight four-o-five from Frankfurt. He will be en route to Cairo. There is a strong possibility that he will be followed on the flight from Frankfurt, but it is our intention that he not be under surveillance when he continues on to Cairo. He is not one of us, but he serves our interests. You will contact him at the airport and instruct him to take a taxi to the Statler-Hilton in New York City. Identify yourself as 'Karl.' It is your responsibility to see to it that he is not followed into the city. How you accomplish this is entirely up to you."

Dietrich handed Ritter a snapshot of a nondescript man in his thirties wearing horn-rimmed glasses.

"That is Braun. Memorize his appearance and destroy the photo."

Ritter nodded, slipped the picture into his pocket and looked at Dietrich impassively, though questions were flooding his mind. Who was Braun? Who would be following him? How would Ritter recognize the man following Braun and prevent him from following Braun into the city? But if Dietrich was not going to volunteer more information, he wouldn't ask for it.

"We don't have the manpower to spare to cover you," Dietrich said. "If something goes wrong at the airport, you will be on your own. Do you have any questions?"

"No."

Dietrich nodded with a hint of satisfaction. "*Auf Wiedersehen,* Ritter," he said. Then he turned and walked briskly away, breaking into a run as it began to rain in earnest.

After Dietrich had gone, Ritter walked aimlessly along the boardwalk, ignoring the pelting rain, trying to sort out his whirling thoughts. An old Gypsy woman beckoned to him from her fortune-teller's booth and then followed him with a doleful stare as he passed by. Whatever his future, he thought, it was not in his hands. He was caught like a rat in a maze, compelled to follow the path laid down for him. He would have to try to carry out Dietrich's assignment. But how?

"Hey, mister. Come on in out of the rain," a stunted, middle-aged man called to him from behind the counter of a shooting gallery. "It's dry in here. Try one of these machine guns. Only a quarter and you can cut loose just like Eliot Ness."

Ritter shrugged and stepped into the shelter of the shooting gallery's awning. Rainwater trickled down the back of his neck from his soaked hair. He wiped his face with his handkerchief and tossed the little man a quarter.

"That's the ticket, mister," the man said, handing Ritter one of the compressed-air machine guns attached by a chain to the counter.

Rows of wooden ducks and rabbits moved in line across the back of the gallery. Ritter's fingers curled about the pistol grip of the toy weapon, and long-buried memories surged to the surface of his mind. He had not fired a gun — even a toy — for nearly twenty years.

"Go on. Don't be shy. Let's see what you can do."

Ritter smiled thinly and swung the gunbarrel toward the parade of wooden ducks, automatically locking the butt against his side. He pressed the trigger and held it down as he traversed the barrel in a smooth, practiced motion. The ducks fell, row by row, like scythed wheat until the gun was empty. Ritter put the gun down and walked back out into the rain.

"Jesus, mister," the open-mouthed attendant called after him, "where'd you learn to shoot like that?"

Ritter arrived at Idlewild Airport an hour before Lufthansa Flight 405 was due to land. He had no trouble finding a space in the open parking lot in front of the International Arrivals Building. He switched off the engine, rolled down the window and lit a cigarette, hoping that his nervousness would subside and knowing it wouldn't.

Ritter couldn't be sure who Max Braun was, or who would be following him, but he could guess. For months, the Israeli government had been raising a storm of protest over renegade German engineers who were secretly building rockets in Egypt. If his guess was correct, Braun was one of those engineers, and the man following him would be an Israeli agent. Ritter would be an amateur going up against a professional.

Jet engines thundered from behind the terminal buildings as one of the new DC-8s left a runway and rocketed skyward in a steep climb, sunlight flashing on its wings. Ritter watched it until it became a bright speck in the cloudless sky. Then he dropped his cigarette out the window and got out of the car. Sitting in the car, thinking about what might happen, only made him more nervous. He ground out the cigarette butt under his heel and reached into the back seat of the car for a short pair of aluminum crutches wrapped in his trenchcoat. They were an integral part of his makeshift plan.

Carrying the concealed crutches under his arm, he started across the parking lot toward the Arrivals Building, a hangarlike structure with a front wall entirely of glass. The crisp, clear air was tainted with the faint odor of jet fumes and filled with the rumble of distant aircraft on the ground and in the sky. When he reached the grass beside the curving roadway between the parking lot and the line of connecting terminal buildings, he paused and waited for a break in the traffic. He stifled the urge to turn back and return home. Whatever the risks he was about to run, they were less than those he would face if he crossed Werewolf. There was no exit from the maze. He walked across the road and up the ramp to the terminal entrance.

The concourse of the International Arrivals Building was flooded with light and color. Above the concourse, a large rectangular opening had been left in the second floor, and one could look straight up to the arched roof high overhead, from which was suspended a huge, multicolored mobile. The flags of the world's nations hung from poles projecting out from the balcony that ringed the opening.

By day, with light streaming in through the expanse of glass at the front of the building, Ritter's impression of the terminal was quite different from the one he had formed when he had checked its layout three nights earlier. At night, the building, lit only by fluorescent lights, had seemed cold and impersonal. But the warmth and color did little to cheer him.

At the rear of the concourse was a long, windowless wall separating the concourse from the U.S. Customs Hall. As Ritter entered the terminal, members of a Japanese tour group were emerging through the wide exit doors in the wall to join their fellow tourists milling about on the concourse. Although they were obviously exhausted from their long flight, their faces still reflected excitement and anticipation. Ritter envied them — he envied everyone around him. They were ordinary people leading ordinary lives.

Ritter checked the Arrivals board and saw that Flight 405 was on schedule. Then he took the escalator to the second floor to check its layout once again. As he stepped off the escalator he was facing the rear of the building. Ahead of him and to the right were observation windows through which one could look down on the Customs Hall. On his immediate right was a cafeteria. To his left, opposite the cafeteria, was a row of shops.

He turned to his right and walked back toward the front of the terminal, past the cafeteria entrance, to the balcony overlooking the ground-floor concourse. Along the balcony was a long line of seats with a view of the exits from the Customs Hall below. Ritter chose one, sat down, laying the coat and crutches across his lap, and took out an envelope addressed to Passenger Max Braun, Lufthansa Flight 405. He removed the written instructions he had prepared for Braun and read them over once again.

As he read, he loosened his tie and unbuttoned his collar. Although the building appeared light and airy, to Ritter the atmosphere seemed hot and stuffy, and he felt the prickle of sweat on his neck and forehead. He glanced at his watch and was surprised to see that he had been in the terminal only five minutes. He was about to slip the message back in its envelope when it suddenly occurred to him that Braun might not understand English. In fact, he could not be certain what Braun's nationality was. He cursed under his breath. It was a detail he should have checked with Dietrich when he'd had the chance.

He took out a pen and carefully drafted a German translation of the short message on the bottom half of the page, appended the signature, Karl, and inserted the note in the envelope.

He got up, made sure that the crutches were still hidden in the folds of his coat, and returned to the ground floor. Tour guides were patiently herding their Japanese charges toward the front exits. Ritter skirted the group and walked to the Lufthansa counter at the east end of the concourse. A blond girl behind the desk gave him a plastic smile.

"May I help you, sir?"

"Yes, please," Ritter said, placing the envelope on the counter top. "This note is for a passenger coming in on Flight four-o-five.

It is vital that he receive it, but I will be unable to deliver it personally."

"You can leave it with us, sir. We'll page Mr. — er — Braun and request him to come to this desk for the message."

"Could you page him in German as well as in English? I'm not sure he speaks English."

"Certainly."

"You won't forget. It's very important for him to receive this message." The note of urgency in Ritter's voice was real.

"I'll see to it personally."

"Thanks. Thanks very much," Ritter said.

"You're welcome, sir."

Ritter returned to the second floor to wait. Flight 405 was not due for another thirty-five minutes. This time he took a seat next to the escalator, facing the cafeteria, and lit a cigarette. From the seats around him came a low, incoherent babble of voices speaking several different languages. Soft, syrupy popular music played over the loudspeaker system. It was intended to be soothing, but it got on Ritter's nerves. A pair of sexy Spanish girls in skintight slacks and spiked heels clicked by. Ordinarily they would have snared his attention, but now he looked at them without a flicker of interest. Time dragged by, and the butts of Ritter's cigarettes began to accumulate in the ashtray beside him.

Ritter stood at an observation window overlooking the Customs Hall, watching the passengers from Flight 405 as they entered the security area. To his relief, Ritter had no trouble spotting Braun, who was among the first to appear. Evidently Braun cared little for his personal appearance. A twenty-four-hour growth of dark stubble shadowed his pale face, his uncombed hair needed trimming, his shoes were scuffed and his wrinkled suit was ten years out of date. From time to time he absently pushed his horn-rimmed glasses higher on the bridge of his nose, but they immediately slipped back down again.

Ritter turned his attention to the other passengers, hoping he might see someone displaying an obvious interest in Braun, but no one appeared to take any notice of him. Ritter was not surprised; he had not really expected it to be that easy. The amplified click of a microphone switch cut off the background music, and a woman's voice began to page passenger Max Braun. Ritter saw him react. Satisfied that Braun had heard the message, Ritter turned away from the window and headed back toward the front of the terminal. He still had to identify the man following Braun, and logic dictated that anyone following Braun would make every effort to precede him through Customs.

Ritter again took a seat on the balcony overlooking the concourse, from which he could see both the Customs exits and the Lufthansa counter. The only person near him was a scruffy college boy with a backpack, who was catching some sleep in a seat ten feet away, but Ritter looked carefully around to be sure no one farther away was observing him before he unwrapped the crutches and placed them on the floor beneath his chair. Now all he could do was watch, wait and hope that his crude plan would work.

The first passenger through Customs was a dark-haired young woman carrying only a shoulder bag, but she did not linger. She walked briskly toward the street exits and out of Ritter's line of sight. The emergence of the first passenger had served to identify which of the two exits would be used by passengers from Flight 405, and a crowd of relatives and friends began to assemble in a rough semicircle surrounding the doorway.

Ten minutes passed before the next passengers, who carried luggage, were cleared through Customs. The doors opened, and an elderly couple came through and were immediately engulfed by their excited grandchildren. Next came two businessmen, who threaded their way through the crowd and went directly to the street exits. A family of four appeared, the exhausted parents dragging their complaining children by the hand.

Then Braun came through, carrying a small suitcase. He looked around, peering over the heads of the crowd until he located the Lufthansa counter. Ritter watched him cross the concourse to the

Lufthansa desk and ask for his message. No one else had come through the Customs exit, and Ritter's hopes began to rise. Perhaps no one was following Braun after all.

Braun had opened the envelope and had started to read Ritter's message when the Customs exit door opened again. Ritter held his breath. Two teenagers appeared and were immediately embraced by their smiling parents.

Braun had finished reading. He slipped the note into his pocket and picked up his suitcase, but he continued to stand beside the counter, looking anxiously around, as if he expected some confirmation of the written instructions.

"Come on, move," Ritter muttered under his breath.

More passengers were coming through Customs now, and at a faster rate. Ritter still managed to keep track of them, but it was becoming more difficult. At last Braun walked away from the Lufthansa counter, heading for the escalator to the second floor, where he was to take a table in the cafeteria and wait for five minutes before leaving. No one followed him to the escalator. Ritter began to relax, hardly daring to believe his luck. No one was shadowing Braun.

Then he saw the girl, and his stomach tightened into a knot. Just as Braun reached the level of the second floor, the dark-haired young woman who had been the first passenger to clear Customs appeared again out of nowhere and stepped onto the escalator, her eyes turned upward and fixed on Braun. It hadn't occurred to Ritter that the agent following Braun might be a woman.

Braun entered the cafeteria, bought a cup of coffee and sat down at an empty table. The girl didn't look in his direction as she came off the escalator, but he was well within range of her peripheral vision. She strolled over to one of the shops and looked in the window for a few moments before she turned and walked back toward the cafeteria. She took a seat next to the escalator, facing the cafeteria, and took a paperback book from her shoulder bag. She opened it and made a pretense of reading.

Forty feet away, Ritter nervously studied her in profile. Her clothes were American, but her manner — the way she carried herself — struck him as European. She didn't look older than twenty. Her two-piece tweed suit was intended to be business-like, but the straight skirt and snug jacket only emphasized her slim, well-proportioned figure, and several male passersby gave her an appreciative second glance. Though her hair and eyes were dark, her face reminded Ritter of Ingrid Bergman. To Ritter she seemed an unlikely choice for an agent, for even in a crowd she wouldn't escape notice; but he had no doubt that she was the agent he had been sent to intercept.

Ritter saw Braun glance nervously at his watch. It was time for Ritter to position himself. He slipped on his trenchcoat, picked up the crutches and stood up. No one took any notice of him as he made his way toward the escalator, dragging his right leg as if it were partially paralyzed. He took the long way around the balcony to approach the escalator from the side away from Braun and the waiting girl. Her back was to him when he stopped and looked toward Braun in the cafeteria, who was already getting up from his table, too impatient to wait out the full five minutes. It didn't mat-ter, for Ritter was almost in position; but Ritter hoped Braun would follow the rest of his written instructions to the letter. Braun was to go directly to a street exit and immediately take a taxi to the Statler-Hilton.

Ritter crossed in front of the escalator and turned so that his back was to the cafeteria. Anyone approaching the escalator from that direction would pass between Ritter and the corner of the escalator five feet from where he stood leaning on his crutches. He fumbled in the pockets of his trenchcoat, as if looking for ciga-rettes. Behind him he heard footsteps, and a moment later Braun brushed by him, giving Ritter a whiff of his sour body odor. Ritter resisted the urge to look over his shoulder to check on the girl.

Braun stepped onto the down escalator, and Ritter braced him-self as he heard the staccato click of high heels on the floor behind him. Just as the girl came abreast of him, he lurched forward as if one of his crutches had slipped, and thrust the left crutch directly across the girl's path, tripping her up. Flailing the air with his arms in an apparent attempt to regain his balance, Ritter struck her across the shoulder blades, driving her to the floor. He pitched forward and crashed down on top of her, pinning her to the floor in a tangle of arms, legs and crutches.

"My God, miss, I'm sorry," he cried loudly as he made a pretense of trying to pick himself up, all the while keeping her twisting body firmly pinned beneath him. He heard a rasping sound in her throat as she gasped for breath.

Several men rushed to their aid, and powerful hands seized Ritter under his arms and hauled him to his feet. At the very last moment he remembered not to take his weight on his supposedly paralyzed leg. As two other men helped the girl up, an elderly woman handed Ritter his crutches with an embarrassed look and hurried away.

Ritter knew the girl had been hurt, but he saw no pain in her eyes, only angry frustration. Her flushed cheeks were smeared with grime from the floor. She looked down at the concourse, saw that Braun had disappeared, and started to pull away from the two men who still held her arms. Ritter had to reach out and seize her wrist to prevent her from stepping onto the escalator.

"Are you all right, miss?" he asked.

"Yes, yes. Please let go of me! I'm in a great hurry!"

The girl's English was fluent, but Ritter detected a slight, guttural accent that might have been Israeli, but he couldn't be sure.

"Let go of my wrist!"

"But your stocking is torn, miss. You must allow me to pay for it."

"No, it was my fault."

With a strength that surprised Ritter, she wrenched her arm free of his grip and stepped onto the escalator. As she descended, she turned and forced a quick smile for appearance's sake. "It really was my fault," she said.

Ritter shrugged and smiled helplessly for the benefit of the onlookers, and the small crowd around him began to melt away. He brushed himself off and straightened his clothing. He had delayed the girl long enough for Braun to make his escape, but it gave him no satisfaction. He had done Werewolf's dirty work, and the dirt had rubbed off on him.

A pair of cold, gray eyes followed Ritter's progress down the escalator and across the concourse to the street exit. Five minutes later, the phone rang in Dietrich's New York apartment.

"Dietrich here."

"Kadinsky."

"Well?"

"He completed his assignment."

"Any problems?"

"No. His method was clumsy, but effective."

"Are you satisfied?"

"It was no real test."

"It will have to do," Dietrich replied in annoyance.

"You don't have to use him yet. I could complete your project for you. It is a very high-risk venture."

"No! I must have a specialist of your caliber working for me on a permanent basis. That is why I activated Ritter."

"You must be very sure of him to entrust him with the completion of your project. I hope your confidence is justified."

"He was handpicked, just as you were. You have not seen his record. Ritter's qualifications exceed even yours, Kadinsky."

"We shall see," Kadinsky said and hung up.

Kadinsky *had* seen Ritter's record. On paper, Ritter was a specialist of Kadinsky's caliber. But age could leave a man's talent intact and still erode his nerve — or his loyalty. Kadinsky took nothing for granted, left nothing to chance; it was a necessary state of mind for a professional assassin.

. . . FOUR . . . .

"Kill him!"

The girl's words seemed to hang in the air for a moment before fading into the silence in the room. She blinked as a swirl of cigar smoke drifted into her eyes, but otherwise her dark eyes didn't waver as she looked steadily at Zev Barlev, chief of Israeli Intelligence in the United States. Seated in a swivel chair behind a battered, paper-strewn desk, Barlev coolly regarded the girl standing before him. He smoked his cigar and let the silence stretch out. He was a grizzled, barrel-chested bear of a man, physically powerful and accustomed to command.

"The Mossad is not a murder organization," Barlev said at last. Even when speaking softly, his voice had a resonant bass timbre.

"Since when is it murder to kill a Nazi?" the girl challenged.

"You said he had a German accent. That doesn't make him a Nazi."

"I call any German who works for the Egyptians a Nazi."

Barlev drew on his cigar and blew a perfect smoke ring, following it with his eyes as it drifted up to the ceiling and broke apart among the strips of paint peeling off the cracked plaster.

Barlev's small office was directly above the Naomi Travel Agency, which occupied the ground floor of a converted townhouse on East 52nd Street. The travel agency was a cover for Mossad's New York headquarters. Through the open window behind Barlev's desk came the muted rumble of traffic on Second Avenue and the cooing of pigeons nesting on the fire escape The late-afternoon sun filtering through the slats of the folding wooden shutters screening the window formed a pattern of yellow bars on the worn gray carpet.

"We don't know he works for the Egyptians," Barlev said. "We don't know who he is, or anything else about him."

The girl frowned uncertainly. "I don't understand. If you don't know who he is, how did you get the picture you showed me?"

Barlev sighed. The young ones always had to know everything at once. They were too impatient, too impetuous. What did this girl know of Nazis, or of killing? — not killing in the heat of battle, but the cold-blooded taking of a man's life in a back room or in a dark, filthy alley.

"Sit down, please," Barlev said, waving her into a chair beside his desk.

The girl walked to the chair and sat down, her movements lithe and graceful. She's a beautiful girl, Barlev thought with detachment. Once, a girl like her might have distracted him, but now he admired her beauty as he might admire a flower's beauty. Advancing age made some aspects of life less complicated, he reflected sourly, but it seemed a poor compensation for the loss of youth.

He picked up the photograph he had shown the girl. It was a blurred snapshot of a tall, blond man caught by the camera in mid-stride.

"I obtained this picture by pure chance," he said. "I'm not even sure why I kept it in my desk. But when you described the man who tripped you up at the airport, your description rang a bell. That's when I showed it to you. Since there are no crutches in this picture, it seems safe to assume that he deliberately prevented you from following your man. That does not necessarily mean that he was working for the Egyptians."

"But how *did* you get the picture?"

"Indirectly. Last month an old man named Solomon died on a subway platform of a heart attack. He used to work for me, but he was pensioned off years ago. He had become — unreliable.

"When he died, the police found a gun in his pocket, so there was a brief investigation. It seems he still carried my home phone number on a card in his wallet, and the police called as a matter of routine. Solomon had no living relatives, or any real friends, so I went downtown myself to collect his effects and to arrange burial." Barlev paused and tapped the photograph with his forefinger. "This was in his pocket when he died."

"And you kept it. Why?"

Barlev shrugged. "I don't really know — perhaps because of the gun. I'd never known Solomon to carry a weapon. Are you absolutely sure this is the man who knocked you down?" he asked, handing her the photograph. "That picture is not very clear."

"It's clear enough," the girl said tightly, her cheeks coloring slightly as she looked at the snapshot. Her mind recoiled from the memory of the man's heavy body pinning her to the floor. "The bastard made a fool of me."

"And you want to kill him for that?" Barlev said dryly.

"Of course not! But an example should be made — a warning to those who think they can do Nasser's filthy work without fear of reprisal. Kill him, and . . ."

"Enough!" Barlev broke in sharply. "I'll have no more talk of killing."

The girl's eyes flashed defiantly, but she had the sense to bite off the reply that flew to her lips. Barlev saw her check herself and was satisfied. She was not alone in her desire to strike back at the Germans who were building rockets for Egypt. For months the pressure had been building to make an example of some of the engineers who worked in Nasser's secret Factory 333.

"How long have you been in the field, Elana?" Barlev asked.

"Six months," the girl answered, trying not to sound defensive. Barlev groaned inwardly. The last thing he wanted was an inexperienced, hotheaded Sabra messing up his efficient little operation. But he wanted her help; he wanted to find the man in the picture.

"Would you object if I asked Tel Aviv to lend you to me for a while?"

"No, sir."

"Good. We need someone who can positively identify this man. The picture just isn't that good."

"May I ask how you intend to find him?"

"I can tell you how we'll begin. In the photograph, he's entering an office building. The street number above the doorway is visible, and there is enough detail to check the picture against existing buildings. Once we find the building, we'll stake it out and hope he shows up."

"And if he doesn't?"

"Let's hope we're lucky. In the meantime I'll send a copy of the photograph to Tel Aviv. Maybe they can get a line on him. Now, go downstairs and tell Naomi you're on the payroll. She'll fix you up with a place to stay, money for clothes and anything else you need."

After the girl had left, Barlev picked up the phone and dialed a Brooklyn number. He had to wait seven rings before a sleep-drugged voice finally answered.

"Yoel, this is Zev."

"For God's sake, Zev, I was up all night in Washington — as you very well know. Let me go back to sleep."

"I want you here tomorrow morning at seven sharp. I have some legwork for you."

"I have some time off coming, remember?"

"Life is tough all over," Barlev said. "But there is one bright spot you can focus on."

"What?" the voice asked suspiciously.

"You'll like your new partner."

"Partner! What the hell are you talking about?"

"I've got her on loan from Tel Aviv — or soon will have. She's real pretty, Yoel."

"And new at the job, I suppose," the voice groaned.

"Yes."

"And eager?" The groan became a sob.

"Very."

Barlev held the phone away from his ear just in time. The voice on the other end of the line was still stringing curses together when Barlev hung up. He was smiling as he replaced the receiver, but the smile vanished as he thought again of Solomon.

Solomon had been useful in the old days, but the past had haunted him. On his own time he had begun to assemble files on former Nazis spotted in the United States — small fish that had slipped through the net of the War Crimes tribunals. Some of them were as evil as Mengele or Eichmann, but not as notorious. Tel Aviv had not been interested, but Solomon had been unwilling — or unable — to give it up. It had become an obsession that had begun to affect his work. Finally, Barlev had been forced to let him go.

If the man at the airport turned out to be a former Nazi, that would explain Solomon's interest in him. But why the gun? Had the old man been afraid, or had he decided to release his pent-up hatred by killing some of the men whose dossiers had slowly yellowed in his dusty files?

Barlev did not speculate long; only one question was important now: who was the man who had intercepted Elana at the airport?

Ten days later, a dossier on Erich Ritter lay on Barlev's desk. It consisted of a single typewritten sheet. The Israeli stared at it through a thick cloud of cigar smoke swirling in the cone of light from his desk lamp. It was past midnight, and Barlev's office lay in semidarkness. Slouched in an armchair near the desk sat Yoel Arnon, Barlev's lieutenant. He was a thin, ascetic-looking man in his thirties, with dark, mournful eyes and curly, black hair. He watched Barlev in silence. Arnon knew the contents of the file by heart.

Subject:	Erich Ritter
Age:	46
Birthplace:	Koblenz, Germany
Nationality:	USA (Naturalized 1948)
Occupation:	Business executive
Marital status:	Widower
Political:	No affiliations
Relatives:	None

History

Ritter educated in Germany. Completed secondary schooling, but did not enter university. Parents killed in auto accident in 1937. In 1938, at age 21, Ritter emigrated to Venezuela. Employed by Banco Nacional, Caracas, 1940–46. U.S. Immigration visa issued 1946. Ritter became U.S. citizen in 1948. Employed by Rupert Brewery 1946–50; Chase Manhattan Bank 1950–57; J. M. Garcia Exports Co. 1957– Married Jane R. Martin in 1951. No children. Wife died of cancer in 1958. No living relatives.

Remarks

Ritter is a successful, respected businessman. He speaks fluent German, Spanish and English. He has few close friends. There is no evidence that he holds extreme political views.

"Shit," Barlev growled, looking up and scowling at Yoel Arnon.

"I know it's thin," Arnon said, "but it was the best we could do. Hell, we were lucky even to find him."

"I need information, not excuses."

"When you do the legwork, Zev, you can do the complaining."

"Maybe I will next time," Barlev said, arching his back and stretching. His biceps bulged as he flexed his thick arms. "How much of this do you believe?"

"His employment record here in the States. As for his history before he became a U.S. citizen, all I can tell you is that U.S. Immigration is satisfied."

"So, why does an apparently solid citizen take it into his head to intercept one of our people? — And why was Solomon carrying around his photograph? Who is he? *What* is he?"

"Nothing from Tel Aviv?"

Barlev shook his head. "The file-shufflers came up empty."

"If he's an intelligence agent, his cover is good — damned good."

"Yeah," Barlev muttered absently. He ground out his cigar and stared blankly into the surrounding gloom.

Arnon broke the silence. "What do we do now?"

"I want to know about this man. Tel Aviv is also curious. They want us to follow it up."

"What, exactly, do they expect us to do?"

"I was advised to proceed on my own initiative."

Arnon raised his eyebrows fractionally. "And what does that mean?"

Barlev smiled crookedly. "It means that if I go out on a limb, they'll be happy to saw it off."

"So?"

Barlev's smile stretched into a mirthless grin, revealing a set of chipped, tobacco-stained teeth. "So, we'll have a chat with Mr. Ritter."

"A snatch?"

Barlev nodded.

"Don't do it, Zev. Not yet. We have no idea who this guy might be, and once we've snatched him it won't be so easy to let him go again. If this blows up in our faces, the Americans will close down our whole operation, and the brass in Tel Aviv will chop you off at the ankles. I've never known you to go off half-cocked before, so why now? Let's keep Ritter under surveillance for a while."

Barlev shook his head and laid a blunt forefinger alongside his nose. "I smell something, my friend. I want to know all about Mr. Ritter, and I want to know now."

"Don't go mystical on me. Your instinct isn't reason enough to risk blowing our whole operation sky high."

"Set it up, Yoel."

"All right, but it's your funeral. Don't blame me if this guy turns out to be CIA or something equally sticky."

"I won't. And if I do get the sack, you can count on me to recommend you for my job."

"Thanks," Arnon said sarcastically. "I'll get Moshe back from Chicago. Will you be coming along on this one?"

"Yeah. With Elana, that will make four. That should be enough to handle him."

"I thought you were sending her back to Tel Aviv."

"I changed my mind. You said she worked out okay."

"She did all right."

Barlev nodded. From Arnon, that was high praise. "This will give her the chance to even the score with Mr. Ritter."

"An eye for an eye?"

"Something like that."

For a time after Arnon left the office, Barlev continued to sit behind his desk, wondering where the chase would lead. He opened the desk drawer and took out Solomon's picture of the man they were after. The man had a strong, intelligent face, but one couldn't read a man's character from a snapshot or a one-page summary of his life. Perhaps it was just as well, Barlev thought. Arnon was right. Once they kidnapped Ritter and interrogated him, it might not be possible to let him go free. Barlev didn't want to know too much about a man he might have to kill.

. . . . FIVE . . . .

Thunder rumbled in the dark evening sky, but Ritter couldn't hear it above the roar of cascading water below him. He locked the door to his summer cabin, which was built on the side of a wooded ravine beside a rushing, boulder-strewn brook, and crossed the wooden bridge that spanned the stream. He was completing a yearly ritual. Each spring, Ritter drove up to Connecticut to open the cabin, and in the fall he came up again to close it for the winter. With his wife gone, he seldom stayed at the cabin, but she had loved the place and he couldn't bring himself to sell it.

He had driven up that morning and had worked all day, sweeping out the cabin, putting up the storm shutters and clearing fallen limbs from the brook. The work had been good for him, draining away the tension that had become part of his daily existence ever since he had received Werewolf's summons. Over two weeks had passed since the incident at Idlewild, and Dietrich had left him in peace. But Ritter knew it wouldn't last, and he jumped each time the phone rang.

Ritter walked through a gap in a thick stand of fir trees into a small, grassy field where his car was parked. With the coming of darkness, loneliness had closed in on him, and he was anxious to leave. He drove the car across the field and out through a narrow gate in the rail fence bordering his property. As he got out to close the gate, he heard the rustle of rain beginning to fall into the trees above him.

He closed the gate, returned to his car, switched on the headlights and drove out onto a narrow, winding road that led west toward the Wilbur Cross Parkway. As the car emerged from beneath the canopy of leaves, heavy raindrops splattered the windshield, and he turned on the wipers. At first, each stroke of the wipers left behind a greasy smear on the glass that made a blur of the road ahead, and he was forced to drive slowly.

As the windshield cleared, Ritter increased his speed, the headlights cutting a swath through the darkness. He had driven less than two miles when a vehicle came up behind him fast with its headlights switched to high beam. Ritter squinted as the reflected light from his rearview mirror dazzled his eyes. A moment later, a gray VW van swerved around him and swept by, forcing him off the road onto the shoulder. He cursed and leaned on his horn. The van accelerated and raced on ahead, and soon its taillights disappeared around a bend in the road.

Ritter swung the car back onto the road and had just settled back in his seat again when the storm broke loose in full fury. The sudden torrent of rain reduced his visibility to thirty yards, and Ritter eased up on the accelerator. He drove on with his eyes fixed on the yellow stripe running down the center of the glistening asphalt. He switched on the car radio, but all he could pick up as he dialed across the band was static and a confusion of overlapping transmissions. He turned it off and reached for the cigarettes in the pocket of his windbreaker. He was trying to extract a cigarette from the pack when he came over a sharp rise in the road.

His headlight beams dipped down and splashed against the side of the gray van, which was broadside to him and blocking the road one hundred feet away. Ritter stamped on the brake pedal and steered into the skid as his car slewed sideways on the slick asphalt. The tires shrieked as the rubber finally grabbed the road, but it was too late. Ritter gritted his teeth and braced himself for the crash.

His car's right front fender slammed into the side of the van. The hollow bang of the impact was followed by the tinkle of shattered glass falling onto the road. Both vehicles rocked back on their suspensions, quivered, and were still. Ritter took a deep breath and switched off the engine. He had bruised his chest on the steering wheel, but otherwise he was unhurt. In the sudden silence the rattle of rain on the car roof seemed unnaturally loud. He peered through the streaming windshield, but he could see no one. The van, illuminated by his car's surviving headlight, seemed deserted.

He frowned, opened the door and started to get out of the car. As he set his left foot onto the road, his arm was seized from behind and he was yanked from the car. A man's leather-jacketed forearm clamped down on his windpipe, and a knee drove into the small of his back, arching him backward. Cold steel was thrust against his left temple, and he didn't need to be told that it was a gun barrel. He stopped struggling. Rain lashed his upturned face and ran into his eyes.

"My money's in my wallet. Right hip pocket," Ritter said through clenched teeth.

"We don't want your money," a woman's voice said harshly from behind him. He had heard that voice somewhere before . . . and suddenly he understood. He couldn't guess how they had tracked him down, but it didn't matter. He couldn't let them take him.

A man wearing a hooded poncho appeared in front of him and ran his hands over Ritter's body. "He's clean," Poncho said.

The man wearing the leather jacket grunted and swung Ritter around, keeping him off balance. As Leather Jacket pulled him toward the rear of the van, the girl moved into Ritter's line of vision. Her trenchcoat was soaked through, and her black hair clung wetly to her cheeks. Cradled familiarly in her arms was an Uzi machine pistol.

"Please," Ritter gasped, rolling his eyes and plucking spastically at the leather sleeve on the arm across his throat. "Please don't hurt me!"

Ritter saw the girl's eyes narrow with contempt, and he felt the arm loosen its grip slightly. He began to make sobbing sounds. The girl brushed past him and opened the van's rear door. Ritter couldn't see Poncho, but he heard him opening the door to the driver's seat, far enough away for Ritter's purposes. Leather Jacket spun Ritter around and shoved him against the van's rear bumper.

"Climb in, you!"

"No, please! Don't hurt me!"

"Get in, damnit!" Leather Jacket cried, prodding Ritter in the back with his pistol.

It was only a momentary mistake, but Ritter was waiting for it. He spun around, his left arm sweeping aside the pistol that an instant before had been pressed against his back, and delivered a vicious judo chop to the side of Leather Jacket's neck. The girl had jumped back, her Uzi at the ready, but Leather Jacket was in her line of fire. As Leather Jacket collapsed, Ritter caught him under the arms and tore the pistol from his grasp.

He put the gun to the man's lolling head and backed away from the van. Poncho, in the van's driver seat, had twisted around and drawn a pistol, but he, too, was afraid of hitting the semiconscious man Ritter held in front of him as a shield.

"Get rid of your guns or he's a dead man," Ritter demanded. "You can try again another day. You — in the front seat — throw away that pistol. You, girl, throw your weapon into the woods." Ritter could feel the man in his arms recovering. "Now!" he shouted.

Behind him, Ritter heard the scuff of a shoe on some loose gravel, and his instinct shrieked a warning; but he reacted a split-second too late. A stunning blow behind his ear sent him spinning down into darkness.

Zev Barlev slipped his blackjack into his coat pocket and stooped to help the man in the leather jacket to his feet.

"Moshe, can you drive?" he asked the man, who was swaying drunkenly, his hand over his bruised neck. "Moshe, snap out of it!" Barlev ordered, shaking the man roughly by the shoulders.

"Yesh — yes — I can drive."

"Okay. Get Ritter's car out of here. Stay off the main highways. I don't want a cop stopping you because of that damned headlight."

Yoel Arnon came up to them, his sheepish expression hidden by the shadow of his poncho hood. "Sorry we made a mess of it, Zev."

"Shit," Barlev growled. He reached down and seized Ritter's inert body by the shoulders. "Come on, let's get him in the van before someone comes along this road. Elana, get that broken glass off the road."

The man called Moshe had started Ritter's car and was turning it around as Arnon and Barlev heaved Ritter into the back of the van. The car headlights swept over Ritter's pale face, and his eyelids flickered. "Give him the hypo," Barlev said to Arnon. "The son-of-a-bitch is dangerous."

Ritter opened his eyes as he felt someone seize his arm and push back his sleeve. He started to struggle up as a needle jabbed him, but a knee pressed against his chest pinned him to the floor of the van. As consciousness began to slip away again, he wondered vaguely if the shot he'd been given was fatal. It didn't seem to matter.

Ritter awakened slowly to a dull, throbbing pain behind his eyes. His tongue was sore and swollen, and he tasted blood in his mouth. Dazedly he opened his eyes, squinting against the light from fluorescent lamps on the ceiling above him. When he tried to move, the pounding in his head increased and a wave of dizziness washed over him. He closed his eyes again and waited for the pain to subside. Gradually his mind cleared.

With the return of full consciousness came fear. Ritter assumed that he had been seized by Israeli agents as an act of reprisal. Since they had not killed him out of hand, they apparently intended to interrogate him, but that gave him little comfort. He could play for time and watch for a chance to escape, but he doubted that the chance would come. It didn't occur to him to tell them the truth; he was sure they would never believe it.

The only sound in the room besides his own breathing was the buzz of the fluorescent lamps. He opened his eyes again and waited for them to adjust to the light. He was lying on his back on a leather sofa with his wrists and ankles bound. The cords bit into his flesh, but the circulation had not been cut off and he still had feeling in his fingers and toes. He twisted awkwardly onto his side and looked at the large, windowless room in which he was imprisoned.

It appeared to be a recreation room in the basement of a private home. A mahogany bar ran the length of one wall. In front of the bar were a half-dozen chrome and leather bar stools, and behind it, built into the wall, was an elaborate liquor cabinet. A stereo system and a large-screen television were built into wooden cabinets in two corners of the room. A clock above the bar read 3:15, but Ritter had no idea whether it was day or night.

Gritting his teeth against the pain in his head, he swung his legs off the sofa and struggled up to a sitting position. He leaned forward, intending to slip off the couch and onto his knees on the floor, so that he could reach the bindings on his ankles; but a small sound behind him stopped him, and he twisted around. Sitting quite still in a chair beside the sofa was the girl. The Browning 9mm automatic in her hand told him to stay where he was.

It was the same girl; he was sure of it, even though his memory of her had been blurred by his nervousness at the airport that day. She was dressed in black toreador slacks and a loose, gray sweater, and she looked even younger than he remembered, less sophisticated; but she was just as beautiful. She still reminded him of a dark-haired, dark-eyed Ingrid Bergman.

He swallowed to relieve the dryness in his throat and said, "Are you Israeli?"

"Don't play games," she snapped.

"Are you or aren't you?"

The girl started to reply, but she stopped as a door opened at the top of a carpeted staircase leading to the first floor. Two men descended the stairs. The one in the lead was a dapper little man with a pencil-thin mustache. He carried a glass of water in one hand and a black leather doctor's bag in the other. He walked across the room to Ritter and held the glass to Ritter's lips.

"I expect you need this," the little man said. "The drug they used leaves one quite thirsty."

Ritter nodded and began to drink greedily, not caring that water spilled out of the corners of his mouth and dribbled down his chin. The man saw that Ritter was having difficulty swallowing, and when Ritter had drained the glass he said, "Open your mouth, please. I'm a doctor."

Ritter did as he was asked.

"Ah, bit your tongue, I see. Probably when you were struck. Headache?" the doctor said, looking closely at Ritter's eyes.

"Yes."

"Nausea?"

"No."

"Good." The doctor turned to the other man who had come downstairs. "It would be simpler to examine him if his hands weren't tied."

The second man nodded, slipped his hand into his trousers pocket and handed the doctor a penknife. "Go ahead, cut him loose — his feet, too."

Ritter looked at the second man, who, from his bearing, was obviously in charge. He had the build of a weight lifter and the face of an aging journeyman prizefighter, but the eyes didn't match the blunt-featured, leathery face. They were intelligent and coldly analytical.

The doctor dropped to one knee and cut the cords binding Ritter's ankles. Then he freed Ritter's wrists. With just the girl to deal with, Ritter might have tried to seize the knife and use the doctor as a hostage, but he knew he wouldn't get past the Israeli leader.

"You were the one behind me in the road," Ritter said to him.

The man nodded. "I am Barlev."

Out of the corner of his eye, Ritter saw a flicker of surprise on the girl's face. Apparently Barlev was not worried about Ritter learning his identity; it was a bad sign.

"Are you Israeli?" Ritter asked.

"Of course. Didn't you know?"

"I guessed."

"An excellent guess," Barlev said dryly. "Why did you intercept our agent at the airport?"

"I was ordered to."

"By whom?"

"That's a long story."

"We have time."

The doctor had opened his bag and taken out a stethoscope. "Please remove your shirt, Mr. Ritter."

Ritter didn't ask the purpose of an examination; he did as he was told.

"Didn't you know she was an Israeli agent?" Barlev asked.

Ritter shook his head.

"You follow orders blindly?"

"Not by choice."

Ritter ached for a cigarette, but he wouldn't ask for one. He winced as the cold metal of the stethoscope was pressed against his chest. The doctor listened to Ritter's heart, checked his lungs and pulse rate and asked some questions about his medical history. When he had completed his brief examination, he casually grasped Ritter's right arm and twisted it slightly to reveal the scar on the underside of the upper arm.

"How did you get that scar?" he asked coldly.

Ritter looked up and locked eyes with Barlev. "You know what it is," Ritter answered.

"SS pig!" the girl spat out.

Barlev's expression didn't change at all. He just stared at Ritter in silence.

"You *were* SS," Barlev said at last, the words rumbling out of his deep chest. "What are you now?"

Ritter didn't answer, and Barlev, watching him, felt a growing puzzlement. Ritter's reactions were somehow off-key. They didn't fit with Barlev's experience with former Nazis, who had either groveled shamelessly or had maintained a disdainful, hate-filled defiance. He sensed fear in Ritter, but not cowardice, and there was no hatred — or even real anger — in his eyes. Ritter was not reacting to his captors as *Jews*.

Barlev could see that neither the girl nor the doctor had noticed, which didn't surprise him. The girl was too inexperienced, and the doctor was a physician, not an intelligence agent. Doctor Weiss was an American Zionist, who had helped Barlev's group before. The Mossad's small cadre of professionals relied on the part-time but dedicated help of non-Israeli Jews abroad.

"Please understand, Ritter, that we must have answers to our questions," Barlev said. "We have time, but we do not intend to waste it. The doctor will explain your options."

Weiss cleared his throat. "You appear to be in good health, which means that we can use either of two drugs at our disposal. Pentothal is safest, but to be effective, it must be used in conjunction with hypnosis, which requires your cooperation. The second drug does not require cooperation, as it is more effective in breaking down the subject's resistance. Unfortunately, it can have rather nasty and long-lasting side effects. The choice is yours."

Barlev frowned as he detected a sudden glimmer of hope in Ritter's eyes, a hope Barlev couldn't understand.

"Pentothal," Ritter said without hesitation.

"All right, Mr. Ritter," Weiss said, "you can put your shirt back on, but roll up your left sleeve."

Weiss took cotton and a bottle of alcohol from his bag and swabbed the inside of Ritter's elbow. Next he tightened a rubber tube about Ritter's arm above the elbow to raise the vein. He removed a prepared syringe from its sterile packing, depressed the plunger to squirt a little of the clear fluid through the tip of the needle, and said, "Please look away, Mr. Ritter." Then he deftly slipped the needle into Ritter's vein and slowly pressed home the plunger. When he had finished and removed the tourniquet, he taped a Band-Aid over the tiny puncture wound.

"That should do it," Weiss said. "Lie down on the couch and relax. The Pentothal will take effect very soon."

Ritter stretched out on the couch, closed his eyes and waited for the drug to invade his brain.

"Your first name is Erich, isn't it?" he heard the doctor ask.

Ritter nodded drowsily. A heavy weariness was settling over him.

"You are tired, Erich, and you want to sleep. As you listen to my voice, you feel peaceful, so very peaceful. Your pulse is steady and your breathing is regular. Your pulse is beating steadily as you listen to the steady, steady rhythm of my voice. You feel so peaceful and relaxed as you listen to the steady, steady rhythm of my voice. You are slipping into sleep; slipping into sleep. Slipping into sleep to the steady, steady rhythm of my voice. Calm, peaceful sleep. Sleep. . . . Sleep. You are asleep, Erich. You are asleep. . . ."

Weiss's voice trailed off, and he stepped back from the couch. Ritter lay quite still, his breathing deep and regular, his facial muscles slack. "He's ready," Weiss said softly.

"Are you sure?" Barlev whispered.

Weiss nodded. "The drug did some of the work, but I'm not sure it was even necessary. He wanted to be hypnotized. Still, the drug should make it easier to keep him under if our questions put him under stress. Shall I begin?"

"Yes."

"Listen to me, Erich," Weiss said soothingly. "You are asleep, but you can still hear my voice. It calms you and relaxes you. You can hear my voice, can't you, Erich?"

"I can hear you," Ritter mumbled.

"That's good, Erich, very good. You will remain asleep, Erich, but you will answer my questions. You want to answer my questions. Answering my questions makes you feel even more relaxed and peaceful. You want to answer my questions, don't you, Erich?"

"Yes," Ritter said in a clearer voice.

"What is your name?"

"Erich Ritter."

"Was that always your name, Erich?"

"Yes."

"Very good, Erich. Answering my questions is so relaxing. You feel so calm and peaceful as you listen to my voice. Are you an American citizen, Erich?"

"Yes."

"When did you come to the United States?"

"In nineteen forty-eight."

"Very good, Erich. It's so very pleasant to answer my questions. Were you ever a German citizen?"

"Yes."

"Were you in the war, Erich?"

"Yes."

"What did you do in the war, Erich?"

"I fought," Ritter said in a louder voice, and he stirred restlessly.

"You are doing very well, Erich, and you feel peaceful. Listen to how calm my voice is. My voice soothes you. Did you fight for Germany, Erich?"

"Yes."

"Were you in the Wehrmacht?"

"No."

"What branch of the armed services were you in?"

"Waffen–SS."

Weiss frowned and repeated the question. Ritter gave the same answer.

"What was your rank in the Waffen–SS?"

"Hauptsturmführer."

"You are sure that you were in the SS. Is that right?"

"Yes."

"Very good, Erich. You will sleep now. You are in a deep, deep sleep."

Weiss turned away and beckoned to Barlev and Elana to follow him to the other side of the room, out of range of Ritter's hearing.

"Why did you stop?" Barlev said. "I thought we have a strictly limited time before the drug wears off."

"He is fully hypnotized, and it may not matter if the drug wears off. That's not the problem. The problem is, he's lying."

"What!"

"Keep your voice down!" Weiss whispered urgently.

"How can he be lying?"

"Hypnosis — even with Pentothal — doesn't guarantee the truth, though spontaneous lying is rare. But we have something quite different here. Someone has been in his head before us."

"What the hell are you talking about?"

Weiss compressed his lips in annoyance. "Give me a chance, and I'll explain. I would never have caught it if I hadn't seen something like it before. I think he has been hypnotically trained to give specific answers to certain questions — untruthful answers. Lying produces psychological stress in almost everyone, even if the lie is for a moral purpose, and the stress shows up physically — a flush of embarrassment, a quickened pulse rate, or, more subtly, a change in the skin's electrical resistance. A lie detector is designed to register those physical signs of stress. But some involuntary responses to tension — a facial tic, for example — can be suppressed by hypnotic conditioning. The trick is to program the subject to release the tension in a less noticeable way, to provide him with a psychological relief valve."

"What kind of relief valve?"

"In Ritter's case, the twitching of a finger. When he responded to certain of my questions, the little finger on his left hand twitched violently. If he had been awake, he could easily have hidden that twitch. He would be able to look you straight in the eye and lie like a trooper. I doubt that even a lie detector would catch him at it."

"But if he's been hypnotized to give false answers to specific questions," Elana put in, "he must believe the answers to be true. There would be no need for a relief valve."

"I don't mean that lies have been implanted in his mind as the truth," Weiss said, "just the ability to give the false answers without turning a hair. He knows the truth, and he knows when he's lying; but under hypnosis, he apparently lies automatically."

"Do you know that, or are you guessing?" Barlev demanded.

"Call it an educated guess. I've seen just that kind of finger-twitching in patients who had been cured hypnotically of a facial tic, but in those cases the twitching occurred at random. Ritter's finger twitched only when he answered certain questions."

"Which questions?" Barlev asked. "When was he lying?"

"I know this is hard to believe, but I think Ritter was lying when he told us he was in the Waffen–SS."

"But that's crazy," Elana objected. "Why should anyone want to lie his way *into* the SS?"

Barlev looked over at Ritter lying asleep on the couch, and he felt a cold prickling at the back of his neck. Who was this man? What was he?

"Assuming you are right, can you get straight answers out of him?" Barlev asked Weiss.

The doctor shrugged. "Maybe. At least the finger-twitch will warn us when he's lying — if I'm right."

"Then try again. Now."

They walked back to the sofa and Weiss took up the questioning again. This time they didn't watch Ritter's face; they kept their eyes fixed on the little finger of his left hand.

"What did you do in the war, Erich?"

"I fought for Germany."

Ritter's finger remained still.

"What branch of the armed forces were you in?"

"Waffen–SS."

Ritter's little finger twitched violently.

Barlev reached out and touched the doctor's arm. "Ask him if he takes orders from the SS now," Barlev whispered.

"I don't understand," Weiss whispered back.

"Neither do I. Ask."

Weiss shrugged and asked Barlev's question.

"Yes," Ritter muttered, and this time his finger did not twitch.

"But the war is over, Erich," Weiss said. "The SS no longer exists. Do you work for ODESSA?"

"No." Again the finger remained still.

"What organization gives you orders?"

Ritter's response was inaudible, and he shifted restlessly on the couch. His breathing became more rapid.

"The drug may be wearing off sooner than I had thought," Weiss whispered. "I'll have to rely on technique to keep him under if my questions disturb him."

"You are sleeping, Erich. You are in a deep, peaceful sleep. You hear my voice and it relaxes you. Answering my questions is pleasant. Answering makes you feel at peace. You want to answer my questions, don't you, Erich?"

"Yes," Ritter said, but his breathing did not return to its earlier slow rhythm.

"You work for an SS organization. What is that organization?"

"Werewolf," came the response, sharp and distinct.

"Werewolf? What is Werewolf?"

"Secret."

Beads of sweat broke out on Ritter's forehead, and his eyelids fluttered.

"Relax, Erich, sleep. You hear my voice and it soothes you."

Weiss turned to Barlev. "He's coming out of it. Shall I try for more?"

"When can we use the Pentothal again?"

"I wouldn't want to hit him with it again for at least six hours."

"Damn! See if you can get some more."

"Erich, you can hear my voice, and it calms you. You want to answer my questions."

Ritter was still in a trance, but his lips moved restlessly, forming soundless words. Weiss shook his head pessimistically.

"What is the secret of Werewolf, Erich?"

Abruptly, Ritter's eyes flew open, and Barlev saw them snap into focus. It was over. Barlev gestured for Weiss and Elana to go upstairs and they left quickly.

Ritter sat up and massaged a crick in his neck. Barlev went to the bar and picked up a bar stool. He returned with it to the sofa, sat down facing Ritter and produced a pack of Lucky Strikes.

"Smoke?"

Ritter nodded. He could think clearly enough, but his senses seemed strangely distorted. Small sounds snared his attention: the whir of the electric clock above the bar, the soft sigh from the cushion on the stool when Barlev had sat down. He accepted a cigarette and a light from Barlev and gratefully inhaled a lungful of smoke. Barlev lit one for himself and exhaled twin streams of smoke through his nostrils.

"Did you get what you wanted?" Ritter asked.

Barlev shook his head slowly. "Not yet, but we will eventually."

"What time is it, day or night?"

"What's the difference?"

Ritter's eyes flicked around the room, and Barlev saw a slight, telltale tensing of his body. "Don't try it," Barlev said quietly. "Don't even think it. You might get past me, but the exits upstairs are covered. My boys underestimated you once, but they won't again."

"I suppose not," Ritter said tiredly.

"Look, Ritter, why waste time? You agreed to hypnosis readily enough. Why not spill your guts now?"

"No."

"Goddamnit," Barlev shouted, lunging forward and seizing Ritter by the shirt. "Who the hell are you?"

Ritter blinked, but that was his only reaction. He knew Barlev was only putting on a performance. Barlev smiled crookedly and released him. "You don't scare so easily, do you?"

"I scare," Ritter said.

"But you won't talk."

"I'll wait for another dose of Pentothal. You'll have to dig your information out of my mind, Barlev. Maybe then you'll believe it. That's what I'm counting on."

"Why?"

"Because then you may realize that I'm not your enemy."

Six hours later they went to work on Ritter again. Flanked by Barlev and Elana, Dr. Weiss sat in a chair beside the sofa where

Ritter lay in a hypnotic trance. Weiss had increased the Pentothal dose, and they were prepared for a long session. The doctor was about to try a different approach to the interrogation, designed to avoid direct questions that would trigger automatic lies, but he had no idea if it would work.

"Erich, I want you to let yourself go back in time — to Germany and the war. You remember it so clearly. You will tell me what you see and hear. You fought for Germany in the war, didn't you?"

"Yes, I fought."

"And you remember your last battle. You remember it very clearly."

"*So eine Verschwendung,*" Ritter said.

Weiss looked inquiringly at Barlev.

"What a waste," Barlev translated. "Keep going, doctor. I understand German. Elana?"

"Enough to follow what he says," the girl said.

As she looked at Ritter lying helpless on the sofa, she found herself unable to summon up the hatred she had felt for him earlier. As her uncertainty about the man they had kidnapped had increased, her reactions to him had been thrown into confusion.

"You remember that last battle, Erich, and you will tell me about it," Weiss said. "You can see it, hear it, feel it. . . ."

Elana saw Ritter's expression change. The trance-induced slackness in his face gave way to a grim tension. His breathing quickened, and his right hand tightened into a fist. She glanced at Barlev, who was watching Ritter with unfeeling eyes. She recalled Barlev's anger when she had talked so glibly of killing a man she did not know. It had been her glibness that had angered him, she realized, not the thought of killing. She might have second thoughts about Ritter, but his life was in Barlev's hands now; and Barlev would do what he thought was necessary, without hesitation and without pity.

"You are in that battle now," Weiss said quietly, insistently. "Tell me about that battle, Erich. You are there now. You are there. . . ."

. . . . SIX . . . .

"Run for it, Herr Hauptmann!"

Ritter, crouching behind the burning hulk of a Russian T-34 tank, turned and looked out over the bridge he would have to cross, squinting against the sleet and snow being driven into his face by the wind sweeping over the river. At the far end of the bridge, his sergeant continued to call to him, the man's hoarse shouts rising above the rattle of small-arms fire. The ancient stone bridge was littered with shapeless, snow-dusted bundles — the bodies of Ritter's men who had been cut down in their own attempt to reach the German lines on the other side of the river. Sparks from ricocheting bullets flared in the gathering darkness as Russian machine gunners raked the bridge from end to end.

Ritter set the timer of the detonator at his feet for a delay of thirty seconds and glanced at the Panzerfaust team huddled beside him behind the burning tank. "We'll make the run together. All set?"

The two youths, with straggly, adolescent beards and old men's eyes, nodded grimly. They knew as well as he did that they had little chance of making it across the bridge. The sudden revving of an engine and the ominous clank of treads stopped Ritter from pressing the detonator switch. Fifty yards away, a Russian tank pushed out from behind a brick factory building and wheeled toward them. They would have to kill the tank before they could risk the run across the bridge. Ritter gestured to the two men, and the Panzerfaust team slithered into firing position at one end of the hulk.

As the man carrying the rocket launcher settled the tube on his shoulder and sighted toward the attacking tank, Ritter raised his head to see if the tank was supported by Russian infantry. Oily smoke blew back into his eyes, and his vision blurred, but he could see that the tank was coming on alone. The monster was only thirty yards away now, its turret cannon fully depressed and pointed directly at them. Just as he ducked back into cover, Ritter saw the bright, flaring muzzle flash as the tank gunner fired.

The crack of the cannon, the whoosh of the shell and the blast as it slammed into the hulk's forward quarter merged into one deafening bang. Ritter recoiled as splinters sang over his head and the shock wave took his breath away. The man with the rocket launcher winced, but his eyes remained locked on the tank as he coolly waited for the range to close. Finally, with the tank so close its clank and roar filled their ears, shutting out the other sounds of battle, the man pressed the trigger. The rocket howled from the tube and exploded against the base of the turret.

The T-34 lurched to a halt, its racing engine screaming, and black smoke belched from its vents. "Now!" Ritter cried, pressing the detonator switch. Ritter's men scrambled to their feet and dashed past him out onto the bridge. Seizing his machine pistol, Ritter turned and raced after them. Behind him he heard a sharp clang as the stricken tank's turret hatch was thrown open by a desperate crewman. An instant later the tank was blasted apart by the explosion of its magazine.

Ritter's boots flew over the slippery cobblestones as he and the two men in front of him sprinted through a hail of Russian bullets.

The icy wind cut through his battle dress and seared his throat as he sucked air into his lungs in ragged gasps. Steel-jacketed bullets sang off the stones at their feet and hummed in the air around them as they pounded across the bridge. Cover was only one hundred fifty feet away, but for Ritter's men it was too far.

The two men were hit simultaneously, and they collapsed like marionettes with their strings cut. They were dead as they hit the cobblestones, and Ritter leaped over their bodies without breaking stride. One hundred feet to go. He could see the remainder of his company fanned out along the opposite bank, firing back across the river, trying to cover him, but the Russian fire didn't slacken.

Sixty feet. A bullet plucked at the sleeve of his white camouflage smock. Fifty feet. A second bullet smashed into the receiver of his machine pistol, driving it from his grasp. His lungs burned, and his thighs felt like great lumps of lead. He could feel himself slowing down even as he desperately sought to run faster.

"Come on, Herr Hauptmann! Faster!" his sergeant yelled, standing exposed at the end of the bridge, waving him on.

"Get down, Meyer!" Ritter shouted uselessly, wasting precious breath. Behind him he heard the grinding shriek of tearing steel as yet another Russian tank, trying to advance across the bridge, plowed aside the burnt-out hulk that blocked its path. He was almost across. He could see Meyer's round, mud-streaked face clearly. So close. Run! His foot slipped in the muddy slush at the end of the bridge, and he pitched headlong into Meyer's outstretched arms. Together they tumbled into the snow behind the stone bridge abutment.

"The tank!" Ritter cried, but his voice was drowned out by the thunderous explosion of the demolition charges. Chunks of stone and steel rained down around them, rattling on the cobblestone roadway and burying themselves soundlessly in the snow and mud on the riverbank. Abruptly, the Russian fire from directly across the river slackened, and Ritter, panting for breath, raised his head above the level of the abutment to assess the damage to the bridge. For a moment smoke and dust from the explosion shrouded the bridge, but the wind quickly shredded the veil. The fifty-foot center span of the bridge had disappeared into the dark river below, taking the attacking Russian tank with it.

Ritter looked to his left and right at the survivors of his company, who were spread out along the riverbank on both sides of the bridge, their rifles trained across the river. He twisted around and sat down in the snow with his back against the abutment. He was bone weary, and it was a struggle to think clearly.

"Night is closing in fast," he said to Meyer. "We'll drop back as soon as it gets a little darker. How many did we lose, Stabs'?"

"Twenty-five killed, eight wounded, Herr Hauptmann. We have thirty-five men in condition to fight."

"*Scheisse!* What a goddamned waste," Ritter burst out. "Regiment never did intend to counterattack. They left us on the other side holding that damned bridge for nothing. Nothing! The bastards didn't . . ."

Ritter ducked as a stray bullet chipped stone above his head and whined off into the darkness.

"Cigarette, Herr Hauptmann?" Meyer said carefully, holding out a crumpled pack.

"Thanks, Stabs'," Ritter said, getting a fresh grip on himself. Stabsfeldwebel Meyer was more than a good sergeant, he was a friend. Ritter accepted a crushed cigarette, and Meyer deftly lit it before the match was snuffed out by the driving wind. Meyer was Ritter's highest-ranking subordinate; in the last two days of fighting, Ritter had lost his two lieutenants. He didn't need them now, for his company was down to little more than platoon strength.

A Russian onslaught at Korosten had driven the Wehrmacht LIX Corps into a reeling retreat, dragging with it a battalion of the elite Brandenburg Division, to which Ritter and his men belonged. That day they had been driven back into Gorodnitza on the Sluch River, along with elements of the LIX Corps and a mixed bag of Waffen-SS units. The Germans now held the west bank of the Sluch.

"I've been on the radio to Battalion, Herr Hauptmann," Meyer said. "Second Company is on our left flank, and an SS unit is on our right."

"We're still in the gap between the SS and the Third Division?"

Meyer nodded.

"Then if Ivan comes across the river tonight, he'll hit us. The Popovs never fail to attack the line at a point between units under separate commands. What's the word from Battalion?"

"We're to hold the river line until dawn. No reinforcements," Meyer added in a neutral voice.

"Christ, that's perfect," Ritter growled. "We're stretched so thin, a gang of kindergarteners could walk through us."

With a grunt of weariness, Ritter got to one knee for another look at the Russian lines. Directly across the river it was quiet; only occasional muzzle flashes winked fitfully in the darkness. But to the north and south, crisscrossing tracer streams arced across the water, and the flashes of mortar shells marched up and down the banks on both sides of the river.

"Move the men back now," Ritter said. "We'll fall back to those buildings behind us. We'll have a clear field of fire right down to the riverbank. Set up MG positions in the center and on each flank."

"*Jawohl*, Herr Hauptmann," Meyer said, moving away to pass the word.

Ritter's men began to fall back from the river in twos and threes, flitting like ghosts over the low rubble piles between the river and an irregular line of brick factory buildings. Although they were exhausted, the men moved swiftly and silently, the occasional clink of metal or the rattle of loosened masonry masked by the distant small-arms fire and the *crump-crump-crump* of mortar shells.

Ritter watched them with a mixture of pride and bitterness — pride in their discipline and courage, and bitterness for the way the High Command misused them. The Brandenburgers were commandos, volunteers trained to raid behind enemy lines.

Brandenburg commandos had seized bridges in Holland and Belgium in advance of the main German assault, and they had done the same in Poland; glider-borne troops and parachute units had raided behind enemy lines in North Africa and in Russia. But now the High Command squandered their lives in useless attempts to plug gaps in disintegrating German lines of resistance, caring nothing for the commandos' specialized training. The High Command only valued their uncommon willingness to fight and to die.

Ritter chose a small two-story brick building for his command post. It would be in the center of his company's firing line, which was stretched along a seventy-five-yard front. A heavy wooden door, hanging askew on rusted hinges, blocked the entrance. He kicked it open and pushed his way inside, followed by a radioman and a machine-gun team. The stale odor of machine oil hung in the damp, frigid air, mingling with the smell of animal decay.

Ritter switched on a hooded flashlight and swept the empty room with its feeble beam. The building had once housed a machine shop, and a rusted, antiquated drill press still stood in one corner. In another corner lay the carcass of a cat, as yet undiscovered by rats. Ritter climbed a flight of rough wooden stairs that led to the second floor, where he found another large empty room with two low windows facing the river. The windowsills were only inches above the floor.

"Stahl!" Ritter called. "Bring your radio up here. And I want the MG team up here, too."

As the three men stumbled up the stairs in the darkness, Ritter heard Meyer call to him from below, and he went back downstairs. Meyer's bulk was silhouetted in the doorway against the fading light from a distant star shell. He was a beefy giant whose size was unusual even in the Brandenburg Division.

"Are the men in position, Stabs'?"

"Yes, Herr Hauptmann."

"If the Popovs do come across, it'll be the same drill as at Bryansk. Tell the men that no one is to fire until I send up a flare. No shooting into the darkness — not one damned shot. When the flare goes up, we all fire together, and for Christ's sake tell them to make every shot count. We don't have ammunition to waste. When the flare dies, no one is to fire until the next one goes up."

"*Jawohl*, Herr Hauptmann," Meyer said, but he made no move to leave.

"Well?"

"The men already have those instructions, Herr Hauptmann."

"When the hell are you going to stop anticipating my orders?" Ritter burst out in annoyance.

"At once, Herr Hauptmann," Meyer answered earnestly, and the heels of his boots slammed together as he snapped to attention. In spite of himself, Ritter laughed.

"I have a weapon for you, Herr Hauptmann, to replace the MP you lost on the bridge."

Meyer handed Ritter a rifle and an ammunition pouch. It was a lightweight Mauser carbine designed for parachute troops and fitted with a telescopic sight. Brandt, their sniper, had not made it across the bridge.

"I'd rather have a machine pistol," Ritter said.

"There was only one available, and I gave it to Schmidt, Herr Hauptmann. He can't shoot straight and needs a squirt gun. Besides, Herr Hauptmann, an MP wastes your talents," Meyer said, his grin dimly visible in the gloom.

Ritter ignored the flattery. "Flare pistol?"

"Right here, Herr Hauptmann."

Meyer pressed the flare pistol and a sack of flares into Ritter's hand. For a few moments the two friends stood together in the darkness without speaking. There was no need to voice the obvious. If the Russians came across the river in force, Battalion's order to hold at all costs might be the company's death warrant.

"Send two men down the riverbank to set up a forward observation post," Ritter said, breaking the silence. "If we don't watch out, Ivan will be on our doorstep before we know he's out there."

Ritter stared through the splintered panes of his second-story window at the dark mounds of rubble near the riverbank, watching intently for a hint of movement. Despite the forward observation post, he was taking no chances. It was nearly two A.M., and sleep threatened to overwhelm him; he hadn't closed his eyes in thirty-six hours.

To keep himself awake, he gnawed on a piece of dry sausage

from his ration pack, even though it increased his nagging thirst. No one had taken the time to boil snow for water, and Ritter's canteen was nearly empty. Even after two winter campaigns, it still seemed strange to him to be tormented by thirst while shivering with cold.

Ritter cursed softly as the meat slipped from his grease-coated fingers and fell to the floor. He knelt and picked it up again. Dirty or not, food was food. The thick grease on his hands was an annoyance, but it was necessary. In the first Russian campaign, thousands of German soldiers, unprepared for the arctic cold, had developed deep fissures in their fingers, which had quickly become infected.

At the other window, the machine-gun team waited beside their Spandau, its tripod resting on the rough floor planking. Ritter had sent the radioman down below to support Meyer on the ground floor. To the south, the Russians were pounding the German positions with a heavy rocket barrage, but in Ritter's sector it was quiet — too quiet. The ominous stillness frayed his nerves as he waited for the attack he was sure was coming.

A star shell burst high above the river to the north, and Ritter peered more intently in the direction of the riverbank. Just before the light from the star shell faded, he caught a flicker of movement at the base of a rubble pile fifty yards away, and he felt a familiar tightening in his stomach. They were coming.

"Did you see that, Herr Hauptmann?" the machine gunner called softly.

"I saw it," Ritter answered, checking his flare gun. In his mind he wrote off the forward observers. A Russian advance party must have caught them by surprise and silenced them.

Across the room, the machine gunner worked the bolt of his weapon as his partner arranged the ammunition belt for a smooth feed. The man at the machine gun was an old hand, a four-year veteran of the Brandenburg Division — like Meyer and Ritter himself. There weren't many of them left.

Ritter poked the flare pistol out through a jagged hole in the window glass and tensely waited for the moment to fire. He would let the Popovs get a little closer yet. He ignored the tightness in his stomach, knowing it would pass once the fighting started. Night actions were the worst. Meyer was the only man he knew who could calmly await a night attack. Ritter could visualize him at a window on the ground floor, alert but relaxed, a stubby briar pipe clamped between his teeth. Thank God for Meyer, Ritter thought. He heard a faint scuffling sound on the ground outside, and he fired the first flare.

A harsh white light burst upon the rubble-strewn area between the line of factories and the river. The area was alive with Russian assault troops in bulky, brown overcoats scrambling over piles of smashed masonry toward Ritter and his men. The nearest Russians were only thirty yards away when the flare caught them, and they were immediately cut down by the opening fusillade from Ritter's company.

The sharp cracking of carbines punctuated the ripping bursts from machine pistols and the steady, staccato rattle of machine guns. The Russians surged forward, their battle cry, shouted from a hundred throats, rising above the din. "Oorah! Ooorah!"

On they came, firing their burp guns and hurling grenades as they ran. The first wave fell like scythed wheat, cut down at point-blank range. Then the second wave began to fall. The sound of gunfire and the crash of grenades rose to a deafening intensity, drowning out the screams of the wounded thrashing on the ground as their comrades leaped over them and raced on, only to be cut down in their turn.

Ritter put his eye to the telescopic sight of his carbine, and the terrain jumped toward him in sharp relief. The cross hairs settled on the chest of a Russian officer waving his men forward. Ritter's forefinger curled around the trigger, taking up the slack in the firing mechanism. With a final increase in pressure, the carbine cracked, and the butt slammed back into Ritter's shoulder. Seventy-five yards away, the Russian officer threw his arms wide and toppled backward into the snow.

Ritter worked the bolt and settled on a new target. Again the carbine cracked, and a second Russian officer died. The Spandau at the other window momentarily fell silent as a fresh ammunition belt was inserted. Cordite fumes swirled in the room. Ritter fired again, and a third Russian fell. The light from the flare faded, and instantly Ritter's men ceased firing. The muzzle flashes from Russian burp guns winked in the darkness, marking targets, but the Germans held their fire until Ritter's second flare burst in the air.

The Russians were falling back, breaking off the attack. Ritter's machine gunners held their fire, conserving ammunition, while the men with rifles picked off stragglers. Ritter raised his own carbine and began to search out Russians who had found cover among the rubble and were not retreating. Each time he fired a man died, he never missed. Not once.

The second flare died, and darkness closed in again. As his men stopped firing, Ritter became aware of the sound of battles raging in other parts of Gorodnitza. The Russians were pressing hard all along the line. The lanky youth who handled the ammunition for the Spandau was laughing excitedly, almost hysterically. He was a replacement fresh from training camp, and this was his first night action.

"We showed the Popovs, didn't we, Max," he burbled.

"Sure, kid," the veteran answered. "But they'll be back. You can count on it. And this time they'll know what to expect. You can only surprise Ivan once."

Ritter turned away from the window and went downstairs to check with Meyer. His hands were shaking, whether from adrenaline or fear he didn't know. It had not happened to him in a long time.

"Stabs'?"

"Yes, Herr Hauptmann."

Meyer's shadowy bulk detached itself from the darkness and moved into the faint light coming in through a window. He carried a machine pistol. The radioman crouched at another window, a carbine cradled in his arms.

"How did we weather the storm?" Ritter said.

"Okay, I think, Herr Hauptmann. I can check the casualties, if you want."

"No," Ritter said, nervously lighting a cigarette. "It makes no difference. The orders are to stand and hold."

"*Achtung, Zigarette!*" the radioman called out as Ritter moved in front of the window without shielding the glow of his cigarette.

Ritter cursed himself silently for his carelessness. He wondered suddenly if he was losing his grip. He had seen it happen to better men.

"They'll be coming again soon, Herr Hauptmann," Meyer prompted quietly.

"Right," Ritter said and walked back to the stairs, his boots crunching on the spent cartridges from Meyer's machine pistol.

Five minutes later, the Russians attacked again — hundreds of them. This time the assault was supported by heavy machine guns firing from concealed positions on the riverbank. Ritter winced as bullets chewed up the window frame beside him, and he had to fight down the urge to duck out of the line of fire. But he continued to shoot into the oncoming waves of Russian troops as fast as he could work the bolt of his carbine. They were mowing down the Russians in droves.

"Oorah! Oorah! Ooorah!" On and on they came, directly into the guns of Ritter's company. The men held their ground, firing coldly and efficiently, but here and there a German rifle fell silent as a random Russian bullet found its mark.

Ritter fired flare after flare. Russian bodies covered the ground outside, but more kept coming; there seemed to be no end to them, and Ritter could detect a slackening of his company's defensive fire as more of his men were hit. The boy feeding the Spandau spun onto his back with a gurgling cry and flopped about on the floor, a crimson jet of blood spurting from his torn jugular.

"Herr Hauptmann, the belt!" the machine gunner yelled, ignoring the boy's death throes and continuing to fire controlled, deadly bursts.

Ritter sent up another flare and rushed to the gunner's side. He dragged aside the boy's body and helped the gunner load a fresh belt of ammunition. As the gunner opened fire again, Ritter remained beside him to be sure the belt was feeding smoothly. Outside on the killing ground, the attacking waves of assault troops had coalesced into one great mass that now surged forward in a final, desperate attempt to close with the Germans slaughtering them.

Ritter's throat was raw and burning, and his ears rang from the unremitting din. Suddenly the Spandau fell silent, and the gunner slumped to the floor, a neat round hole punched in the front of his helmet just above the rim. Ritter pulled the gun from the dead man's grasp and jumped to his feet. Cradling the machine gun in his arms, he pressed the trigger and held it down, firing into the mass of charging Russians.

His whole body shook with the recoil of the gun, which jumped and bucked in his arms like a wild beast. Ritter, himself, was a beast with bared teeth, bellowing at the top of his lungs, his voice lost in a crescendo of grenade explosions as the attacking wave, its ranks decimated, broke against the company line. Ritter saw one Russian directly below him hurl a grenade an instant before Ritter shot him down.

Two seconds later, the floorboards beneath Ritter's feet jumped as the grenade exploded in the room below. "Meyer!" Ritter cried. "Meyer!"

Suddenly it was over; the attack was broken. The sound of gunfire sputtered and died in a scatter of isolated shots as darkness reasserted itself and blotted out the scene of slaughter. Ritter ran for the stairs. "Meyer!" he shouted again, but there was no answer. He stumbled down the stairs to the ground floor and swept the room with his flashlight.

Dust from the grenade explosion swirled in the faint yellow beam. The radioman's body lay sprawled beneath one window, his helmet thrown back and dripping blood and brains. Ritter heard a thumping sound from the opposite corner of the room, and he swung around. Meyer was still alive. He lay on his back, his remaining eye rolling wildly. Grenade splinters had torn out his other eye and had ripped open his abdomen. Bloody excrement squelched from his torn intestines with every breath he took. The thumping was the agonized pounding of Meyer's fist on the floor. Ritter came across the room and knelt beside him.

"Help me," Meyer gasped.

"I can't," Ritter choked out.

"Please! For God's sake, do it!"

Thump, thump, thump, thump. For Ritter, the insistent pounding of Meyer's fist was worse than the sound of screaming.

"Please!"

Ritter reached for Meyer's machine pistol lying on the floor nearby. The floor began to vibrate, and from outside came the roar of a tank engine. A scatter of cheers drifted in through the windows as the survivors of Ritter's company greeted the arrival of a Tiger tank that had been sent up at last to support them.

Ritter's fingers closed on the cold steel of Meyer's gun, and he picked it up. Tears flooded his eyes and ran down his cheeks as he worked the bolt. Meyer heard the snick of the bolt, and the thumping of his fist stopped. Something like a sigh escaped the dying man's lips. Ritter placed the gun muzzle close to the back of his friend's head, closed his eyes, and pulled the trigger.

Ritter stumbled as he descended a rubble-choked flight of stairs leading down into the cellar of a gutted department store, in which Ritter's commanding officer, Major Bernheim, had set up his command post. Ritter had snatched three hours of sleep before the runner from Battalion had found him, but he was still numb with fatigue. He paused at the bottom of the steps to allow his eyes to adjust to the gloom, and then advanced down a narrow passageway toward a glimmer of light, ignoring the scrabbling sound of rats scurrying out of his path.

At the end of the passage was a doorway screened by a crude burlap curtain. He pulled aside the curtain and entered a dank, dimly lit storeroom. As he stepped through the doorway, he collided with a girl with straw-colored hair, who brushed by him and hurried away, her diminutive form swallowed up in a Wehrmacht overcoat. She was weeping.

Major Bernheim stood behind a makeshift desk of wooden planks supported by empty ammunition cases. The room was illuminated by a sputtering candle on the desk and a gasoline lamp-heater on the concrete floor, its reflector aimed at Bernheim's feet. The major was a tall, scrawny man with close-cropped, bristly gray hair, an undershot chin and a great beak of a nose. His ability, age and experience should have made him at least a colonel, but his unbridled tongue had cost him the chance of promotion. Ritter approached the desk and snapped to attention.

"I suppose you're wondering about the girl," Bernheim said.

"Herr Major?"

"Brought her with me from Korosten. Didn't want to leave her behind. I suppose I'll have to now, though; the Field Police are getting edgy. She'll be all right; she's undoubtedly a Red Army spy. Why else would she stick with an ugly old buzzard like me, eh?"

Ritter blinked tiredly, wondering why he'd been summoned. Bernheim picked up a sheet of paper and handed it to Ritter, who stared at it listlessly. The print was difficult to read in the dim light, and his eyes refused to focus.

"Wake up," Bernheim said impatiently. "That's your ticket home. It came in two hours ago, and I sent a runner for you the first chance I got. I didn't want you to get killed now that you can get the hell out of here."

At last the words on the paper swam into focus, and Ritter stared at them in disbelief. The paper was an order transferring him back to the Brandenburg's 5th Regiment in Germany. Attached to the transfer was an order for Ritter to proceed directly to Berlin to report in person to Admiral Canaris, chief of the Abwehr, German Military Intelligence.

Originally, the Brandenburg commando force had been created

as a single battalion under the control of the Abwehr's Sabotage Section; but the demands of the war had swelled the Brandenburg force to division strength, and command of the division had been taken away from Military Intelligence. Now, only the 5th Regiment was still controlled by the Abwehr.

"I don't understand, Herr Major," Ritter said dazedly. "Why should the admiral send for me? I've never even seen him."

"Your guess is as good as mine, but don't look a gift horse in the mouth. I hate to see you go, Ritter; I'll have the devil of a time replacing you."

"Thank you, Herr Major."

"Before you go, I do have a bit of advice for you."

Bernheim crossed the room and looked out into the passage, to make sure no one was within earshot.

"I just received a message from Heinz. They're going to try again."

Bernheim's words cut through the fatigue clouding Ritter's mind; suddenly he was fully alert.

"How do they intend to do it?"

"A bomb again — in fact the same bomb that was planted on Hitler's plane in Smolensk. They think they know why it failed to explode that time, and they've replaced the fuses."

"When?"

"I don't know. I only know that a staff officer named von Stauffenberg is pushing for another attempt as soon as possible. This time I'm staying clear of it, and my advice to you is to do the same. Canaris has managed to protect this amateur conspiracy for longer than I would have thought possible, but he's skating on very thin ice now. The Gestapo has arrested Oster and two other Abwehr officers in Berlin."

"What!"

"They're holding them on trumped-up charges — some sort of currency offenses — because they can't prove treason, but that may just be a matter of time. I don't think the Gestapo suspects Canaris, himself, but one false step and the old fox is finished. Stay clear of it, Ritter. It's too late now, anyway. What difference will it make if we do manage to kill the Führer? We're fighting on the Sluch River now, but it won't be long before we're fighting on the Oder. Ivan won't quit just because we rid ourselves of Hitler."

As if to emphasize Bernheim's point, a clutch of mortar shells exploded nearby, rocking the cellar command post. Dirt rained down from the low ceiling and drifted into their eyes. Bernheim irritably brushed away the debris that had fallen onto his desk and growled, "I thought we were out of range of their mortars. They must have forced a bridgehead on this side of the river. We won't be holding this city much longer. It's a hell of a way to start nineteen forty-four."

"What about my men, Herr Major?"

Ritter and Bernheim ducked involuntarily as a howling shell slammed into the ruins above them with a deafening explosion.

"They'll be absorbed by Second Company," Bernheim said, coughing in the dust-filled air. "Dorn!" he yelled. "Where the hell is everybody? Dorn!" A door to an adjoining room flew open, and Bernheim's radioman and two runners rushed in. "Start packing up," Bernheim ordered. "We're going to have to move back."

"My men could use a rest, Herr Major," Ritter said quickly. "Just a day or two out of the line."

Bernheim's only answer was a bitter, twisted smile and a shake of his head.

"I have a motorcycle waiting for you outside — if it's still in one piece. The driver will take you as far as Rovno. Hang on to your orders, Ritter, and be sure your equipment is in order. The MPs are shooting deserters first and asking questions afterwards. Now, get the hell out of here before the Popovs take back their city."

Ritter saluted and left the command post. Outside he spotted the motorcycle driver sheltering with his machine under the entrance arch of a bombed-out building across the street. The driver was watching a cat tear flesh from the hand of a corpse buried beneath a mound of ice-glazed bricks.

"Let's go," Ritter yelled to the man.

The driver kicked the starter and drove the motorcycle out into the street. Ritter jumped into the BMW's sidecar just as a fresh round of mortar shells began falling in the street fifty yards behind them, throwing up gouts of frozen mud and snow. The driver popped the clutch, and Ritter's head snapped back as the motorcycle shot forward.

Ritter didn't need to tell the driver to step on it; the man drove as if the Devil himself were behind them. With the machine in low gear and the throttle wide open, they raced through the city, careening around corners and swerving madly to avoid the knots of haggard infantrymen trudging up from the rear to be thrown into the disintegrating German line.

On the outskirts of Gorodnitza, motorized units were already preparing to withdraw, but in the confusion of wood and straw hovels surrounding the town, their vehicles had become locked in a hopeless traffic jam. The driver gunned the engine and shot through the gaps between stalled lines of vehicles and the snowbanks bordering the twisting streets. They cleared the traffic jam, swerved around a clapped-out Russian Tatra truck carrying German wounded to the rear, and raced out onto the rutted highway of frozen snow leading west away from Gorodnitza.

Ritter heard the hum of approaching aircraft and twisted around to look up into the gray sky behind them. A flight of Ilyushin fighter bombers broke out of the cloud cover to the east and swept in on a bombing run, diving straight for the tangle of tanks and half-tracks on the edge of the city. Seconds later, thundering explosions ripped through the mass of armor and helpless men. The Russian planes screamed low over Ritter's head, climbed steeply and disappeared back into the clouds.

The motorcycle sped on down the road, out into the limitless, white expanse of the Ukraine. As he was carried away from the hopeless battle, Ritter felt no relief at all, only bitterness.

At Rovno, Ritter was issued a fresh uniform and new boots; and after a thorough delousing, he received what he needed most: eight hours of uninterrupted sleep. When he boarded a west-bound train the following day, he was clean and free of lice for the first time in months.

There was little joy to be seen in the faces of the officers and enlisted men boarding the train. They were going home on leave, but it would only be a brief respite before they returned to the Eastern Front and to a war that was lost. Even their new uniforms bore mute testimony to Germany's dwindling strength. The material was rough and of poor quality, and the new boots were made of cheap, brittle leather that cracked as soon as it was flexed.

Ritter slept through much of the slow, halting journey out of Russia into Poland, caring nothing for the bleak, wintry landscape sliding past the window. Once, just south of the Pripet River, the train was stopped by an SS unit pursuing partisans into the desolate Pripet marshes. One hundred enlisted men were summarily ordered off the train and pressed into a bloody attack on a partisan group trapped two miles from the railway line. Three hours later, sixty of those men returned, and the train moved on.

As Ritter was carried westward and the Front began to lose its grip on him, his thoughts turned to Major Bernheim's warning and to what might await him in Berlin. While at the Front, Ritter had been drawn into a military-civilian conspiracy to overthrow Hitler, a conspiracy in which Admiral Canaris's Abwehr was deeply involved. For years, Canaris had used his power as Hitler's intelligence chief to cloak the conspirators in a protective mantle of secrecy, without which they could not have survived in the Nazi police state. General Oster, Canaris's chief of staff, had been the driving force behind the Abwehr's participation in the German Resistance; but with Oster arrested, it was possible that Canaris, himself, was assuming a more active role.

Ritter did not know why he had been summoned to Abwehr headquarters by Canaris, but Bernheim had hit on an obvious possibility. Although Bernheim had been told that a bomb was to be used in the renewed attempt on Hitler's life, both he and Ritter knew why Ritter might have been singled out from among the many line officers connected with the Resistance: Ritter was an expert sniper.

Bernheim had warned him to stay out of it for good reason. Oster's arrest could only mean that the Gestapo net was closing. It was a question of who would strike first, the conspirators or the Gestapo. Ritter asked himself what he would do if Canaris wanted him to strike the blow upon which a coup d'etat depended, but he had no answer. He would not know until the time came.

The troop train pulled into Lublin station in the dead of night. Commands barked over loudspeakers greeted the groggy, gray-faced soldiers stumbling out of the train onto the platform. The enlisted men were formed into lines and marched into a great hall at one end of the station. On an adjacent track, an eastbound train was being loaded with fresh-faced boys in their early teens. Some of them looked dazed, but most of the boys were excited — particularly the Hitler Youth contingents.

A Wehrmacht officer, who happened to be walking down the platform alongside Ritter, shook his head. "Jesus, look at them. Babies. Most of them won't survive their first battle."

Inside the hall, the veterans were greeted warmly by young women in Wehrmacht uniform, who smilingly pressed little packages of food into their hands. Most of the men tucked the presents into their packs to save for their families at home. Ersatz coffee and spoonfuls of jam were dispensed in great quantities, and gradually some luster returned to the tired soldiers' vacant eyes. They were going home, if only for a short time, but they were going home.

At the far end of the hall there was a sudden bustle of activity, and an officer climbed up onto an improvised platform. He picked up a microphone, and his amplified, metallic voice cut through the babble of five hundred voices.

"*Achtung, achtung! Achtung, achtung!* All men with leave papers are to return to their units at once. All leaves have been canceled. I repeat, all leaves have been canceled."

A disbelieving, shocked hush fell over the hall, followed by a rising swell of protest. Military Police appeared from nowhere and waded into the angry crowd; and German march music suddenly blared from the loudspeakers, drowning out the angry shouts of the soldiers. Some of the younger men were unable to hold back their tears, but most of the veterans just gritted their teeth in bitter resignation as the MPs roughly herded them back into lines and marched them out of the hall — this time onto the platform where the child-soldiers were boarding the train bound for the Front.

Ritter worked his way to the edge of the crowd, showed his orders to a suspicious MP, and was waved off to one side. In a matter of minutes, the MPs cleared the hall and loaded the waiting train. *Sieg Heil*, Ritter thought bitterly as he watched the train pull out of the station. *Sieg Heil*.

SEVEN

Ritter awoke with a start to the shriek of a locomotive whistle. He straightened up and disentangled himself from a lieutenant sleeping beside him. The ragged snores of his fellow officers in the crowded compartment continued unabated as the troop train jerked forward and began to crawl over a final stretch of track into Berlin's Silesian Station. The troop train had been stalled for hours in the early-morning darkness, awaiting repair crews to replace the rails torn up by the night's British air raid.

The air in the compartment smelled of stale cigarette smoke and closely packed bodies, and the stuffy atmosphere had given Ritter a dull, throbbing headache. He needed fresh air. He checked his watch to be sure it was past dawn, stood up and pulled down the window, which had been painted over for the blackout. The sight that greeted him was worse than he had expected.

With each succeeding air raid, the destruction had been spreading out from Berlin's rail centers in ever-widening circles, and for blocks and blocks around the station, buildings had been blasted flat or gutted by fire. A pall of smoke hung over the city, darkening an already overcast sky, and the smell of wood smoke tainted the cold, moist air streaming in through the window. Ritter shivered slightly and closed the window. He had no family, and his friends had all fallen in combat; for Ritter, it was a cheerless homecoming.

Minutes later, the train pulled into the station. Ritter wound his way through the milling crowds of soldiers and emerged from the station just in time to press his way onto a bus jammed with soldiers and civilians bound for the center of Berlin. As the bus passed through street after street lined with heaps of rubble that had once been apartment buildings, private homes, and stores, depression settled over him.

Tacked to gateposts and doorways in front of bombed-out apartments were countless scraps of paper bearing names and addresses, so that friends and relatives could locate the survivors. Seeing them, Ritter thought of Loni, a girl with long, blond hair and laughing eyes, whom he had met in Berlin two years before, during a two-week furlough. Their affair had been as intense as his leave had been short, but her letters had stopped coming a long time ago. He could try to find her by going to her old address, but he put the thought aside. He didn't want to know why her letters had stopped.

As the bus passed a high school, Ritter watched a group of schoolboys in the yard behind the building. They weren't playing. Dressed in oversized Wehrmacht uniforms, they were readying a flak battery for the American daylight raid that would come in the early afternoon. Flak guns were everywhere — in the schoolyards, on terraces and in the parks, and they took their toll of enemy aircraft; but they couldn't stop the waves of bombers that pounded Berlin day and night.

Ritter got off the bus at a stop in downtown Berlin and walked toward the Tirpitz-Ufer, a street running along the old Landwehr Canal. Large, delicate snowflakes had begun to float lazily down from the smoky sky, melting as they touched the wet pavement, which had been warmed by a mid-January thaw. It was a relief to stretch his legs after days of sitting in a cramped railroad-car compartment.

As he rounded the corner onto the Tirpitz-Ufer, he saw that buildings all along the Landwehr Canal had been bombed out, but the old, three-story apartment building that housed Abwehr headquarters was still undamaged. Ritter quickened his pace, suddenly anxious to have his interview with Canaris over and done with. He showed his orders and paybook to the sentry at the entrance and was passed through.

The ground floor of Abwehr headquarters was a maze of corridors connecting rooms of varying size and shape that had been converted into overcrowded offices. From all directions came the clatter of typewriters and the ringing of telephones. After being cleared by the duty officer, Ritter had to ask directions twice more before he finally located the ancient elevator in the rear of the building which took him directly up to Canaris's office on the top floor.

It was hot and stuffy in the elevator, and Ritter unbuttoned his overcoat. He wiped away a trace of perspiration on his upper lip, wondering whether it was due to the heat or to his growing nervousness. A part of him looked forward to meeting Canaris, for Germany's spymaster was something of a legend; but that feeling was overshadowed by wariness. He still did not know the reason behind his strange recall from the Front.

The rickety elevator jerked to a stop, and Ritter stepped out into the anteroom to Canaris's office, the door to which was flanked by two middle-aged secretaries at work at their desks.

"May I help you, Herr Hauptmann?" said one of the women, looking up from her typewriter.

"My name is Ritter. I was ordered to report to Admiral Canaris."

The secretary nodded and pressed an intercom switch. "There is a Hauptmann Ritter to see you, Herr Admiral."

"Ritter? *Ach,* of course. Please ask him to come in," came the response from the intercom.

"You may go in, Herr Hauptmann," the secretary said with a smile and gestured toward the door.

Ritter knocked once and opened the door. Admiral Canaris was seated at his desk, but he rose as Ritter entered the office. Ritter walked briskly forward, snapped to attention and started to salute, but Canaris forestalled him by coming around from behind the desk and extending his hand.

"Welcome home, Hauptmann Ritter," Canaris said, grasping Ritter's hand and looking up at him with a friendly smile.

"Thank you, Herr Admiral."

Ritter towered over Canaris. The lines around the little admiral's eyes and mouth that years of tension had etched into his face made him look older than his fifty-eight years. His blue eyes were alert and probing, and Ritter suspected they learned more than they gave away.

"Take off that coat, son," Canaris said, returning to his chair behind the desk. "You don't want to catch a cold when you go back outside. This is the worst season for colds. Your first name is Erich, isn't it?"

"Yes, Herr Admiral," Ritter said, bemused by Canaris's informal, fatherly manner.

"Well, sit down, Erich," Canaris said, gesturing toward a worn leather chair beside his desk. "We don't stand on ceremony around here. In the old days I used to know all my Brandenburg officers, but I don't need to tell you that times have changed. Cigar?"

"No, thanks, Herr Admiral."

Canaris selected a cigar from a box on his desk and lit up. During the short silence, Ritter glanced about the Spartan office. Besides the desk and a few chairs, there was a single file cabinet and a steel safe. The rug at the base of the file cabinet was badly stained where Canaris's dachshund had used the file cabinet as a substitute for a tree. In one corner stood a military cot, which Canaris used for occasional naps. On the wall, opposite the desk, hung a large map of the world; and a photograph of Count Nicolai, the World War I chief of the Abwehr, hung above the mantelpiece of a small fireplace. There was no photograph of the Führer.

The only personal touches in the office were on Canaris's desk:

a model of the cruiser *Dresden,* on which he had served as intelligence officer in World War I, and the small bronze figures of three monkeys mounted on a stone base. One monkey was shading his eyes, peering into the distance; the second monkey held his paw cupped to his ear, listening; and the third held his paw over his mouth. They symbolized Canaris's watchwords for his Abwehr: watch, listen, and keep silent.

Canaris took several puffs on his cigar and looked at Ritter through a thin veil of blue smoke. Strangely, Canaris's frankly appraising eyes did not make Ritter uncomfortable.

"Of course you're wondering why I sent for you," Canaris said.

"Yes, Herr Admiral," Ritter said, tensing slightly.

"I need a man to do a very special job for me — a man with special qualifications. He must be a line officer; he must be a genuine expert with small arms and the techniques of unarmed combat; he must be physically fit and Aryan in appearance; and, finally, he must be an anti-Nazi. That last requirement, as you can imagine, considerably restricted our search. Only one file came to my desk for consideration. Your file."

Ritter could not refrain from interrupting with the question uppermost in his mind. "Does this have anything to do with Operation Flash, Herr Admiral?"

Canaris looked momentarily surprised, but then he nodded in understanding. "I see. Naturally that would occur to you. No, Erich, this job has nothing to do with a rerun of Operation Flash. At this point, even if I weren't convinced that it is too late for a putsch, there would be very little I could do to help. I will have enough difficulty keeping the Gestapo from hanging Oster and his two friends. For that matter, it wouldn't surprise me if the Gestapo has already measured my neck for a noose, as well; and that is why the job I want you to do for me must be done quickly, while I'm still in control of the Abwehr.

"It concerns a secret Action Group that is being formed within the SS. Himmler has given the group's leaders a blank check, and they are authorized to draw upon the full resources of the SD, the Gestapo and the Waffen-SS. The group's mission is to carry on the war after the final collapse of Germany's organized military resistance. Himmler has visions of fanatical guerrilla bands, called Werewolves, fighting on to the death, even after Germany is occupied."

"But that's absurd, Herr Admiral. After a military collapse, guerrillas would have no safe haven from which to launch attacks, no outside source of supply. Sustained guerrilla action would simply not be possible."

"I quite agree. Himmler, of course, is a fool; and Goebbels, who has also seized on the idea, is interested in it only as propaganda. He is constantly seeking fresh propaganda to bolster public morale, and once the Allied ring begins to tighten around us, he'll start broadcasting threats of guerrilla war. Unfortunately, there is more to Action Group Werewolf than either Himmler or Goebbels realize. One of our contacts in the SS — a high-ranking officer in the SD — has discovered that the Werewolf plan Himmler has endorsed is merely camouflage. It is a cover for an entirely different operation which Himmler knows nothing about. The Action Group is preparing to carry on the war after formal hostilities have ceased, but not by means of guerrilla warfare. The officers involved are a tightly knit, determined group, using Himmler to their own ends, and their actual plan is known only to them."

"But what could they possibly have in mind, Herr Admiral? They must be crackpots."

"I wish I could believe that. I only know the identity of one of the SD officers in the Action Group, but that is enough to worry me. He is a middle-echelon officer who was recruited by Heydrich, and he is cast in Heydrich's mold: ruthless, fanatical, and highly intelligent. He is not the sort of man to waste his time with crackpot schemes."

"Is it possible that these officers are just organizing an escape to neutral territory before they're caught in the trap, Herr Admiral?"

Canaris shook his head. "I don't think that's it. Our contact is convinced that Action Group Werewolf is preparing to carry on the war. Consider the cover they have chosen; it's perfect for their purpose. When the Allies march into Germany and discover that Werewolf guerrillas were never anything but empty propaganda, the Occupation Forces will laugh off any references to Werewolf that might turn up in interrogations or in captured SS documents. The Action Group's leaders have chosen the best way to hide: by parading before the world in a clown's mask."

Canaris crushed out his half-smoked cigar in an ashtray. "Something is brewing, and my instinct tells me that it's dangerous."

Absently, Canaris picked up a fresh cigar and lit it. Ritter could see that Canaris no longer smoked for pleasure; he smoked for the same reason as did the men at the Front: to keep a grip on his nerves. The admiral had walked the tightrope of high treason for too long.

"I want to send you into their camp," Canaris said. "I want you to penetrate Werewolf and discover the men behind it and what they are up to."

Ritter tried to ignore the warning of his own instinct, a sense of hidden danger he had only experienced behind enemy lines. He didn't ask Canaris how he was expected to penetrate Werewolf; he waited for the admiral to tell him.

"The group's leaders may be clever," Canaris said, "but they have already made one mistake: they approached our contact. He was asked to help recruit specialists for the group, Waffen-SS officers who are experts with small arms and the techniques of unarmed combat. I intend to provide them with a candidate."

"You want me to impersonate an SS officer, Herr Admiral?"

"Only if you agree. There is some danger, and it must be your decision."

"I still don't see . . ." Ritter broke off, unsure if he should put his thoughts into words.

Canaris smiled tiredly. "You were about to say that you don't see why I'm concerned about a handful of SS fanatics with some half-baked, desperate scheme for salvaging the Final Victory."

"Yes, Herr Admiral, that's the gist of it."

Abruptly, Canaris pushed back his chair and stood up. "Come with me. I have something I want you to see."

Puzzled, Ritter rose and followed Canaris through a side door that connected the office with a small conference room. A film projector rested on one end of the long conference table, and a projection screen had been erected at the opposite end of the room.

"You are about to see a film prepared for the SS archives," Canaris said. "I obtained it from the same man who warned us about Werewolf. This film was shot at one of the SD concentration camps in Poland, K.L. Auschwitz, and I warn you that even your front-line experience will not have prepared you for what you are about to witness. I have already seen the film. Forgive me if I do not stay to see it again."

Canaris switched on the projector, and a series of numbers appeared on the screen as the film leader was fed past the projector lens. Canaris left the room, turning off the ceiling light and closing the door behind him. A moment later the first frame flashed onto the screen, and Ritter began a visual descent into hell.

Three interminable, horrifying minutes later, the film ended with a shot of an SD officer turning away from the slaughter to smile and wave at the camera. For several seconds Ritter continued to stare blindly at the bright, blank rectangle of light on the screen as the projector whirred on, the free end of the film slapping against the projector housing. He swallowed, trying to clear the taste of bile from his throat, and turned off the projector. He stayed alone in the darkness for a moment longer to steady himself and then opened the door and reentered Canaris's office.

The admiral was standing beside a window overlooking the Landwehr Canal, watching the snow falling into the black water below. He turned away from the window and looked at Ritter.

"My God," Ritter said hoarsely, "I didn't think men could . . . I didn't think such things were possible."

"Sit down, Erich," Canaris said.

Ritter walked numbly to the chair beside Canaris's desk and sat down. Canaris, who remained standing, waited until some of the shock left Ritter's eyes before he spoke again.

"That film is over a year old, and the scenes of slaughter are outdated. Machine-gun fire is not as efficient as gas, and the SS prizes efficiency. They are much more efficient now. In that camp alone they gas to death two thousand men, women and children each and every day. It is our Führer's final solution to the Jewish Problem."

"Two thousand? It's not possible."

"Not possible?" Canaris said harshly. "It's not only possible, it's happening right now." Canaris had begun to pace restlessly, and as he became progressively more agitated, a lisp crept into his speech. "This war will not end until the Allies have ground us into the dust, and Germany may never recover; but whatever happens, not a trace — not one spore — of the Nazi fungus can be allowed to survive. If there is only one chance in a million that Action Group Werewolf has a viable plan to preserve the spores of Nazism, that chance is too great."

Canaris paused and returned to his chair behind the desk. When he spoke again, his voice was firm and insistent. "I must know what is behind Werewolf."

Ritter struggled to regain his mental equilibrium. Random scenes from the ghastly film continued to flash before his eyes.

"I want you to become the Waffen-SS officer Werewolf is so anxious to recruit," Canaris continued. "You have the physical characteristics, the combat skills, and the combat experience that are required. Once we have prepared you for the role, our contact will submit your name to the Action Group for consideration. With the record we will provide you, they won't be able to turn you down. Once you discover the Werewolf plan and the identity of a few of the key men, we'll pull you out. I'll do the rest.

"All I need are a few names, Erich — names to whisper in Himmler's ear. Our Reichsführer-SS guards his power jealously. If he discovers that a group of his officers has been conspiring behind his back — for whatever reason — his reaction will be swift. He will eliminate Werewolf for us. If it turns out that the Action Group is nothing to worry about, then we'll let sleeping dogs lie."

Ritter started to speak, but Canaris held up his hand.

"I don't want your answer until you have heard me out. I said this could be dangerous, and I was not exaggerating. The men you will be dealing with are fanatics, and by going behind Himmler's back, they have chosen to play a very dangerous game. Their lives are on the line. If you should make a slip, or if something in official records should betray you, I don't think they would hesitate to kill you out of hand. The Action Group has access to the full investigative apparatus of the SD and the Gestapo, and we must expect them to run an extensive check on any potential recruit, so your cover must be airtight.

"You will not simply impersonate an SS officer, you will become one.

"Agents from our Section Three will pull every last one of your military and civilian records — birth certificate, school records, church confirmation — the lot. Officially, you will cease to exist. We will prepare an entirely new personal history for you, staying as close to the truth as possible, but making certain that your racial history qualifies you for the SS. Our agents will insert the false records in files wherever they are needed — including SS and SD files. You will be provided with an immaculate Waffen-SS service record consistent with your actual abilities and combat experience. Waffen-SS units will be selected which have suffered one-hundred-percent losses, to minimize problems with 'old comrades.' You will become an SS captain — Hauptsturmführer Erich Ritter, and no one will be able to prove you are not the man you claim to be. Absolutely no one.

"In the meantime, you will be trained by specialists from Section Two. They will drill you day and night until you can talk, act and think like an SS officer. Not until the transformation is complete will we have our SS contact submit your name to the Action Group."

"And when the masquerade is over, Herr Admiral?"

"We will reverse the process and restore your identity to you. You must understand that the forged documents will be indistinguishable from genuine records, and only I have the power to issue the orders necessary to reverse the process. Your identity will be entirely in my hands."

Ritter's throat went dry as the implications of Canaris's words sunk in. Ritter had no living relatives, nor anyone else whose testimony could stand against the evidence of a complete set of official records. If Canaris should die — of a heart attack or in an air raid — Ritter would remain forever the SS officer Canaris had made him.

Canaris, watching Ritter's expression, nodded slowly. "Now you understand it all. I wouldn't go to such extremes if I didn't think it was necessary. Will you do it?"

Ritter understood, and he understood as well why Canaris had shown him the SS film. Canaris had shown him a glimpse of the horror of a world under SS control. Even as he hesitated to give his final answer, he knew he had no choice. He looked into Canaris's world-weary but unyielding eyes and nodded.

"When do we begin, Herr Admiral?"

"Today."

Dressed in the black uniform of the SS, Ritter sat on a cot in a three-room air-raid bunker in the cellar of Abwehr headquarters. He was trying to listen to his instructor, who was having difficulty making himself heard over the thunder of bomb explosions. The bunker was sealed off from the outside world by a pressure door, and the air in the reinforced-concrete shelter was hot, humid and laced with the pungent smell of a chemical toilet. High above, British Lancasters droned in on their bombing runs, heedless of the furious antiaircraft fire tearing at their formations.

The instructor's pale, scholarly face was coated with a sheen of sweat, and his watery eyes blinked furiously behind their spectacles as a wave of explosions swept toward the Tirpitz-Ufer. The shrill whistle of a falling bomb pierced the thick concrete walls of the bunker, cutting through the thundering crescendo of detonations, and the instructor stopped speaking and held his breath. Ritter gritted his teeth as the nerve-tearing whistle grew louder and louder. *This one is going to be close! It's going to be* . . .

Both men winced as the bomb exploded in the street in front of headquarters, rocking their shelter and blasting a huge crater in the pavement, but the succeeding bomb explosions diminished in intensity as the remaining bombs in the stick fell farther and farther away. The instructor swallowed with relief and wiped his shining forehead with a handkerchief.

"I suppose you're used to this sort of thing," he said to Ritter. "You must think me a coward."

Ritter shook his head. "No one gets used to it."

The instructor swallowed again and looked at his watch. It was just past midnight. "Are you tired?" he asked.

"Not yet. We can keep at it for a while longer."

"Good," the instructor said with an academic's satisfaction at a determined pupil. He opened a small black book and began to read aloud a series of questions. The book was the SS catechism.

"Why do we believe in Germany and the Führer?"

"Because we believe in God," answered Ritter. "We believe in Germany which He created and in the Führer whom He has sent us."

The instructor frowned.

"I thought I got that right," Ritter protested.

"The words were right, but not your tone. Himmler created these rituals in order to bind SS men together in a sacred cult with its own pseudo-traditions, mythology and rigid code of conduct. He lifted most of his ideas straight from the Order of the Jesuits. You may find this mumbo jumbo ridiculous, but you must cultivate a new attitude; you must create a new personality for yourself. In recent years, many SS recruits have ignored this crap, but not you, Ritter. You joined early — in nineteen thirty-eight — and you are a true believer.

"You received your ceremonial dagger in nineteen forty-one. That, in itself, is unusual. Very few officers of your rank ever receive that honor. You are proud, Ritter, remember that. Your physique and coloring fit the very top SS specifications. The ancestral tree we've manufactured for you is clean as a whistle all the way back to seventeen fifty; there's not a trace of non-Nordic blood. You are proud and you *believe*. I want to hear that in your voice — always."

"All right, I'll work on it. Let's have some more questions."

"Whom do we serve?"

"Our people and our Führer, Adolf Hitler."

"And why do we obey?"

"From inner conviction, from belief in Germany and the Führer, and from loyalty."

The questions went on and on amid the background rumble of bomb explosions and the *crack, crack, crack* of flak guns, and Ritter gave the answers he had learned by rote. For over a week, he had spent most of his waking hours in the bunker, cramming into his head the details of his bogus personal history and the bizarre rituals of the SS. The stark concrete walls of the bunker were covered with charts of the SS hierarchy, charts of the command structures of battle groups with which he had supposedly served, and with pictures of high-ranking SS officers he would be expected to recognize.

"Let's have the oath again," the instructor said. "You muffed it last time."

Ritter rubbed his eyes. He *was* beginning to tire. "I swear loyalty and bravery to you Adolf Hitler, as Führer and Chancellor of the German Reich. I vow obedience unto death to you and to the superiors whom you appoint. So help me God."

"Good," the instructor said with a smile. "I liked your tone of reverence. It was just right. Now, let's go over some dates. When is an SS candidate accepted as an applicant and first allowed to wear the SS uniform?"

"November ninth, the anniversary of the Munich beer cellar putsch."

"With or without collar patches?"

"Without."

"When do you receive collar patches?"

"When the cadet swears the oath: April twentieth, Hitler's birthday."

"No!" the instructor snapped. "Not 'Hitler'; never 'Hitler.' 'The Führer,' or 'Adolf Hitler.' Don't make a slip like that again. Remember, Hitler is a god and Himmler is his pope."

"Christ," Ritter groaned, falling back on the cot. "I've had it; let's call it a day."

The instructor nodded and began to collect his things. There was a metallic clank as the latch on the pressure door was turned, and a squat, jovial man with medical insignia on his Wehrmacht uniform came into the bunker. Ritter got up and stretched wearily.

"Burning the midnight oil while the Tommies burn Berlin, eh," the doctor said. "It's time for another session, Erich."

"We're through anyway," the instructor said. "He's doing well. Another day or two should wrap it up."

"You look tired," the doctor said to Ritter as the instructor left the bunker. "I'll put you under right away, and when I'm finished I'll leave you asleep. You'll have a good night's rest even with that racket going on outside. Take off your boots and stretch out on the cot."

Ritter pulled off his boots and settled himself on the cot, lying on his back, his hands at his sides. The doctor took out a gold pocket watch, sat down beside Ritter and began to swing the watch back and forth on its thin chain.

"You know the drill, Erich. Relax and keep your eyes on my watch. See how rhythmically it swings, in time with your pulse; it makes you drowsy. You're very sleepy."

"I'll say I am," Ritter muttered.

The doctor pursed his lips in annoyance. "Let's not waste time. Concentrate. Concentrate on the watch. Follow its swing."

Two minutes later, Ritter was in a deep hypnotic trance, and the doctor began the training session. He took out a small notebook and consulted a list of questions.

"You're asleep, Erich, but you can hear my voice. We are going to play the game. When you were on the Eastern Front, what unit were you with?"

"First Brigade, Ninth SS Panzer Division," Ritter answered, and the little finger on his left hand twitched spasmodically.

"Very good. Remember, when you are awake you can play this game any time you wish. We have given you a new personality and a new history to enable you to play the game. When you must give false information about yourself, you won't be lying, you'll just be playing the game; and to show that it's just a game, your little finger will twitch. We'll continue the game now. When did you join the SS?"

"In nineteen thirty-eight."

"When and where did you receive your commando training?"

"November, nineteen forty-two; Waffen-SS Special Training Course at Oranienburg."

The doctor continued the questioning for an hour, and then he let Ritter lapse into a deep sleep. He covered him with a blanket, turned off the overhead light and left the bunker.

The doctor from Section II had not been told why his subject was being given deep cover as an SS officer, and although it made no sense to him, he had not asked. Canaris had clamped a lid of secrecy on the case, and the doctor knew better than to ask unnecessary questions.

He had been glad of the opportunity to continue his experiments with hypnotic conditioning, but he doubted that there would be a follow-up. Only twice before had he seen deep-cover cases handled with such secrecy and thoroughness, and neither of those agents had ever returned.

.... EIGHT ....

SS–Hauptsturmführer Erich Ritter strode up the Prinz–Albrechtstrasse toward Gestapo headquarters, his polished jackboots shining in the bright winter sunlight. Pedestrians gave way to the arrogant blond officer wearing the sinister black uniform, who walked straight up the middle of the sidewalk as if he owned it. As he climbed the broad front steps to the entrance of the massive Gestapo building, a female clerk emerging from the building gave him an openly admiring glance. His eyes were hidden by aviator's sunglasses, but she saw the hint of disdain in the thin smile he gave her. She flushed and hurried past him.

He paused inside the entrance, removed his sunglasses and checked his watch. The message he had received at his hotel had instructed him to report to Room 205 at 1300 hours. He was right on time. He walked through the cavernous ground-floor hallway, past the padlocked elevator to the infamous cellar prison, to a wide stone staircase leading up to the second floor.

A long corridor ran the length of the second floor, lined on both sides with office doors. Anxious civilians huddled on wooden benches in the corridor, awaiting their turn to be interrogated. They averted their eyes at Ritter's approach. One old man in a threadbare coat cringed as Ritter strode by, like a dog expecting to be kicked.

At the very end of the corridor, Ritter found Room 205. There was no lettering on the door's frosted glass, only the number. He knocked sharply.

"*Herein!*" called a high, nasal voice from within.

Ritter opened the door and entered a windowless cubicle furnished only with a military desk and chair. Seated behind the desk was a fat, pink toad of a man stuffed into the gray uniform of an SD Standartenführer, a rank equivalent to an army colonel. The SD man's body was a soft mass of pink flesh, and his oversized head, covered with curls of fine, reddish-blond hair, seemed to have grown directly out from his thick, rounded shoulders without the benefit of a neck. His pale blue eyes protruded from between folds of fat.

Ritter saluted, and the SD officer languidly raised his arm in response. His wet, rubbery lips twitched into the semblance of a welcoming smile. "You are prompt, Hauptsturmführer. I am Standartenführer Werner, formerly of *Amt* Six, now attached to Action Group Werewolf."

Already on his guard, Ritter became even more wary. *Amt* VI was SD Counterintelligence; Werner would be no fool. "I've never heard of Action Group Werewolf, Herr Standartenführer," Ritter said.

"Nor should you have."

"May I ask the purpose of my recall from my combat unit?" Ritter said, with the arrogance of a man who held desk officers in contempt.

"You may ask," Werner said, and there was a long silence as the two men stared coldly at each other. Having made his point, Werner continued. "I appreciate your reluctance to leave your comrades at the Front, but you were recalled for a very special purpose. You have the honor of being considered for service in Action

Group Werewolf, an elite, top-secret unit. I have studied your service record carefully, and on paper, you have the qualifications we are seeking."

Ritter raised his eyebrows fractionally, but made no comment.

"This is an all-volunteer unit, and only those men serve with us who are absolutely dedicated to our unique mission. This is a preliminary interview, and you are completely free to refuse service with us and return to your unit at the Front."

From somewhere down the corridor, Ritter heard a man cry out, followed by a woman's short wail of despair. Werner appeared not to have noticed.

"How would you assess the progress of the war?" Werner asked abruptly.

"We are in an increasingly precarious position, Herr Standartenführer," Ritter responded in a neutral tone.

"Do you think the war is lost?"

Ritter returned Werner's unblinking stare. "We still have the Führer, Herr Standartenführer."

"But one man — no matter how inspired — can only do so much."

Ritter failed to respond, and there was another long silence.

"Well?" Werner prodded.

"I was not aware that your statement required a response, Herr Standartenführer."

Werner's lips managed to produce a smile. "I appreciate discretion, my dear Ritter. In fact, it is essential in the men we select. Still, there are times when one must speak frankly, and this is such a time. I am not testing your loyalty, I am testing your intelligence. Do-you-think-the-war-is-lost?"

"Of course it is lost, Herr Standartenführer."

Werner expelled his breath in a hiss of satisfaction and leaned back in his chair, his body's fat rippling as it rearranged itself.

"Given the inevitability of military defeat, Ritter, what do you intend to do?"

"Do, Herr Standartenführer? I intend to do my duty."

"Very commendable," Werner said dryly. "The difficulty is, of course, to determine precisely what one's duty is in such a situation. If you were given the opportunity to fight on after a military collapse, would you take it?"

"If you are referring to guerrilla warfare, Herr Standartenführer, I'm afraid I would not consider that a realistic option."

"Nor would I. I am suggesting something quite different — a prolonged, undercover struggle with a global strategy, the end of which we might not live to see."

Ritter put on a deliberate smile of condescension. Werner stared at him for a moment and then nodded.

"I understand your skepticism. You are obviously a realist — another trait we consider essential. But your skepticism will evaporate when you learn what we have in mind. The leaders of Action Group Werewolf are neither dreamers nor fools."

"Even intelligent men can do foolish things when they are desperate, Herr Standartenführer."

Werner compressed his lips impatiently. "You have not answered my question."

"Then I will answer it, Herr Standartenführer. If there were a genuine opportunity to carry on our struggle, I would seize it."

"Even if it meant taking action not sanctioned by the SS High Command?"

Ritter made it appear as if the question surprised him, and he did not answer immediately.

"The orders recalling me to Berlin were signed by the Reichsführer–SS, himself," Ritter said.

"Himmler has authorized the formation of Werewolf, but its true operational plan is known only to officers in the group. Our work is too important to suffer the interference of leaders who have brought us to the brink of disaster."

"And the Führer?"

"He has been betrayed no less than we," Werner said, his voice rising sharply. "It will be for his vision that we will continue to fight. We will never surrender. Never!"

Werner's body actually quivered with emotion, revealing some of the personal force that lay buried beneath the layers of fat.

"I have no taste for surrender either," Ritter said as fervently as he could. "Show me a way to continue the struggle, and I will fight to my last breath."

"We will show you the way, Ritter, believe me," Werner said, pushing a button on his desk. "You have already taken the first step."

The door to the office opened, and a plainclothes Gestapo agent appeared.

"This man will drive you to your hotel," Werner said to Ritter. "When you've collected your gear, he will take you to Tempelhof. A plane will be standing by to fly you to our indoctrination center outside of Munich. There you will learn more of Action Group Werewolf. *Heil Hitler.*"

"*Heil Hitler,*" Ritter responded, snapping out the Nazi salute. He turned and followed the Gestapo agent from the room.

As the door closed behind Ritter, Werner lifted the receiver of the phone on his desk. "This is Standartenführer Werner. Hauptsturmführer Ritter is to be allowed to leave; you may dismiss the arrest squad."

Ritter wriggled his toes and alternately tensed and relaxed his calf muscles to keep the circulation going in his cramped legs. After two hours in the light observation plane's unheated cockpit, he was shivering with cold.

"How much longer?" Ritter shouted to the pilot over the roar of the engine.

For an answer, the pilot banked the plane to the left and pointed. To the west Ritter saw a lonely airstrip on the snowy plain below. The pilot eased his stick forward, and Ritter's ears popped as the aircraft lost altitude. He began to massage his thighs vigorously; he didn't want to fall flat on his face when he tried to climb out of the cockpit.

The pilot circled the airstrip to check on its condition, and Ritter wondered how long it had been since it had been used. A tattered wind sock hung limply from a pole beside the runway, but there was no control tower, not even a radio shack. A lone military staff car was parked at the western end of the strip.

The pilot brought them down smoothly onto the runway and cautiously applied the brakes, wary of the possibility of ice on the snow-dusted tarmac. With the engine throttled back, he taxied down the strip and brought the plane to a stop thirty feet from the car.

"End of the line," the pilot said.

Ritter nodded, opened the cockpit door and jumped stiffly to the ground. He reached back in behind the seat and pulled out his kit bag. "Thanks for the ride," he yelled and slammed the door shut. The pilot waited for Ritter to get clear before he swung the plane around and ran the engine up to full throttle for takeoff. Ritter hunched his shoulders against the blast of propeller-driven snow and walked toward the car as the plane roared off down the runway.

An SS Scharführer had emerged from behind the wheel of the car and stood stiffly to attention as Ritter approached. He saluted Ritter, took his bag and opened the rear door for him. Ritter climbed in and was immediately enveloped in warm air from the car's heater. Without a word, the driver climbed in behind the wheel, put the car in gear and drove them away from the airstrip.

Five minutes later, the car came over a rise in the country road they were following, and Ritter saw a tiny farming village nestled in a hollow between three low hills. Tidy white-washed cottages with red tile roofs clustered about a church with a gilded steeple. As they approached the village, the taciturn driver slowed the car and pulled up in front of a cottage on the village outskirts. Smoke curled lazily up from its chimney. The driver switched off the engine, got out and opened the door for Ritter.

"This is it?" Ritter said in surprise. He had expected to be taken to an SS installation, not a country cottage.

"Yes, Herr Hauptsturmführer," the driver said in a gravelly voice.

Ritter shrugged and climbed out of the car. Carrying Ritter's bag, the driver led the way to the cottage's front door and entered without knocking. Ritter followed the driver through a narrow hall and up a creaking staircase to a tiny, low-ceilinged bedroom at the rear of the cottage.

"This is your room, Herr Hauptsturmführer," said the driver, setting down Ritter's bag on the floor beside a narrow, rustic bed. He saluted and left the room, closing the door behind him.

"What the hell?" Ritter muttered to himself, looking around the room. On the wall above the bed hung a crucifix, an odd ornament to find in an SS "Indoctrination Center." An enameled washbasin and a water pitcher rested on an antique bureau. Poking out from under the bed was a chamber pot.

Hoping that the cottage was not really as rustic as that, Ritter left the room in search of a bathroom. To his relief, he found one at the end of the hall and made prompt use of it. Then he went downstairs.

Hearing sounds from the front of the cottage, Ritter went to investigate. In the cottage's living room, he found a bulky, red-faced woman in a house dress and apron setting out a supper on an oaken table before an open hearth. The fire crackled softly.

"Ah, there you are, sir," the woman said with a wide, gap-toothed smile. "I was just about to call you. I thought you would be hungry. It's suppertime, you know."

"Thank you, Frau . . ."

"Frau Brecht, sir. I take care of all the young gentlemen who stay here."

"Are there others here now?"

"Oh, no, sir. You young gentlemen always come here one at a time. Now come sit here by the fire and have your supper. The Professor will be along shortly."

"The Professor?"

"Yes, sir. He'll be along shortly," she said, going to the windows to close the blackout drapes. Outside, darkness was falling. "*Guten Appetit*," she said cheerfully and left Ritter alone.

It was still early for supper, but when Ritter looked at the food on the table, his mouth watered. It was a black-market feast, with fruits and vegetables he had not seen in years. There was real butter — at least a quarter pound of it — and, incredibly, real coffee. The significance of this meal so casually presented to him did not escape Ritter, even as he greedily began to eat. It was a simple, but graphic demonstration of Action Group Werewolf's power.

"Good evening, Hauptsturmführer."

Ritter, who had been standing before the fire, smoking an after-dinner cigarette, turned and looked toward the door. A round-shouldered, potbellied elderly man in a rumpled tweed suit came into the room and carefully closed the door behind him.

"Good evening," Ritter said.

"I am Behrens," the man said, coming across the room to shake hands. His eyes blinked myopically at Ritter from behind round, rimless spectacles. "Professor Behrens. I'm in charge of indoctrination."

"Erich Ritter."

"Yes, yes. I've read over your record. Excellent. Shall we sit down?"

Behrens seated himself in one of the two armchairs flanking the fireplace and gestured for Ritter to sit opposite him. "Now, let me see," Behrens said distractedly. "I seem to have misplaced my pipe."

"In your pocket."

"What?"

"Your pipe. It's in your breast pocket."

"Ah, yes. Thank you."

Behrens patted his coat pockets, located his matches and tobacco, and began to stoke his pipe, spilling a good deal of tobacco into his lap in the process. Ritter wondered if his bumbling manner was a pose. Behrens looked like a caricature of the absent-minded professor. His bald head was fringed with unkempt tufts of gray hair that stuck out from his scalp in random directions. His vest, with one button missing, was streaked with gray smears of tobacco ash.

"You must be puzzled," Behrens said. "No doubt you expected to be taken to an SS military installation. Instead, you find yourself here, talking to a clapped-out professor."

"Impatient would be a better word," Ritter said. "My men are fighting at the Front while I sit on my backside eating black-market food. It's time I learned what this Action Group is all about. I am not interested in wasting time on what may be a fool's errand when my men are out there dying."

"Blood and iron, eh? Just what we need, my boy. The very reason we're interested in you — in addition to the special talents you possess."

"Let's cut the crap," Ritter said coldly. "Just who are you, and what's all this about?"

"Don't be fooled by appearances," Behrens said, dropping his jovial tone. "I am an SD officer, and I outrank you by a considerable margin."

Behrens struck a match and sucked furiously at his pipe until it was fully alight. Then he clamped the pipe into the corner of his mouth, sat back in his chair with a contented sigh and looked at Ritter. The firelight was reflected in his glasses, hiding his eyes, an effect Ritter found disconcerting.

"You know why you are here," Behrens said. "You are a candidate for service in Action Group Werewolf. Our mission is to win for Germany what now appears to be lost: Final Victory."

"How?"

"To understand that, you must first understand the origins of Werewolf. We must go back to the spring of 'forty-one. It was then that Reinhard Heydrich created Section L, a top-secret special unit of the SD.

"Section L was Heydrich's brainchild, the product of his highly original mind. Most men were terrified of Heydrich, so they misjudged him; but in his own way he was brilliant. It occurred to him that the combined efforts of economists, political scientists, psychologists and experts in related fields might be as effective in war as the efforts of teams of physicists and engineers, so he created Section L.

"The members of the section were recruited from universities, research institutes, and the business world. There are twenty of us in all, each of us personally recruited by Heydrich. Each man was a recognized expert in his own field, and each man was a dedicated Party member.

"Heydrich began by proposing to us specific problems to be solved, usually involving the manipulation and control of hostile populations in the occupied countries. But later he allowed us to go off on tangents of our own, and whenever we came up with a plan of action, he did his best to put it to the test. Europe became a laboratory in which to test our theories. It was exhilarating."

Behrens's pipe had gone out, and he paused to relight it. Spit gurgled in the bowl as he sucked on the stem.

"Heydrich's administration of Czechoslovakia is an excellent example. When the Führer first ordered him to Prague to clean up the mess there, the Czech Resistance was a nightmare for our Occupation Forces. Heydrich's own inclination was to try to crush the Resistance with overwhelming military force and to cow the population with a reign of terror, but we advised instead a two-pronged strategy.

"In addition to military action and harsh reprisals against proven supporters of the Resistance, we persuaded Heydrich to exploit the latent hostility of the Czech workers toward their ruling class, in order to win support for the Occupation. Following our recommendations, Heydrich instituted sweeping economic and social reforms, sharply upgrading the wages of workers and breaking down social barriers. At the same time, he proceeded ruthlessly against the Resistance. We were applying both the carrot and the stick. In a matter of months, Heydrich had the Czechs eating out of his hand.

"In the end, of course, it worked too well, and the British parachuted in those Czech assassins to kill Heydrich. His death was a tragedy for all Germany, but particularly for us in Section L. We lost our reason for existence.

"When Kaltenbrunner took over the SD after the assassination, he learned of Section L for the first time. He was determined to ape Heydrich in every possible way, but the brute has the mind of a vicious five-year-old, and he never understood our purpose or value. We continued to meet and to exchange ideas, but for a long time it was an empty exercise."

Behrens's thoughts seemed to drift away, and he turned to stare at the fire. "I admired Heydrich. He was both a man of action and a man of intellect — a rare combination. In all the time I knew him, I only heard him say one foolish thing. The Führer had just decided to annihilate European Jewry once and for all. It was a sensible decision, yet Heydrich had misgivings. He told me that he thought the idea was extreme. It's the only time he disappointed me."

Ritter looked at the placid, reflective face of the harmless-looking professor and had to suppress a shiver of revulsion.

Abruptly, Behrens turned away from the fire, and his eyes lost their faraway look. "Stalingrad changed everything. By the summer of 'forty-three, not one man in Section L believed the war could be won. Without ever resolving to do so, we found ourselves looking to the future, and we began to discuss ways in which the seed of National Socialism might be preserved. Was it possible, we asked ourselves, to formulate long-range plans that might one day restore a National–Socialist Germany to world leadership?

"At first, our discussions were purely theoretical; but as our ideas crystallized, we decided to act upon them. We contacted those few SD officers who knew of our existence and understood our work and described to them the plan that was rapidly taking shape in our minds. Their response was gratifyingly enthusiastic. They, in turn, recruited others — in the SD, in the Gestapo, and in the Waffen–SS. Action Group Werewolf was born.

"We worked in secret, for to acknowledge the possibility of defeat was to invite the charge of treason from the very fools who have led us to disaster. But we needed sweeping powers to implement our plan, so we devised a cover operation to sell to Himmler — and to mislead the Allies. Very soon now, it will become an open secret that Action Group Werewolf is preparing for a last-ditch guerrilla struggle against the Allied invasion of Germany. Our actual plan, of course, will remain absolutely secret; we trust no one outside the Group."

"You must be dreaming," Ritter said. "The Allies will tear National Socialism out by the roots. Our armies will be disbanded and the Party destroyed. We will be lucky to survive as a nation."

"If the Russians would have their way, I would agree with you," Behrens responded. "They would destroy us as a people, not just a nation. But the British and Americans will not let the Russians have a free hand in Europe, and the Russians will not be the sole occupiers of Germany. The nation will survive, lick its wounds, and eventually recover. Then our time will come. Werewolf will see to it."

"You still haven't answered my question," Ritter said. "How?"

"The answer lies in our picture of the postwar world. We have no crystal ball, but political, economic and military realities can be perceived and analyzed. With Germany and Japan defeated and the British exhausted, there will be only two great powers in the world: Russia and the United States.

"Once the war is over, the Americans will remember that the Bolsheviks are their natural enemies. Stalin, of course, has never forgotten that. The world will divide into two armed camps, polarized by these two great antagonists. Sooner or later, Russia and America will go to war with each other, a war so cataclysmic that even the victor will lose. It will be out of the ashes of the next great war — not this one — that Germany and National Socialism will rise again to establish a new world order."

Ritter looked at Behrens incredulously. "Is that what your great brain trust has come up with?" he said, unable to suppress a smile. "Is that your secret plan? — to await another war?"

Ritter felt relief wash over him, and with it, almost a sense of anticlimax. The whole charade had been a waste of time; Canaris had sent him on a wild-goose chase.

Behrens regarded Ritter coolly for a moment and then shook his head, as if he were dealing with an earnest but disappointingly dull student. "You misunderstand me, Hauptsturmführer. When I said that America and Russia will go to war with each other, that was not a prediction, it was a promise."

Ritter frowned. "I don't understand."

"Werewolf was created for a very specific purpose," Behrens said, his eyes burning with a sudden, feverish intensity. "Action Group Werewolf will precipitate World War Three."

. . . . NINE . . . .

The hairs rose on the back of Ritter's neck as he looked into Behrens's eyes and saw the glint of madness — not the madness of a raving lunatic, but the insane purpose of a twisted mind. Behrens smiled slightly.

"You are thinking that it's not possible to precipitate a war between two great powers, but you are wrong. It will not be easy, but it *is* possible."

"Even if I grant you that," Ritter said, "why do you assume that Germany would escape such a war unscathed?"

"I did not say we would escape unscathed, but the odds of survival will be in Germany's favor. With America and Russia utterly prostrate after such a war, Germany will emerge as the dominant world power. We in Section L are convinced of that."

Outside, a siren sounded, its low moan rising to an undulating wail. Behrens glanced at his watch and nodded. "The British are right on schedule."

A muttering rumble came from the sky, gradually increasing in intensity until it became a droning roar; a British bomber stream passed overhead, flying toward Munich.

"And just how do you think Werewolf can bring about World War Three?" Ritter said, not bothering to keep the skepticism out of his voice. He still had heard nothing that really worried him.

Behrens ignored Ritter's tone and began to explain, leaning forward in his chair as if to bridge physically the gap between his own confidence and Ritter's disbelief.

"We must assume that both Russia and the United States will realize the suicidal folly of a war between them. They will endeavor to keep the peace by maintaining a balance of power. Our problem, then, is to destabilize that balance — a difficult task, but not an impossible one. Imagine a gigantic boulder balanced on the edge of a cliff. A hundred men could not lift it, but allow the base upon which it rests to erode, and eventually a child could lean against the boulder and plunge it into the abyss.

"Werewolf will erode the base of equilibrium between East and West; Werewolf will plunge Russia and America into war. To accomplish this we must have three things: the knowledge, the time, and the manpower. Section L has the knowledge, secrecy will give us the time, and we are already recruiting the manpower.

"We are recruiting specially selected young men and women who will be infiltrated into target countries throughout the world. Most of the recruits are the children of marriages between Germans and foreign nationals, with a command of the target country's language. Each agent is well educated and fully capable of becoming a productive citizen of the target country.

"These agents will settle into their new lives and work toward positions of influence in government, in the financial world, in educational institutions, and in the military. Our worldwide network of agents, monitored and guided by experts like those in Section L, will be the source of erosion, the destabilizing force that will trigger World War Three.

"Wherever we have agents, we will tear at the fabric of society. In countries that are strong, we will seek out weakness; where there is peace, we will stir up conflict; we will sabotage alliances that foster world stability and help create alliances that increase tension. We will keep the world in ferment, Ritter, and watch for our chance to precipitate the final conflict. It will come, as surely as the sun rises."

Ritter shook his head obstinately. "I can't believe that a handful of agents scattered about the world can accomplish all that you seem to think they can," he said, but already doubt had begun to creep into his mind, like a snake slithering out of a dark corner.

"You don't believe, because you think in terms of positive action. Only rarely can an individual exert a positive influence on his country or on the world. But we do not seek to build or to create, or to spread new ideas; we have the very opposite objective: to erode and to undermine. The destructive potential of individuals is enormous — particularly when they are intelligent and armed with the proper expertise.

"It takes a team of engineers and thousands of man-hours to produce a complicated piece of machinery, but an individual can jam a safety valve or a governor, and the machine will tear itself to pieces. Like a machine, society has its vulnerable points at which individuals can exert destructive pressure. I'm speaking of sabotage, Ritter. Our agents will carry out social, political, economic and educational sabotage around the world, and sabotage is the work of individuals.

"For decades political scientists, historians and economists have studied society in an attempt to understand its workings, and psychiatrists have studied the minds of individuals and the motivations of the masses. The social sciences are still in their infancy. We cannot make a sick mind well; we cannot always revive a failing economy; we cannot devise the perfect educational system. But we have come far enough to know how to be destructive. We can destroy a mind, sabotage an educational system, ruin an economy or move the masses to rage with propaganda."

Ritter listened to Behrens with a growing, sick fascination. The muffled thunder of bombs falling on Munich in the distance provided an eerie background to Behrens's words. Even as Germany was being destroyed in a nightmare of its own making, Behrens and his colleagues were busily plotting to engulf the world in yet another holocaust. Ritter wished he could dismiss it all as nonsense, but he could not; Behrens had begun to frighten him.

"Werewolf's experts have the required knowledge," Behrens was saying. "They will guide and coordinate our agents' efforts all over the world. Many of our actions will be so slight as to pass unnoticed, but even small disturbances, when brought into resonance with each other, can shatter the strongest structures. And we will not be working with a 'handful' of agents, as you suggested; there will be hundreds.

"We have the full power of the SD and the Gestapo to aid us in the identification and recruitment of potential agents, and our requests receive top priority. It is not an easy thing we ask of the young people we recruit: to go into voluntary exile, to dedicate their futures to Werewolf's eventual success. But you would be amazed at how many young Germans, hard and true, are willing to accept that challenge.

"We have begun with Eastern Europe and the Baltic States, which the Russians will certainly reabsorb. Our occupation of these countries makes infiltration a simple matter. As our armies fall back in the East, we will concentrate on countries in Western Europe. More difficult, but already under way, is our infiltration of Britain, South America, the United States and Canada. Submarine transport is inefficient and extremely hazardous, but we will continue right up to the moment the last of our seaports is closed.

"Even if we do not succeed in dispersing a sufficient number of agents before the final collapse of our military resistance, that may not be fatal to our purpose. Once the chaos of the Allied Occupation subsides and Allied vigilance wanes, we may be able to continue to recruit and disperse our agents. Steps have already been taken to preserve the necessary equipment and personnel for clandestine operations in Germany after the war."

"And where do I fit in?" Ritter said, swallowing back the sour taste in his throat. "My own education is limited. I'm a soldier, nothing more."

"You underrate yourself, Ritter. Your intelligence is well above average, and your record indicates a talent for languages. Had you not joined the Waffen–SS, you could easily have entered a university and completed your education."

"But I didn't."

"And we did not recruit you to become one of our normal agents."

"Then why *did* you recruit me?"

"Because you have special talents we require. Werewolf agents will be manipulators, subtle and indirect. They will precipitate action, not undertake it themselves. Nevertheless, there are moments in history when a single, precisely timed act of purposeful violence — an assassination, perhaps — can produce a shock wave of sufficient force to warrant the risk of direct action. There may also be instances when treachery or cowardice within our own ranks threatens our operations. We will need men who can dispose of such threats."

"You want a professional killer."

Behrens sucked noisily on his pipe and frowned. "More than a killer. We need men who can kill expertly but who also possess intelligence and judgment. If you agree to join us, you will be a member of a very small, select group. Now that you have heard our plan, you are in a position to make that decision. If you join us, you will be trained and infiltrated into another country, where you may live out your life without ever being called upon for service. Yet you must always be ready. From the moment you agree to join us until the day you die, you will belong to Werewolf."

Circumstances dictated Ritter's response.

"I accept," he said firmly.

Behrens smiled broadly and rose from his chair. He extended his hand. "Then it is done. Werewolf welcomes you."

Ritter stood up and shook Behrens's moist hand. "What happens now?"

"You will remain here for a few days, while we give you a series of aptitude tests to determine a suitable civilian occupation in which to train you. Once the testing is completed and a target country has been chosen, you will be sent elsewhere for training. It will mean at least a full year of extremely hard work before you are ready to be sent out.

"Once you leave Germany, you will be on your own, without the support of comrades. You will not know who your fellow agents are or where they are located. That is the price our agents must pay for absolute security."

The thunder of bombs falling on Munich grew in intensity, drawing Behrens's attention. He turned off the single lamp that illuminated the room, went to the window and drew aside the blackout drapes. To the south where Munich lay, a reddish-orange glow suffused the sky above the horizon. Distant searchlight beams stabbed upward in search of targets among the British squadrons.

"They are pounding us into submission now," Behrens said, "but we will make them pay." Ritter could not see the professor's face, but he could hear the visceral anger in his voice. "The destruction they will unleash on each other in the next war will be infinitely greater than that which we are suffering now."

Behrens seemed to expect no response, and Ritter remained silent. With his face hidden by darkness, he could relax for the moment with no fear of betraying the disgust he felt for the evil little man by the window. Ritter had learned enough for Canaris's purposes, and it was time to get out. At the first opportunity, he would call the emergency contact number Canaris had given him. Once Canaris was informed, it would no longer matter if Behrens's ideas had substance or not; the admiral would see to the destruction of Action Group Werewolf.

Behrens was still gazing fixedly out the window at the distant glow of the burning city. "Even if we are wrong," he said, "and the next war destroys Germany as well as our enemies, we will still have gained something denied to us now."

"What?" Ritter said. "What would we gain?"

"Vengeance, Ritter. Vengeance."

Two nights later, while Ritter slept, the trap sprang shut on him. For two days, Ritter had spent most of his waking hours seated at a portable desk in the cottage's front room, taking a battery of aptitude tests. The tests were administered by a bookish, anemic-looking officer from SD Political Security who now worked for Werewolf.

Halfway through the morning of the third day of testing, Behrens, clearly excited, burst into the room. The SD man looked up in annoyance. "I haven't finished checking his last test results, Herr Professor," he protested peevishly.

Behrens snorted, strode to the desk, and swept the test papers onto the floor. "Out," he commanded. "We've had enough tests. Get out!"

The underling jumped up and scurried out of the room like a startled crab, and Behrens turned to Ritter, who was standing by the window, smoking a cigarette.

"It's a good day — a great day," Behrens exclaimed. "The Führer has finally cleaned house. He's given control of the Abwehr to the SS. Do you know what that means for us?"

Ritter shook his head, and Behrens was too jubilant to notice Ritter's sudden pallor or the unnaturally stiff expression on his face.

"The Abwehr's entire foreign intelligence apparatus is now at our disposal. It will make infiltration of our agents into the Americas ten times easier!"

"When did this happen?" Ritter asked as coolly as possible. He could feel his heart hammering against his ribs.

"The Führer dismissed Canaris yesterday and signed a decree combining the SD and the Abwehr into a single intelligence service under SS control. The news reached me an hour ago," Behrens said, rubbing his hands together in satisfaction.

"But why was Canaris dismissed?"

"Why? The real question is how he managed to hang on this long. He should have been put up against the wall years ago — for incompetence if for nothing else. Last week the Abwehr station chief in Turkey defected to the British, and that proved to be the last straw."

"Is he under arrest?"

"Not yet, but that's bound to come. Now, to the purpose of my visit. You are to begin training tomorrow."

Ritter desperately wanted to know more about Canaris's fate, but he couldn't continue to ask questions without arousing suspicion. "I thought you still had more tests for me," he said.

"We've learned as much from testing as we need to know; the results fell precisely into the pattern we had anticipated on the basis of your record. We have chosen an occupation for you that suits both your aptitudes and our requirements, and tonight you will be flown to Frankfurt. There you will be taken in hand by top personnel in Frankfurt's leading commercial bank, who will teach you the business from top to bottom. By the time they've finished with you, you will be qualified to occupy a junior executive position in a major commercial bank anywhere in the world."

Ritter forced himself to concentrate on what Behrens was telling him. He had to keep his head; he had to keep playing his role.

"How can that be possible? It's too short a time," Ritter said.

"You have the intelligence, and the men who will train you are the best in the business. We've allotted thirteen months for your training, and you will be worked day and night. You will be force-fed the necessary experience. You will make more business decisions — and probably more mistakes — than a man working his way up the ladder would make in a decade."

"But the bank . . ."

"The bank will absorb any losses you may cost them."

"Has the Action Group that much power?"

"Of course," Behrens said, surprised at the question. "In addition, you will be given a crash course in Spanish. Our tests confirmed that your aptitude for languages is quite remarkable. Later, you will also need to improve upon your schoolbook English, but you can deal with that once we've smuggled you abroad.

"When your training is completed here, you will be conveyed by U-boat to Venezuela and smuggled into the country by our agents in Caracas. You will be supplied with flawless documents showing that you emigrated from Germany to Venezuela in nineteen thirty-eight just before the war. You will have Venezuelan citizenship papers dated January, nineteen forty-three.

"We have reliable contacts in a certain Caracas bank which will soon receive a substantial deposit of gold bullion. Employment has already been arranged for you there, and our contacts will look after you until your career is established. After that, you will be on your own. You are to pursue a career in banking or in any other type of business that suits you. After a few years, you are to apply for an immigration visa to the United States. Your ultimate objective is to become a respectable American citizen.

"Do not expect Werewolf to contact you for a very long time. Your only responsibility is to pursue your career and to become an American citizen. We will keep track of you. The signal that we have need of you will consist of a single word: Werewolf. There is a possibility — a very remote possibility — that you will never receive the activation signal, but that must make no difference in your attitude. You must always be ready."

"I understand," Ritter heard himself say.

Behrens looked at his watch. "I must be going. It is doubtful that we will ever meet again, so I will wish you luck now."

"Thank you, Herr Professor," Ritter said, shaking hands. He was still unwilling to believe that what was happening was irreversible. There had to be a way out.

As an afterthought, Behrens said, "The day is young, and you've been cooped up in here for two days. Why don't you go out — take a stroll through the village. These will be the last hours of leisure you will have for a very long time."

"I'll do that," Ritter said.

In the village there would be a telephone he could use.

Thirty minutes later, from a phone in the local inn, Ritter made his call to the Berlin number Canaris had given him. The voice that answered on the other end of the line did not respond to the prearranged code word and demanded to know who was calling. Ritter hung up. His last hope was gone.

He left the inn and walked slowly up the rutted, snow-covered dirt road leading out of the village, trying to restore order to his whirling thoughts. The frigid air was absolutely still and clear, and in the distance, Ritter thought he could see the Alps.

He had a decision to make. He could try to make his way to the border and slip across into Switzerland, a desperate gamble he had little chance of winning, or he could carry on with the charade. There was no third way; he was a prisoner of the identity Canaris had given him.

Two hours later, cold and tired, Ritter returned to the cottage and to Werewolf.

. . . . TEN . . . .

A lone U-boat lay at the end of a deserted pier in Bergen Harbor, waiting for the night that crept ever closer to the Norwegian coast. The mountains ringing the harbor appeared as jagged, two-dimensional silhouettes which were already blending into the darkening sky. The soft lapping of the black, oily harbor water against the U-boat's hull was drowned out by the clang of steel on steel as two shipyard workers, laboring under the glare of an electric utility lamp, hammered on a fitting for the boat's snorkel mast that was jury-rigged to the side of the conning tower. On the boat's afterdeck, crewmen were securing the 20mm antiaircraft gun. U-615 was almost ready for its last war patrol.

Kapitänleutnant Wollmar, the U-boat's commander, stood with his back to the icy shore breeze, watching the repair of the snorkel, upon which their lives would depend. The brass on his battered officer's cap was covered with verdigris, and his soft leather coat was worn and salt-stained. He was as weatherbeaten and battle-weary as the boat he commanded.

The conning tower of U-615 was streaked with red where the

undercoating showed through the flaking gray battle paint. Rust patches spotted the boat's superstructure, and a sheen of green algae covered the deck planking. The U-boat's scars were visible; Wollmar's scars were hidden deep inside him.

A military staff car drew up to the shore end of the pier, and Wollmar twisted around to look. The passenger they awaited was overdue. A door slammed, and as the car drove away, a figure detached itself from the dark background and walked quickly out along the pier toward the U-boat.

"Repairs completed, Herr Kapitän," called one of the shipyard men.

"Very well, go ashore," Wollmar responded.

The workmen gathered up their tools and disconnected the utility lamp, plunging the conning tower into darkness.

"Permission to come aboard, Herr Kapitän," a voice called from the pier, and Wollmar looked down at the shadowy bulk of their passenger. In the darkness, the rucksack the man carried made him look like a giant hunchback.

"Come aboard," Wollmar said curtly. He was in no mood to hide his anger. The Russians were at the gates of Berlin, and he was being ordered to risk the lives of his crew to ferry a single passenger across the Atlantic. It was madness.

Moments later the passenger climbed the ladder to the bridge. He wore a seaman's duffel coat over olive green U-boat fatigues, without insignia of service or rank. Wollmar stepped forward and grudgingly extended his hand.

"I assume you are 'Erich.' My name is Wollmar. Welcome aboard U-615. I hope you know what you're in for."

"Either way, Herr Kapitän, I have no choice."

Wollmar was taken aback by the bleak emptiness in the man's voice. This mission had been forced upon U-boat Command by the SS, and Wollmar had expected their passenger to be a die-hard fanatic.

"We'll be casting off as soon as it's fully dark. You'd better get below," Wollmar said, and he stepped to the edge of the conning-tower hatch. "Seitz! Passenger coming below. Stow his gear in the bunk the doc used last trip, and then give him a quick tour of the boat. We get underway in twenty minutes."

"*Jawohl*, Herr Kaleu," came the reply from below.

Erich Ritter climbed down the aluminum ladder to the control-room deck, ducked under the conning-tower extension and straightened up to find himself surrounded by a bewildering array of tubes, wheels and gauges dimly lit by a tiny light over the chart table. Officers and seamen worked silently and methodically, making their final preparations for departure. One or two of the men cast him quick looks of curiosity.

A chubby, pink-faced ensign grinned at him. "I'm Ensign Seitz."

"Call me Erich."

"If you'll follow me, sir, I'll show you to your bunk."

Ritter followed the ensign through the circular hatch in the forward bulkhead and was immediately assaulted by the lingering stench of sweat, mold and diesel oil from the U-boat's last patrol.

"Radio room," Seitz said as they passed a tiny cubicle, and he continued his terse explanatory remarks as they worked their way forward. "Soundman's station; captain's nook; officers' quarters."

Ritter's sense of claustrophobia grew as he moved farther and farther into the boat. Every available space was crammed with stores for the patrol, and every few steps he had to duck to avoid banging his head on a pipe or valve wheel.

"This is your bunk, sir. We had a doctor along on the last patrol, but he didn't last. He was sick the whole time. Do you get seasick, sir?"

"I never have," Ritter answered, eyeing the impossibly narrow double-decker bunk mounted to the inner hull.

"Good," Seitz said approvingly. "See that door over there? That's the forward washroom. You can use it whenever it's free, but we lock the door when we dive deep. If a man tried to flush the toilet when we're down deep, the back pressure would shoot a jet of water into the boat with the force of a pile driver. Cut you in half and probably sink the boat.

"Upper or lower, sir?" Seitz asked.

"Upper."

Seitz nodded and shoved Ritter's rucksack onto the lower bunk. "We're going out shorthanded this trip," he said, explaining the empty bunk. "Want to have a tour of the rest of the boat, sir?"

"No, thanks. Right now I need some sleep. How the hell do I get into that bunk?"

"Take hold here, like this — and swing up into it."

Seitz swung himself into the bunk with practiced ease; but when Ritter tried, he bungled it, and only Seitz's quick hands saved him from falling onto the steel deck plates. Seitz pushed him into the bunk and secured the guardrail.

"You'll get the hang of it," Seitz assured him with a grin. "Now, if you're all set, I'll get for'ard."

"I'm set. Thanks."

Ritter curled up on his side and closed his eyes, but although his eyes ached and his head buzzed with fatigue, sleep eluded him. Exile. He was going into exile.

A year of his life had slipped by in a blur of feverish work. He had pushed himself even harder than his unrelenting tutors had demanded, using work as a drug to blot out thoughts of the future — while the Reich crumbled about him. Then one day, in January, 1945, his tutors had announced that they were satisfied. They had transformed him into a competent banker, fully qualified for a middle-management position. In addition, he had acquired a working knowledge of Spanish. An anonymous courier had appeared one week later to deliver a complete set of Venezuelan identity papers and orders to report to the submarine base at Bergen, Norway.

Right up to the last moment, Ritter had considered deserting and trying to disappear into the growing chaos of the disintegrating Reich, but in the end he had chosen exile. However uncertain his new life might be, it offered more hope than the existence he would face under the Allied Occupation with the record Canaris had given him. He no longer took the Werewolf plan seriously. Against the reality of Germany's total destruction, Behrens's vision of revenge seemed no more than the fantasy of a brilliant but desperate mind.

He was sure that Werewolf would disintegrate along with the rest of Hitler's Thousand-Year Reich.

Sleep overtook Ritter before U-615 got under way, and he didn't feel the gentle vibration as the electric motors started. The U-boat slipped its moorings and glided stern first out into the bay. The bow swung around as the captain turned the boat toward the fjord, and a low mutter filled the boat as the diesel engines took over. Invisible in the moonless night, U-615 felt its way between the towering mountains of the fjord and crept toward the sea.

At the mouth of the fjord, the U-boat passed through the gap in the rugged coastal cliffs and pushed out into the open sea, into the teeth of a northern gale. The heavy seas crashed into the hull, causing the submarine to pitch and roll violently, and Ritter awoke with a shock as he was thrown against the bunk's guardrail.

He rolled onto his back and tried to ride out the wild gyrations of the bunk, but the violent, erratic motion, coupled with the stink of the dank air in the boat, made his stomach roil. Afraid that he might foul his bunk, Ritter hastily lowered the rail, twisted out of the bunk and dropped to the deck. He seized a handhold as the deck lifted abruptly like an express elevator and then sickeningly dropped away. He could feel the vomit reflex coming and he lunged toward the door of the forward washroom.

He wrenched the door open, pulled himself inside and just managed to reach the toilet as the contents of his last meal spewed from his mouth. Emptying his stomach brought some relief, and after a few minutes he thought it safe to leave the washroom. He was not prone to motion sickness, and he assumed that he would adjust to the heavy seas in time.

To keep his mind off his uneasy stomach, he worked his way aft toward the control room, hoping to observe some of what was going on. Unnoticed by the officers in the control room, he took up a position forward of the radio room where he could see what was happening, but where he did not block the passageway. To maintain his balance, he gripped an overhead pipe with one hand.

"Radar impulses all across both forward quarters, Herr Kaleu," reported a voice in the control room, and Ritter heard the captain's muffled response come down through a speaking tube from the bridge. A moment later the deck canted forward, and the bridge watch, followed by Wollmar, skidded down the ladder into the control room, accompanied by a cascade of sea water from a wave breaking over the conning tower.

"Ease her down to twenty meters, Chief," Wollmar said. "Steer two thirty."

The deck came level again as the U-boat completed its shallow dive, and the boat glided serenely forward beneath the storm-tossed surface, its diesels sucking air down through the snorkel tube.

"Watch those bow planes!" an officer barked.

"Let's hold her steady," Wollmar said quietly. "It's not going to be easy to snorkel in this sea."

"Faint propeller sounds, bearing one ninety."

The captain turned and spotted Ritter. "Please go to your station, Herr 'Erich,'" he said coldly.

"Station?" Ritter wondered silently, and then he realized the captain meant his bunk. Chastened, he turned and made his way forward.

A searing pain in Ritter's ears tore him out of a deep sleep. He gasped desperately for air that no longer seemed to be there; he couldn't breathe. He jerked up off the bunk and cracked his head on the curving hull. Out of the corner of his eye he saw a crewman staring at him with bulging eyes. The crewman's mouth was contorted as he, too, tried to suck air into his lungs. There was a sudden whoosh, and the air pressure returned to normal.

"What the hell happened?" Ritter gasped.

"Snorkel," said the young seaman, holding his hands over his own tortured ears. "A wave passed over the air intake and shut the float valve. When that happens the diesels suck the air right out of the boat."

"Jesus, does it happen often?"

The boy shrugged. "Often enough. Still, it's better than trying to run on the surface. These days that's suicide."

Ritter looked at his watch. Only an hour had passed since the captain had ordered him back to his bunk. Ensign Seitz appeared beside the bunk.

"The captain would like a word with you, sir. He's in the captain's nook."

The sound of Seitz's voice was filtered through the ringing in Ritter's ears, which still ached from the sudden decompression. He nodded, twisted out of his bunk and went aft to the captain's tiny cabin. The air in the confines of the U-boat was heavy with humidity, and Ritter's fatigues had a soggy feel to them. The doorway to the captain's cabin was screened by a green curtain to give a pretense of privacy. Ritter knocked on the metal door frame, which was beaded with moisture.

"Come in," Wollmar said.

Ritter found the captain sitting on his bunk, unfolding a chart of the Atlantic.

"Since the sole purpose of this patrol is to land you on the coast of Venezuela," Wollmar said, "I thought you might be interested in how I plan to go about it."

"Thank you. Thank you very much," Ritter said, stepping forward to look at the chart.

"We're here at this moment," Wollmar said, stabbing the chart with his forefinger. "We'll proceed on a northwesterly course to pass between the Shetland and the Faroe Islands. In this area, here, northeast of the Shetlands, we'll be in the greatest danger from hunter-killer teams. If we survive and make it farther out into the Atlantic, beyond the range of land-based aircraft, we'll be able to run on the surface at night. That will speed our passage considerably."

Wollmar traced a line across the chart. "We'll proceed west, turn south here, and make our run for the Venezuelan coast. We have three opportunities for a rendezvous: at twenty-two hundred hours on the eighteenth, and at the same hour on the nineteenth and the twentieth. After that, it's a washout."

Ritter nodded. Wollmar's orders coincided with the final briefing Ritter had received.

"I have one request, Captain."

"Yes?"

"It's nothing to do with the mission. There is a bunk near the radio room. Might I be allowed to sit there occasionally when it's not in use? — so I can see what's going on. I'd be out of the way, and I don't think I'll panic if things get sticky."

Wollmar looked at Ritter thoughtfully for a moment and then nodded. "All right, but see that you do keep out of the way. That's Kreske's bunk, and he won't mind if you keep it warm for him."

"Thank you. It will keep me from going crazy with boredom."

Wollmar smiled tiredly. "Boredom? If I were you, I'd pray for it."

At noon on the fifth day, eighty miles northwest of the Shetland Islands, U-615 was sighted. Ritter was sitting on the bunk by the radio room, watching Wollmar make a routine scan with the periscope, when suddenly Wollmar stiffened in alarm.

"Open all vents! Take her down fast! Two hundred meters. It's a Liberator coming in on a bombing run."

Dishes in the galley rattled as the deck tilted sharply forward.

"Hang on," Wollmar warned. "He'll be on top of us in a second. He must have spotted the peri —"

A terrific, deafening explosion drove the bow of the U-boat downward, as if it had been struck with a giant sledgehammer, and Ritter was thrown from the bunk and slammed against a bulkhead. He was too stunned to feel fear.

"Bow planes up. Up, damnit! We're going down too fast!"

"Planes are jammed, Herr Kaleu! I can hardly turn them!"

Ritter felt the U-boat tilt farther toward the vertical as its engines thrust it into the depths in an uncontrolled dive.

"Both motors stop!" Wollmar cried. "Blow tanks three and five!"

The captain's voice was loud and urgent, but there was no panic in it. Ritter heard a hiss as compressed air expelled water from the ballast tanks, and the downward angle of the U-boat decreased perceptibly. The U-boat's descent slowed and then stopped. U-615 began to rise.

"I'm having trouble holding her, Herr Kaleu. We're coming up too fast. I can't hold her! Forty meters, Herr Kaleu. Thirty meters. Twenty meters."

"Braun! Give Hempel a hand with those bow planes. Free them up. Without them, we're finished."

Suddenly the U-boat began to pitch and roll, and Ritter realized they had popped to the surface.

"Up periscope," Wollmar said tautly. He clapped his eye to the eyepiece and swung the scope around in an arc. "*Scheisse*. The bastard's dropped a dye marker."

"Radar impulses, bearing three twenty. Strength three and increasing."

"I can move the bow planes now, Herr Kaleu! They're stiff, but they're responding!"

"Take her down again, Chief. Two hundred meters. Port motor fifty revolutions. Starboard motor seventy. Hard left rudder."

Again U-615 slipped below the surface, turning left as it dove. Ritter struggled to his feet and staggered back to the bunk. His head ached where he had hit it against the bulkhead, and blood trickled down from a cut on his scalp, but he gave it no thought. Now that they had been sighted, the hunter-killer teams would pounce on them like a pack of hungry wolves.

"Two hundred meters, Herr Kaleu."

"Both motors twice ahead full. Steer two ten."

The U-boat lurched as bombs exploded astern near the dye marker the first Liberator had dropped.

"Propeller sounds, bearing three fifty. Increasing."

"Silent routine," Wollmar commanded.

"Propeller sounds still increasing."

A moment later Ritter heard the first faint ping of an Asdic, the British Sonar device. *Ping. Ping. Ping.* The high-pitched, nerve-racking sound grew steadily louder, and Ritter found himself holding his breath. Then he heard a new, more ominous sound: the threshing beat of a destroyer's screws. The propeller beat swelled in intensity, and Ritter stared upward, as if he expected to see the ship that would pass directly over them.

Seconds later he heard a sound that would soon become terrifyingly familiar. It was the splash of depth charges dropping into the sea above them. Five seconds passed . . . ten . . . fifteen. A booming concussion heeled the U-boat over, and a split-second later a second detonation shook the boat. And another, and another, clustering together in a continuous, thundering roar.

Abruptly there was silence, and Ritter heard a peculiar whistling sob; it was his own ragged intake of breath. With a conscious effort, he released his death grip on the bunk's guardrail.

"Come right to one sixty," Wollmar said calmly. "Full ahead. Check for damage."

"Propeller sounds. Three targets, bearing one fifty; two ninety; three fifty. Target bearing one fifty closing fast."

Ping. Ping. Ping. Ping. Ping-ping. Ping-ping. Ping-ping.

The deck plates jumped, and the hull groaned as the depth charges bracketed the boat. The glass faces on several control-room dials shattered. Even as the explosions of the first string of depth charges died away, the next destroyer lunged to the attack, the sound of its pounding screws mingling with the probing ping of its Asdic.

"Release bubbles," Wollmar ordered.

A soft, continuous hiss signaled the release of a stream of bubbles that would produce a false Sonar echo. At first the attacking destroyer continued to bear down on them, but in the final seconds the destroyer veered off, and the depth charges dropped off target.

Ping. Ping. Ping. Ping.

"Continue releasing bubbles. Hard right rudder."

But this Asdic operator did not take the bait. A cluster of twenty-four charges exploded around and above them, tossing the U-boat about like a toy. Ritter heard a shriek from the forward torpedo room, where a seaman had been thrown against a bulkhead, snapping his forearm like a matchstick. Suddenly the boat was plunged into darkness.

"Emergency lighting!" Wollmar shouted above the din.

Somewhere in the pitch-dark control room water splattered against steel, and for a terrifying moment Ritter thought the pressure hull had been breached, but then the emergency lights flickered on, and he saw two seamen struggling with the wheel of a leaking valve.

"Two hundred and forty meters, Herr Kaleu."

The depth charges were driving the U-boat steadily deeper.

"Two forty-five. Two sixty."

"Propeller packings leaking! We're taking water aft!"

"Two hundred and seventy meters, Herr Kaleu!"

Wollmar's icy voice cut through the thunder of explosions and the rising confusion in the control room. "Both motors stop! Work party aft; try to slow those leaks." The string of detonations stopped abruptly, and Wollmar's voice sounded unnaturally loud in the silence. "Chief, we can't use the bilge pumps at this depth, so you'll have to blow our tanks gradually to compensate for the water we're taking on. Try to maintain this depth. If we pop to the surface now, we're dead."

Ping. Ping. Ping. Ping.

"Oh, Christ!" a seaman snarled. "Here come the bastards again."

"Silence!" Wollmar barked. "Both motors full ahead."

Ping-ping. Ping-ping. Ping-ping.

It went on and on, hour after hour, until Ritter thought he might go mad. The British destroyers set up a routine one could set a watch by, calculated to wear down the nerves of the crew they were intent on killing. Every fifteen minutes, a single destroyer ran in for the attack and dropped twenty-four depth charges. Near misses dented the hull; rivets burst and bolts sheared, terrorizing the men inside the boat, who expected any second to see black water burst through the hull.

The fifteen-minute intervals between attacks were no relief; they were an agony of suspense, with each man silently ticking off the seconds until the next attack. They avoided each other's eyes, staring blankly at nothing and biting their lips as they waited for that first ping that would signal a fresh attack. After six hours the men began to cough. Battery fumes were contaminating their dwindling supply of oxygen. The stench in the boat was unbelievable.

In the eighth hour, Wollmar ordered everyone to don breathing gear. Now each man sucked his air in through a rubber mouthpiece attached to a metal canister on his chest. The potash filter in the canister staved off asphyxiation, but the chemical reaction that purified the air also heated it, increasing their misery.

Not only their oxygen was running out. Their supply of compressed air to maintain buoyancy was nearly exhausted. The British no longer had to score a direct hit to kill them; they only had to keep them under.

But in the tenth hour of the U-boat crew's agony, the British gave up the hunt. Fifteen minutes passed with no attack; then twenty; then thirty. The soundman pulled aside his mouthpiece and gasped, "Propeller sounds have faded completely, Herr Kaleu."

"Blow all tanks, Chief," Wollmar croaked. "Use all the air we've got left."

The chief grinned and pulled a lever, but the hiss of compressed air rushing into the ballast tanks was frighteningly brief. In the control room all eyes turned to the depth gauge. The needle pointed to 280.

"Up, damnit!" the executive officer cried hoarsely. "Up!"

The needle quivered, and the men in the control room tensed, but it continued to point to 280. Seconds later it quivered again and then began to move: 278 . . . 275 . . . 270 . . . 260. U-615 was rising.

"She's coming to the surface!" cried the young seaman Wollmar had silenced earlier, but this time the captain said nothing. Wollmar was grinning with relief.

". . . coming to the surface," Ritter heard another voice say from far away. "He's coming to the surface now. He'll be out of it soon."

Ritter blinked, and a blurred face swam into view. He blinked again, and the image sharpened. He was looking up into the face of Zev Barlev.

. . . . ELEVEN . . . .

When Ritter came out of hypnosis, he found himself alone with Barlev in the basement recreation room. He had no memory of what had transpired under hypnosis, so he had no sense of disorientation, as one may have after awaking from a vivid dream, nor even the sensation of time having passed. But his throat was very sore, and he guessed that he'd done a lot of talking.

Barlev was looking at him as a man might observe a strange animal in the zoo.

"Apparently," Barlev said, "you were what one used to call a 'good' German."

"Go to hell," Ritter replied hoarsely, swinging his feet off the couch and sitting up.

Weiss had left a glass of water for him on an end table beside the couch, and Ritter drained the glass in four quick gulps. He was surprised by the flash of anger Barlev's remark had provoked in him. Without understanding why, he felt mentally exhausted, yet keyed up. His body was still awash with adrenaline.

"We don't have to like each other to work together," Barlev said.

"Is that what I'm supposed to do now? — work with you?"

"I hope so."

"And if I don't?"

Barlev noted the tension in Ritter's face. "You have a melodramatic imagination. You never had anything to fear from us."

Ritter smiled mirthlessly. "I believe you, but millions wouldn't."

"Let's not waste each other's time. You hoped we'd discover that you're not our enemy, and that's how it turned out."

Ritter kept his expression neutral, hiding his relief. Barlev was a man he could respect, but he would never trust him.

"You told us about Werewolf under hypnosis," Barlev said. "I assume that the organization still exists in some form and that you have been activated. Is that correct?"

"Yes. For nearly twenty years I thought that Werewolf was dead and buried, but three weeks ago a man named Dietrich contacted me. He told me that I was being activated for a special assignment, but he refused to tell me in advance what the assignment is to be."

"Are you sure Dietrich isn't a crackpot? Do you *know* that Werewolf really exists?"

"I've seen Dietrich's type before. He's a fanatic, but no crackpot. He said Werewolf has grown strong, and I believe him."

It didn't seem possible, Barlev thought. Mossad had numerous contacts in Western intelligence services, and not a hint of such an organization had surfaced.

"Why didn't you go to the FBI?"

"I did — back in 'forty-eight. I told the whole story, claiming that I'd heard it from a former SS man I'd met in Venezuela. The young man who took my deposition was very polite — and very skeptical. I never heard from the FBI after that interview, and by that time I hardly believed the story myself."

"But why didn't you try again after Dietrich contacted you?"

"You can figure that out for yourself."

"You might have exposed yourself to deportation, and you also would have run the risk of Werewolf discovering your treachery. In short, you were afraid."

"I knew you could figure it out," Ritter said evenly, and Barlev's respect for him rose another notch.

"Was it Dietrich who ordered you to intercept Elana?"

"The girl?"

Barlev nodded.

"Yes, but not to intercept her, specifically; he wasn't even sure that Braun would be followed. My job was to prevent anyone who might be trailing Braun from following him into the city. I think Dietrich intended it as a warm-up drill for me."

"Did you know who Braun was?"

"I wasn't told, but I assumed he was a German rocket expert working for the Egyptians. Upsetting the power balance in the Middle East would fit in with Werewolf's objectives."

Barlev frowned. "That may be true, but why risk exposing a special agent just to strip a tail?"

Ritter shrugged. "Dietrich couldn't anticipate that you would identify me and run me down — which is something I still don't understand. How did you know I deliberately intercepted the girl? I don't think she realized it at the time. And how did you discover my identity?"

"That's a long story," Barlev said, his tone making it clear that he had no intention of explaining. "You're right; Dietrich couldn't anticipate what would happen, but it was a mistake to use you. If we play our cards right, that mistake will finish the bastards. They have lost their greatest asset; we know Werewolf exists."

"What do you want from me?"

Barlev smiled slightly. "I think you already know. I want you to be our man on the inside."

"Not your man," Ritter said curtly. "I may decide to help you, but I'll not be your man."

Barlev shrugged. "Just a figure of speech. Will you help us?"

"I'll have to think about it."

"Do that; but remember, we're your best hope of getting Werewolf off your back."

Barlev got up from the stool he'd been sitting on, stretched, and gestured toward the staircase. "Why don't you go out and get some air; take a turn or two around the block. This safe house is in Westchester. It's a nice, respectable neighborhood."

Yoel Arnon wrinkled his nose in irritation at the thickening clouds of smoke from Barlev's cigar that were filling the safe house's small library.

"The stink of that cigar will stay in here for a week," Arnon said sourly.

Barlev, rocking back and forth in a cane chair, shook his head. "How did a fastidious soul like you ever survive in a kibbutz?"

"I didn't," Arnon replied. "That's why you have the benefit of my invaluable services. Are you sure you believe what he said under hypnosis? The story of Bridie Murphy was told under hypnosis, and it was one long, colossal lie."

"I believe him," Barlev said grimly.

"So? What are you going to do with him now?"

As if he had not heard the question, Barlev reached out and plucked a book at random from the shelves lining the walls. It was a thin, leather-bound volume of Tennyson's poems. He opened it and looked at the old, yellowed pages. A girl he had once loved had told him that a man who did not love poetry had no soul. He closed the book and replaced it on the shelf. Barlev detested poetry.

"I'm going to throw him back in the water and use him as bait to catch bigger fish," Barlev said.

"Will he go for it?"

"I think so. He needs us as much as we need him. And there's something else: conscience. It's the reason he let Canaris use him in the first place."

"That was twenty years ago."

"He's the same man."

"Are you going to clear this with Tel Aviv?"

For a moment there was silence, save for the rhythmic creaking of Barlev's rocking chair. Then Barlev shook his head. "Not until we need their help."

Arnon whistled softly. "You like to take chances, don't you, Zev."

"I'm not going to risk a leak — not until we have a better idea of what we're up against."

"You don't think Werewolf could have penetrated Mossad?"

"I don't know, do I? Werewolf may be nothing but a gang of crackpots and hot air, but what if it's real? They have a twenty-year headstart on us; they could have agents planted anywhere in the world — including Tel Aviv."

"Are you going to run Ritter yourself?"

Barlev shook his head. "We're going to have to play him very carefully if we're to keep him attached to our line, and I want an edge. We'll use the girl. Elana will run him."

"But she's green."

"She's also very attractive — and Ritter is unattached."

"You play dirty pool, Zev."

Barlev shrugged. "I need that edge, and Elana is going to give it to me."

Early on an evening one week later, Ritter got out of a taxi and walked up East 19th Street in the direction of Grammercy Park, checking the numbers of the brownstones that lined the quiet residential street. The area around Grammercy Park was an oasis of serenity in the midst of Manhattan's bustle and noise, and Ritter walked at an easy pace, enjoying the calm of the evening and the cool, early October air. From somewhere nearby he heard the drowsy chime of a church bell.

Here and there among the conventional tan and rust-colored brownstones were town houses painted unlikely greens or reds — even lavender — colors apparently intended to proclaim that the owners, however wealthy, were not stuffy. The three-story brownstone in which Elana lived was painted red, its windows framed by black-enameled shutters and ornamented with miniature wrought-iron balconies. Ritter opened the gate of the ivy-covered iron fence that separated the brownstone from the sidewalk and climbed the short, steep flight of steps to the front door. The nameplate beside the doorbell read Ellen Miller.

He rang the bell and smoothed back his hair with a quick, nervous movement. He felt more like a young man on his first date than an operative setting up a cover, and the feeling annoyed him. For the girl, this rendezvous was just an assignment, and probably a distasteful one at that.

When Barlev had told him the plan, it had seemed sensible and straightforward. Ritter would continue to play along with Dietrich, feeding the Israelis whatever information he obtained about Werewolf's personnel and operations. Elana would be his contact, and they would establish a cover by making it appear that they were lovers.

This evening they would make their first appearance together in public. Ritter had not seen her since he had been released from the Westchester safe house, and he felt distinctly ill at ease. When he had agreed to Barlev's plan, it had not occurred to him that he might feel awkward taking out a girl who was required to simulate affection for him. He tried to shrug off the feeling, telling himself that he would get used to it in time.

Elana opened the door. She was wearing a white sheath and a single strand of pearls. The white highlighted the jet black of her hair, which she wore swept up.

"Good evening — Erich," she said with a guarded smile.

"You look stunning."

"Thank you." She stepped back and opened the door wide. "Come in."

For a moment after Elana closed the door behind him there was an awkward silence.

"This reminds me of a blind date I once had when I was at Bennington," Elana said.

"You, too?"

"Yes," Elana said, and her smile was warmer this time. "I suppose we'll get used to it. Let's go into the living room and have a drink to break the ice."

"Okay," Ritter responded lamely, cursing his inability to loosen up. As they walked into the living room, he gave a low whistle. The walls were paneled with hand-carved mahogany, and the carpeting and furniture had a comparable richness of style and material. "How did Barlev manage to get you this place?" he asked.

"We have friends," Elana said simply. "What would you like to drink?"

"Scotch would be fine. No water, no ice."

"Then we have something in common," Elana said, going over to a liquor cabinet built into the wall. She fixed two drinks, and they seated themselves at opposite ends of the living room sofa. Ritter raised his glass in a silent toast and took a sip of his drink.

"I may have something to report soon," he said. "Dietrich called me yesterday. I'm to meet him day after tomorrow."

"When and where?"

"At two in the afternoon in a bar across from the Chrysler Building. It's called Brodie's."

Elana nodded. "We'll have a man there to tail Dietrich. Barlev intends to keep him under surveillance. Do you know why he wants to meet with you?"

Ritter shook his head. "He just gave me the time and the place of the meeting and hung up."

Ritter took another swallow of Scotch and felt an alcohol-induced warmth spreading out inside him, and he began to relax a little. "Where would you like to go this evening? I made reservations at a French restaurant up on East Fifty-fifth Street, if that's okay, but I didn't do anything about after dinner. Would you like to go to the opera or to a concert?"

Elana laughed. "You wouldn't voluntarily go to either one."

"How do you know?"

"Well, you wouldn't, would you?"

"No," Ritter admitted. "What about a cabaret? I have a friend —

a neighbor of mine — who suggested the Blue Angel. They have a new young comic there now who's supposed to be pretty funny. Woody Allen I think his name is."

Elana shook her head. "Let's keep it simple. Dinner and a movie. Okay?"

"Okay."

Ritter took Elana to the restaurant Tom Brixton had recommended to him that morning as he and Brixton had come into the city on the train. Brixton had eagerly mapped out what he had termed a Blitzkrieg campaign of conquest.

"I'm giving you this battle plan free of charge," Brixton had said. "Now that you've found yourself a girl, Lorraine will be easier to live with. Christ, what a relief! Just make sure you stick to my plan; I absolutely guarantee success."

Ritter had retained only one element of Brixton's elaborate entertainment plan: the choice of restaurant. As Brixton had promised, the high-ceilinged, brightly lit dining room had an atmosphere of relaxed and cheerful elegance, and the service was expert, without overbearing snobbery. But as Ritter looked at the menu in disbelief, he saw that Brixton had omitted one significant detail in his description of the restaurant. The prices were astronomical.

Elana looked across their table at him and cocked an eyebrow. "Do you eat here often?"

Ritter grimaced. "This is definitely out of my league. Next time we'll have to eat at the Automat to balance the books."

Elana laughed softly, and suddenly, without knowing exactly why, she felt the last residue of suspicion in her mind dissolve. She realized that her ear no longer picked up Ritter's light German accent. His gestures, the way he sat slightly slouched to one side in his chair — even the way he smoked — were distinctly American. Erich Ritter, she realized, had long ago ceased to be a German in thought or manner; he was an American. And he was not her enemy.

Gradually their talk became less forced, and by the time the waiter served them their meal, they were more at ease with each other than either of them would have thought possible. The food was superb, though it would have been impossible for the quality to match the price, and the time flew by. Ritter almost managed to forget the circumstances that had brought them together.

Over coffee, Elana said, "You know, Erich, I don't think I could do what you did — start over in another country and never return to my own. I spent three years in college over here — mostly to escape the kibbutz I had joined — and I was homesick the whole time."

"I thought it was blasphemy to admit that you don't like kibbutz life."

"It is blasphemy — especially for a Sabra. Do you know the word?"

Ritter nodded. "I read *Exodus* like everyone else. Best damned propaganda a country ever had."

"Yes, and it bears as much resemblance to Israeli life as James Bond novels do to real intelligence work."

"Why didn't you like the kibbutz?"

"Why! You should try working in the fields all day like a coolie during a *khamsin* — a heat wave. A kibbutz is like a cloister with manual labor as the religion. Sweating isn't so bad, but the boredom — day after day, week after week, year after year — it drives one mad. If you're not a confirmed socialist, you have to be a fanatical farmer to stand it. There's no personal freedom at all; you trade that away for mutual security."

"So, you took off for college in the States. But how did you get into intelligence work?"

Elana shrugged. "Economic necessity. When I came back from Bennington without a degree, I had trouble finding a job in Tel Aviv. Finally I answered an ad and landed a job as a clerk in Shin Bet — counterintelligence. That was six years ago. My transfer to Mossad was a matter of chance. I speak fluent Arabic, and one day Mossad needed a rush replacement for a routine courier pick-up. Someone pulled my file card, and I was hustled off to Cairo, posing as an American tourist. I didn't trip over my own feet, so someone decided to train me for field work. And here I am."

"It seems a dangerous profession just to stumble into," Ritter said.

"Not so very. And my old kibbutz was not exactly safe. We were near the Syrian border, and the occasional mortar barrage was a fact of life. And if a Syrian raiding party captured a woman . . . well, the result was not pretty to see."

Elana's eyes clouded, and Ritter decided to change the subject. "My wife says that . . ." He broke off in confusion. This was not the first time in recent weeks that he had momentarily forgotten Jane was dead. It was a sign of nervous strain, and it worried him. Automatically he took out his cigarettes.

"What was she like — your wife?" Elana said, accepting a cigarette.

Ritter lit their cigarettes, inhaled deeply, and blew a long, slow stream of smoke up toward the ceiling.

"She was a Midwestern girl. Uncomplicated, honest. Brown hair, brown eyes and freckles. She liked to wear jeans and go barefoot. I loved her, and we were happily married for seven years. Then she died."

Ritter looked away and took another deep drag on his cigarette.

"I'm sorry. I shouldn't have asked."

"Why? Jane died over five years ago. I got over it a long time ago."

Elana nodded, but she knew he was stretching the truth. "I never married," she said. "I was engaged to a boy from the kibbutz, but one day he was driving a tractor in the fields and a Syrian sniper killed him with a head shot." She fingered a round, amber stone attached to a bracelet on her wrist. "This was his, an amulet he got from a Gypsy woman to ward off evil. It didn't help him, but somehow I think it brings me luck. Silly, isn't it?"

"All of us have to believe in a little magic once in a while. I wouldn't mind having a good-luck charm myself," he said, thinking of Werewolf. Barlev would be watching his back, but it was still a dangerous game he had agreed to play. One false step, and Werewolf would snuff him out.

Elana saw the lines around Ritter's eyes and mouth sharpen as his expression hardened. He suddenly looked older, and there was a deep weariness in his eyes. She glanced at her watch.

"Why don't we skip the movie, Erich."

"That suits me. Work in the office is piling up, and I'll have to put in a long day tomorrow." He signaled the waiter for the check. "I can catch the ten P.M. train out to the Island."

"It would be better if you stayed at my place tonight. Barlev said we were to establish our relationship as lovers right away."

"But isn't that rushing things a bit? It's our first date."

Elana smiled impishly. "Times have changed. This is nineteen sixty-three. You'll be able to get a good night's sleep in my spare bedroom, and Barlev has already stocked the apartment with a change of clothes for you, so there's no problem there."

"All right," Ritter said, "you're the boss. Uh-oh, here comes the bill."

Ritter was dreaming. He hadn't had the nightmare in years, but this night it came again. The jump.

Ritter and his men sat in the cramped confines of the boxlike fuselage of a lumbering Ju-52 carrying them to the drop zone. No one tried to speak over the deafening roar of the engines, nor did they look at each other. Each man stared straight ahead, wrapped in his own thoughts and fighting his own fear.

A crewman opened the jump door just behind the wing, and a rush of cold wind whistled into the plane. Ritter looked forward at the jumpmaster, who nodded his head. Ritter swallowed his fear and stood up.

"Make ready!" Ritter bellowed.

He and the eleven other men in the stick hooked their static lines to the overhead cable and checked each other's parachute rigs. Ritter saw Meyer grinning at him, and he gave his sergeant a wink of mock bravado. Meyer was right behind him in line, and if

Ritter should freeze in the jump door, as he had on his first jump, he could depend on Meyer's boot.

The warning claxon sounded, piercing the engine roar, and Ritter stepped into the doorway and gripped its sides with both hands, the wind tearing at his clothes. The jumpmaster clapped his shoulder, and Ritter dove out into space, arms and legs spread wide to stabilize his fall. He began to count. Two seconds . . . three . . . four . . . five . . . six. He waited and waited for the jerk of the parachute straps. Seven . . . eight. The ground rushed up toward him with terrifying speed. Why didn't the parachute open? He was falling . . .

Ritter's inarticulate cry brought Elana out of her sleep with a start. She sat up in bed, not sure that she had actually heard a cry. Now there was only silence. She slipped out of bed and quietly made her way down the hall to the door to the spare bedroom. She tiptoed into the room, which was faintly lit by the light filtering in through the curtained windows from the street. She saw the shadowy outline of Ritter on the bed.

"Are you all right?" she whispered softly, in case he was still asleep.

"Yes," Ritter answered hoarsely. "It was only a dream. Sorry I woke you up."

"What kind of dream?"

For several seconds there was silence. "Combat jump. I always hated the jumps. Go back to bed, Elana."

Elana was still half asleep, and her next question slipped out without thought. "Did your wife know you were a Nazi commando?"

"She didn't know I was in the war," Ritter answered brusquely. "I wasn't a Nazi commando. I was a 'Brandenburger,' and I was proud of it. I know that Barlev can't make the distinction in his mind, but I hoped you could."

Stung by the harshness in Ritter's voice, Elana responded angrily. "And why should I? You fought for Hitler, didn't you? You killed for that monster."

"Yes, and there's no mystery as to why. I fought for the same reasons millions of young Germans fought and died. In the beginning we thought we were fighting for our country, and in the end we fought to survive."

Elana stifled the urge to make a cutting reply and stalked out of the room, angrier with herself than with Ritter. It was her job to run Ritter as their agent, not to goad him. Why should she care what he had done in the past? All that mattered was what he could do for her country now. But she did care, and the realization worried her. As she climbed back into bed, she forced her thoughts away from Ritter. "Don't get involved with him," Barlev had warned. She refused to admit that the warning might have been in vain.

. . . . TWELVE . . . .

Ritter pushed his way through the revolving door to Brodie's Bar on Lexington Avenue five minutes before his scheduled rendezvous with Dietrich. The stuffy air in the dimly lit, cavernous saloon smelled of stale cigarette smoke and stale beer. The massive fifty-foot-long oval bar in the center of the room had been designed for volume business, but at the moment the saloon was nearly empty, and a lone bartender was keeping himself busy by polishing glasses with a rag of dubious cleanliness.

A handful of drinkers was scattered about the circumference of the bar, and two or three of the booths along the saloon's outside wall were occupied, where the intentional gloom in the place was partially relieved by light entering through cheap, stained-glass windows. Dietrich had not yet arrived.

Ritter seated himself at the bar and looked toward the bartender, who condescended to interrupt his polishing and shambled over to take Ritter's order. He was a frail, rickety man with curly, receding hair piling up to a peak at the back of his head. His glasses had slipped down on his nose, and he had to tilt back his head to look through them at Ritter.

"What do you have on tap?" Ritter asked.

"No draft beer, sir. Only bottled."

"Heineken's."

"Yes, sir."

Ritter felt depression settle over him; it was that kind of place. Four stools down the bar, a bald little man was complaining about his wife to a stoic companion seated beside him. From the darkness of the far corner came a woman's shrill cackle, closely followed by the outcry of a drunk who had burned himself with his own cigarette. Behind Ritter, the revolving door sighed, and he turned around. It was Dietrich.

The Nazi was wearing a tight-fitting, cotton-knit sportshirt beneath a tweed jacket. The shirt clung to Dietrich's sagging flesh, making him look older and fatter than Ritter had remembered him. Dietrich glanced at Ritter, nodded fractionally, and went to one of the booths. Ritter waited for his beer and then walked over to Dietrich's table.

"You pick terrific meeting places," Ritter said sarcastically, sliding into the seat opposite Dietrich.

"It will do."

Ritter caught a whiff of alcohol on Dietrich's breath, and he thought he detected suppressed excitement in his ferret eyes.

"Apparently you had no problems at Idlewild," Dietrich said. "No one followed Braun to the Statler. I won't ask you how you managed it; that's your affair."

"The man, Braun. Who was he?"

"He was not one of us, but he serves our interests."

"Which are?"

"To keep the pot boiling in the Middle East."

"Why there? It's a perennial trouble-spot, but the Americans and Russians are hardly likely to go to war over a flare-up out there."

"I quite agree," Dietrich said, looking about for a waitress. Apparently he was anxious for another drink. "Both sides can still afford to let the Arabs and Jews stew in their own juice. But in ten or fifteen years it may be a different story. Our economists have made a study of the growth of the world's oil consumption, and they have made an interesting prediction: there will come a day when the industrial countries will be absolutely dependent on Middle Eastern oil. When that happens, a flare-up in the Middle East could easily plunge the U.S. and the Soviets into war. So we keep the pot boiling and wait."

A bottle-blond barmaid approached their table to take Dietrich's order, cutting off their conversation. Dietrich ordered a double cognac. Ritter was struck by the change in Dietrich's manner. At their first meeting, Dietrich had made a point of treating Ritter as a subordinate, but now he spoke to Ritter as a colleague, and he seemed willing to talk.

"Are our efforts concentrated in the Middle East?" Ritter asked.

"Of course not. We have projects all over the world. Some are small and rather obvious. Others are more ambitious and quite subtle, and they require years to have their effect."

"Why was I activated? Why now?"

"For a number of reasons, but primarily for my own project here in the United States. I have been working on it for more than a year, but I've only just received clearance to put the plan into action; it is a very high-risk operation. Its potential effect, however, more than justifies the risk. The plan requires an expert marksman, Ritter — a man who cannot miss."

"Anyone can miss."

"But you won't. It must be a one-shot, certain kill."

"Who is the target?" Ritter asked, surprised by the icy calm of his voice.

Dietrich shook his head. "I can't tell you that until the last possible moment."

The words of Ritter's Abwehr instructor in Berlin came back to him: You're SS, Ritter; you're proud. Ritter reacted as he thought Dietrich might expect him to.

"What the hell do you mean, you can't tell me?" Ritter demanded. "I'm no man's pawn! You can't just point me like a gun and pull the trigger."

Dietrich's eyes narrowed, but he kept his temper. "If it were up to me, I'd tell you what you want to know. I have complete confidence in you; otherwise I would not entrust you with the final, crucial step of my project. But I take orders just as you must, and Werewolf always places security ahead of all else. That is why we have survived so long without detection."

"And just who is it who gives the orders? Who runs Werewolf?"

"No single man. A directorate controls Werewolf. The directorate approves and monitors each and every project, and it often imposes specific constraints. In this case, I've been ordered to tell you only what you must know in order to prepare for the job. Most of the necessary preparations will be made for you: sniper's nest, weapon, escape route."

"I'm still not to be trusted, is that it?"

"Don't confuse security precautions with mistrust. Follow your orders, use your skill at the appointed time, and in one stroke you will earn a more privileged position than most of our people attain even after years of service. My project is big, Ritter. I only wish I could tell you how big."

Ritter tried to look mollified, but inwardly he seethed with frustration. It looked as if he would learn very little more about Werewolf unless he was willing to kill for Dietrich, and that he would not do. Hoping to come away from the meeting with something more for Barlev, he tried another tack.

"What if something should happen to you?" Ritter said. "You are my only contact. You could drop dead of a heart attack."

The barmaid returned with Dietrich's cognac, and he drank it down in two quick gulps.

"If something should happen to me," Dietrich said evenly, "someone would take my place. The directorate can contact you, with or without me, never fear."

"That's not the point," Ritter said. "You say you trust me. Prove it. Give me a way to communicate with the directorate in the event of an emergency."

Dietrich shrugged. "Very well, if it will make you feel better, I'll give you a number you can call day or night. Identify yourself and leave your message. It will be transmitted to the directorate within twenty-four hours."

As Ritter committed to memory the number Dietrich recited, he felt a small sense of triumph.

"And now I have instructions for you," Dietrich said, passing Ritter an envelope. "Inside is a map and directions to a farm in southern New Hampshire. On the sixteenth — a week from Saturday — you are to drive up to that farm for a refresher course in the sniper's art."

"I don't need a refresher course," Ritter said coldly. "What I need are hard facts — distance to the target, angle of the shot, the time allowed to make the shot. That's what I need."

"You have no choice in the matter. We want to make sure that time has not eroded your skill, and we have engaged a Major Edgecomb, formerly of the British army and now an occasional soldier of fortune, to check you out. He lives on that farm, and he will be expecting you. He has been well paid, and he will ask no questions."

"And after he has checked me out, what then?"

"You must wait for word from me. It could come at any time after you return from New Hampshire, but almost certainly before Christmas. A precise timetable cannot be set, and you must be prepared to fly anywhere in the country on a moment's notice, so keep a quantity of cash on hand. You will be met at your destination and given complete, final instructions then. Your weapon will be provided at the scene, and there will be ample time for you to make final preparations. I can assure you that it will not be an overly difficult shot. We will see to that."

"Am I to expect any further contact from you before it is time for me to go into action?"

"No," Dietrich said, getting up. He dropped a five-dollar bill on the table and held out his hand. "*Auf Wiedersehen*, Ritter."

Outside the bar, Dietrich stepped to the curb to hail a taxi. A yellow Checker Cab approaching on Dietrich's side of the street pulled up beside him. He climbed in, gave the address of an uptown commercial bank and settled back in his seat. He noted with distaste that the driver was a Jew. New York was infested with the vermin, he thought to himself. He didn't dwell on it, not wanting to dampen his high spirits.

The months of painstaking, frustrating preparation were about to pay off. If his project succeeded, he would receive the recognition he was sure he deserved. He sensed a shift in the directorate's priorities, a hint of impatience with some of the more esoteric projects. It was high time, too, Dietrich thought. This afternoon he would have to waste valuable time channeling additional funds to that conceited Professor Hoffmann.

Hoffmann was an educational psychologist who had been planted in the U.S. in 1948, and he had become a leader in a movement to reform the American educational system. Dietrich was sick of listening to the pompous fool's scheme to sabotage American education.

In lectures, articles and books, Hoffmann preached that learning should be fun, not work. He attacked rote learning, claiming that it stifled creativity; he ridiculed standardized examinations as elitist and intrinsically unfair; he fought against the exercise of classroom discipline.

Hoffmann insisted that he was developing a following in academic circles. He actually believed that he could twist educational policies to the point where an entire generation of American students would graduate from secondary schools and colleges without the basic skills of reading, writing and arithmetic.

"Think of what will happen when this generation of untutored, pampered louts enters the work force," Hoffmann had crowed the last time he had met with Dietrich. "Industrial productivity will drop like a stone. American technological and industrial leadership will be a thing of the past."

It was a pipe dream, Dietrich thought with contempt. Sputnik had galvanized America, and there was a nationwide drive for excellence in the schools. The idea that a handful of education professors could reverse that trend was absurd.

The driver hit his brakes and his horn simultaneously, throwing

Dietrich forward in his seat, as another car cut in front of them. *Damned Jew!*

Yoel Arnon caught Dietrich's venomous look in the rearview mirror, and he smiled inwardly. *Your cover is blown, you bastard,* he thought with satisfaction; *you're living on borrowed time.*

Three days later, Elana met with Barlev in his office above the Naomi Travel Agency. It was late in the evening, and as usual the office lay in semidarkness, lit only by the stray light from Barlev's small desk lamp. Barlev was not trying to save electricity, Elana had decided; he preferred the gloom.

"So, Ritter wants to pull the plug," Barlev growled. "That's definite, is it?"

"Of course. You can't expect him to kill for them."

Barlev did not respond. *She doesn't understand. Nazi is only a word to her.* His face was half in shadow, and his eyes were hidden from Elana. His face might have been carved from stone, grim and implacable.

"He won't do it!" Elana said into the silence, and she was taken aback by the stress she heard in her own voice.

Barlev nodded and leaned back in his chair until his face was entirely in shadow. The cherry glow on the tip of his cigar brightened and turned orange as he dragged on the cigar. "You've seen him quite often, then."

"As you ordered."

Barlev expelled his breath in a hissing sigh and leaned forward into the light. The harshness in his expression had gone, leaving only fatigue. "You're right. We can't expect him to kill for them. It's bad luck that they want him for an assassination, but there's nothing we can do about it. At least we have this man, Dietrich, in our sights. It's precious little, but it's something."

"What about the phone number Dietrich gave Erich?"

"A dead end. We traced it to an empty apartment on a long-term lease. Yoel went in last night. The telephone inside is wired into a small radio transmitter that relays calls to God-knows-where."

"Erich asked for specific instructions. What shall I tell him?"

"Tell him to play along with them until the last possible moment. I'd give a month's pay to know who they're after and why, and I've been hoping we'd get the chance to identify one or two others in the network here in the States. Assassinations are tricky and prone to last-minute snags, and I don't want him to pull the plug until the very last moment. If we get lucky, the assassination will be called off and we'll still have our man on the inside."

"That could be dangerous for him — to wait until the last moment to cut and run."

"Dangerous perhaps, but not necessarily for him. I wouldn't want to be the man who gets in his way. When Werewolf recruited him, they wanted a killer, and that's what they got."

"That was twenty years ago," Elana said.

"I told Yoel, and now I'll tell you: he's the same man — slower, perhaps, but the instincts are still there. Look, Elana, he went into this with his eyes open, and he knows the stakes better than you. We'll get him clear when the time comes. That's a promise."

Barlev saw the girl relax, and he felt a momentary twinge of conscience. She still had a lot to learn. It was easy to make promises, but it was not always possible to keep them.

....THIRTEEN....

The born sniper, once trained, is deadly until the day he dies. Ritter needed no refresher course in the art of long-range killing, but obedient to Dietrich's orders, he drove up to New Hampshire on the appointed day. Elana came with him.

The New Hampshire woods, resplendent under a sparkling blue sky, were alive with color. The woods were splashed with scarlet, crimson, orange, and lemon yellow. It was a last flare of life before the northern winds swept down to brown the leaves and strip them from the trees.

Ritter would have missed the turnoff if Elana, seated beside him, had not seen the faded, weather-beaten road sign hidden by an overhanging branch at the side of the highway.

"Bartlett Lane," she cried, pointing, and Ritter swung the car off the highway onto a narrow macadam road winding along the shore of a mirror-surfaced lake.

"If I sent my family a photograph of this," Elana said, "they'd think it was retouched. I can hardly believe those colors are real."

"It's beautiful, all right," Ritter acknowledged distractedly, glancing down at the map he held in his left hand. A half-mile farther on, he made a left turn onto a second country road that climbed the long, steep slope of a hill covered with apple orchards. Beyond the orchards, just over the crest of the hill, they found the white Colonial farmhouse Ritter sought. He slowed the car and checked the rural mailbox at the side of the road. EDGECOMB had been hand-painted on its side.

"This is it," Ritter said, turning the wheel and driving into the semicircular driveway that led up to the front of the house. The front lawn was spattered with tiny crab apples and brightly colored leaves. He stopped the car and switched off the engine. "I'd better speak to Edgecomb alone."

Elana nodded. "I'll just get out and stretch my legs. It was a long drive."

They got out of the car, and Ritter walked up to the house, arching his back as he walked to relieve the stiffness in his muscles. The complete silence gave the impression that the house was deserted, but there was the scent of wood smoke in the air, and wisps of gray smoke curled out of one of the house's two brick chimneys. Either Edgecomb had heard the car drive up or he heard the loud creaking of the floorboards as Ritter came up onto the porch; before Ritter could knock, a rugged-looking bantam cock of a man opened the front door.

"I'm Edgecomb," the little man said with a clipped British accent, sticking out his hand. "You made good time. I didn't expect you until two o'clock."

"Erich Ritter," Ritter said, shaking hands.

Edgecomb wore baggy khaki trousers and a rough, red-checked woolen shirt that matched his ruddy face. He had thinning sandy hair and a reddish, tobacco-stained mustache. Ritter took an immediate liking to him.

Edgecomb looked past Ritter at the girl, who stood by the road, gazing down at the lake at the foot of the hill. He raised his eyebrows questioningly.

"She came along for the ride," Ritter said. "I told her that you run a private shotgun school for hunters. We'll find some motel nearby to stay the night."

Edgecomb allowed his eyes to linger on Elana, and his smile widened. "Very nice, if you don't mind my saying so; very nice indeed. Can you leave her to her own devices for this afternoon? We should get to work right away."

"Sure. When should she come back to pick me up?"

"Around five. By the way, there's a motel up Route One-o-one, two miles west of where you turned off onto Bartlett Lane. You might have her check the two of you in there for the night."

"Thanks. I'll be back in a moment."

Elana turned and smiled at Ritter as he approached, and for the thousandth time he tried to read her true feelings in her eyes. Dressed in jeans and a suede leather jacket, she looked like a carefree college coed. It was hard to think of her as an Israeli agent. But that was what she was, Ritter reminded himself roughly, and soon they would go their separate ways. What difference did it make what she was thinking, what she felt?

"Edgecomb wants to start right in," Ritter said, "so you'll be on your own until five. You can pick me up then."

"Okay. I think I'll just find a place to lie in the sun and breathe in all this fresh air. I'd forgotten what New England can be like."

"Edgecomb told me there's a motel two miles beyond where we turned off. If it looks all right, why don't you check us in there."

"Will do," Elana said.

Ritter walked her to the car and opened the door for her. She got in, closed the door, and then rolled down the window. "One or two nights?"

"Just for tonight. Edgecomb's job is to check me out. He'll soon see that I don't need a refresher course."

"You're that sure of yourself?"

Ritter's eyes became bleak and distant. "Yes," he said. "I'm sure."

Impulsively, Elana reached up through the window and pulled Ritter's head down to her and kissed him. "For Edgecomb's benefit," she said softly as she released him. Then she started the engine, waved to Edgecomb, who was watching from the porch, and drove off.

Ritter turned, walked back to the porch and followed Edgecomb into the house.

"Want something to eat?" Edgecomb asked, leading the way into a cozy, low-ceilinged living room.

"No, thanks. We stopped for lunch in Massachusetts."

A single log burned slowly in a stone hearth. That and the sunlight streaming in through the windows warmed the room. The light odor of gun oil mingled with a hint of mustiness from the room's antique furnishings. On a wide oak table in the center of the room rested five bolt-action rifles. Each was fitted with a telescopic sight.

"Rented this place for a song," Edgecomb said. "A bit drafty, but I love it. Those windowpanes are one hundred fifty years old. And the door latches — they were all handmade by the same blacksmith."

Ritter nodded politely. It seemed odd to him that an Englishman should be impressed by a history of a mere one hundred fifty years.

"There is one thing I'd like to get straight before we begin," Edgecomb said, fixing Ritter with a stern look. "I was a soldier once — before a damned nigger got me in the Congo and my lung packed up. Now I'm a 'consultant,' and I'm not too fussy about my clients, if you get my meaning. But I won't work for bloody Communists or rag-tailed revolutionaries."

"And you'd like my assurance that we aren't in that category."

"Precisely."

"You have my word on it. In fact, I can promise you that I would never do anything against the interests of either the United States or Great Britain."

Ritter was afraid that his last words had come out a bit pompously, but Edgecomb seemed satisfied. Edgecomb nodded and went to a cupboard in the corner. He took out a bottle of Scotch and two glasses.

"Sun's over the yardarm, what? Some say that shooting and drinking don't mix, but I say that it depends on the man."

Edgecomb poured two generous whiskeys and handed a glass to Ritter. "No ice," he said without apology. "Can't abide diluting good Scotch whiskey."

"Suits me. Cheers."

"Luck to your enterprise."

They downed their drinks, and Edgecomb sighed with satisfaction. "That's better. I don't mind telling you, Ritter, that I like the look of you. Couldn't help noticing a bit of an accent, though."

"German. I'm an American now."

"The other chap — the one who made the arrangements with me — he said he was Swiss."

"He was lying. I'm not."

Edgecomb grinned and took out a pipe and tobacco from his shirt pockets. He filled the pipe carefully and lit up. Trailing a cloud of smoke, he walked over to the gun table.

"As I understand it," Edgecomb said, "my job is twofold: to provide you with an untraceable, accurate rifle, along with ammunition, and to check you out with the weapon you choose. I must verify that you can make a sure kill on a stationary or slow-moving target at ranges up to three hundred yards. If necessary, I am to give you the benefit of my experience and ability to bring you up to scratch."

Ritter walked to the table and looked down at the five rifles. Their oiled barrels gleamed dully in the light. In skilled hands, any one of them would be lethal at long range.

"The one on the left is a modified Springfield — with a Star barrel," Edgecomb said. "The other four are all Mauser actions I worked up myself."

Ritter recognized one rifle as a customized Czech version of the Model 98 Mauser, with a light, small-ring action; it had been a favorite of German paratroops. The bolt knob was hollow, and excess steel had been milled away from the receiver to minimize weight. Ritter picked it up and snicked back the bolt. The rifle was chambered for a 7mm bullet.

"You favor a light weapon?" Edgecomb said. "I would have thought a big fellow like you might have wanted something heavier."

"As long as the barrel is properly bedded, I don't need the weight."

Ritter closed the bolt, lifted the rifle to his shoulder and sighted out the window, settling the cross hairs of the scope on the magnified image of an apple on a tree across the road. He squeezed off a dry shot. The trigger had a military two-stage pull, but once the slack was taken up, the second stage was crisp enough. "This one will do," Ritter said.

Edgecomb nodded. "It's been sighted in on a bench rest for dead on at two hundred fifty yards. I used 139-grain factory loads."

"If it's bench-rest sighted, it will shoot three inches high for me at two fifty."

"I can provide factory loads or hand loads to your specification, whichever you prefer."

"Factory loads will do."

Edgecomb nodded approvingly. The better the marksman, the less he quibbled over ammunition.

"How many shells shall I send along when I deliver the rifle?"

"Three."

Edgecomb smiled slightly. "That's an odd number. Why three?"

"One for the target; one more in case of a misfire; and the third — well, that's just because life is never certain."

Edgecomb pointed to a rifle similar to the one Ritter held, except that it was heavier and was fitted with a much longer scope.

"I'll have to check you out on that one, too."

"Why? I've got the rifle I want. Besides, that scope must be at least a twelve-power — a target scope."

"I know," Edgecomb said. "Needlessly high magnification with a resulting drastic reduction in the field of view. But my instructions were explicit on this point. Your superiors want you checked out on the target scope in case your target is stationary."

"That's just stupid," Ritter said.

"I agree, but . . ." Edgecomb shrugged.

"Okay, to hell with it. We'll keep them happy."

"Then we might as well get to it," Edgecomb said, picking up the second rifle. "The range is out back."

Edgecomb had set up a firing range in a meadow a quarter of a mile back from the road. Ritter lay in a prone firing position and looked through the rifle scope at a distant silhouette target. The dry meadow grass beneath the tarpaulin on which he lay rustled softly as he shifted his position slightly. Edgecomb was kneeling beside him, peering at the target through a spotting scope mounted on a tripod. The air was absolutely still, and the sun soaking into Ritter's back made him drowsy. He brushed away the mental cobwebs and made a final adjustment of the scope focus.

"I'm set," Ritter said

"Range?"

"I'd say between two fifty and two sixty."

"Two fifty-eight, to be exact. Give me a group of five. Between the eyes."

Ritter snapped the bolt closed, chambering the first round, and pulled the rifle butt tightly into his shoulder. He took up the slack in the sling and settled the scope's cross hairs three inches below the eye level of the target's head. He began to squeeze the trigger.

The rifle cracked, shattering the stillness of the meadow, and in the woods beyond, a flock of birds were startled into the air. Ritter worked the bolt, noting with satisfaction the positive ejection of the Mauser action, and fired again. When the five rounds were spent, he laid the rifle aside and looked up at Edgecomb, who was frowning as he looked through the spotting scope.

"Call it," Edgecomb said.

"Two-inch group. One shot a little high and to the left."

"Mm," Edgecomb said. "It looks good from here, but let's go up and take a look to make sure."

They got up and walked out to where the target stood before a neat, ten-foot-high stack of sandbags. The bullet holes were so tightly grouped that they merged into a single ragged hole in the target paper — right between the eyes.

Edgecomb sucked noisily on his empty pipe. "I thought you said the rifle would shoot high for you. Or did you compensate?"

"I held three inches low, but now I'll drop the scope setting a few clicks."

Edgecomb put up a fresh target and they walked back to the firing line. Edgecomb tried Ritter out with both rifles at two hundred, two fifty and three hundred yards, and Ritter's groups just kept getting tighter. It wasn't until Edgecomb upped the range to four hundred yards that the bullet holes started to show some scatter.

Next Edgecomb tested Ritter on moving targets. At a range of two hundred yards, Edgecomb had set up cables running on a slant between a network of poles thirty yards apart. Targets sliding on pulleys along the cables could be released by tugging on wires back at the firing line. Once released, the targets would traverse Ritter's field of fire from left to right, right to left, and diagonally away from him.

"The target speeds are in the range of twenty-five to thirty feet per second — twenty miles per hour," Edgecomb said. "That's the speed your superiors specified."

"Okay. I'll try a sitting position and see how it goes. Let me have them one after the other — bing, bing, bing. I'll give them one round apiece."

Edgecomb waited until Ritter had settled into position and had adjusted his sling. Then he released the first target. Two hundred yards away, a silhouette of a man's head glided from left to right at twenty miles per hour, swaying gently back and forth. Ritter's rifle traversed with the target. He fired when the target reached the midpoint of its run, and Edgecomb immediately released a second target, which ran in the opposite direction and diagonally away from Ritter. Ritter worked the bolt, followed the target for less than a second, fired and immediately worked the bolt again, for Edgecomb had released a third target before Ritter had fired at the second. They went through ten rounds and ten targets in less than thirty seconds.

"That should do it," Ritter said, putting down his rifle. Together they walked out to inspect the targets. Each one had been holed between the eyes.

"Someone has been pulling my leg," Edgecomb said. "You don't need any help from me. But of course you knew that; you're a natural."

"The people I work for are a nervous lot, and they needed reassurance. Sorry we wasted your time."

"Nonsense. I get paid one way or the other. Still, there's little point in your coming out here again tomorrow. There's nothing I can teach you, and you don't need practice. Consider yourself checked out. We'll go back to the house and settle down for some conversation and decent whiskey while we wait for your lovely lady to come and collect you. Your weapon and ammunition will be delivered when your people request it."

On the way back to the house, Ritter decided to take a chance on Edgecomb. Ritter wanted a handgun, and for reasons he couldn't explain, even to himself, he didn't want Barlev to know about it.

"I have a favor to ask, Major. I need a weapon now. A handgun, preferably an automatic — and silenced."

Edgecomb gave Ritter a quick, inquiring glance, and then looked away. "That wasn't in the contract."

"I know. I would pay for it myself."

Edgecomb looked embarrassed. "Look, old boy, it isn't a question of money. I've been paid enough to give you ten handguns. It's a question of propriety. I assume you want the men who are paying me kept in the dark, and I'm not sure I can . . ."

"Major, they're forcing me to work with blinders on, and I have no idea how things will sort themselves out. I'd like to have an edge when the time comes. I suspect there were times when you needed one, too."

"There were," Edgecomb said quietly. They had reached the back porch, and Edgecomb opened the back door and led the way inside. "Wait in the living room," he said. "I'll be down in a minute."

Edgecomb went upstairs, and Ritter walked into the living room.

He could hear the clump of Edgecomb's boots overhead. When Edgecomb returned, he was carrying a flat, leather pistol case, which he handed to Ritter. Inside was a Walther 9mm automatic. The end of the barrel was threaded to accept a four-inch tubular silencer that rested in the case beside the pistol.

"It's not as quiet as a single-shot pistol would be with that silencer, because of the gas leakage when the bolt blows back," Edgecomb said, "but it will do. I can also give you a holster for it, with a loop to hold the silencer. The holster is designed to fit into the small of your back, and with a suit jacket on, no one is going to spot it."

"Thanks," Ritter said.

"Forget it. As you said, there were times when I needed an edge myself. Now, let's have a drink."

That evening, just after dark, Edgecomb was toiling beneath his kitchen sink, wrestling with the ancient plumbing, when he heard a rapping at the front door. He gave the rusted pipe joint one last bang with his wrench and crawled out from beneath the sink. He stood up, wincing at the crick in his back, and went through the house to the door, muttering in irritation at the interruption.

He opened the door, and the light from the hallway illuminated the face of a stranger. The stranger's gray eyes had a cold, empty look.

"Yes? What can I do for you?" Edgecomb said.

"I take it that Mr. Ritter has already completed his business here."

"Ah, I see. You are a colleague of his. Did you see him, then?"

"From a distance only."

Edgecomb frowned slightly. "Well, your man is an accomplished marksman. There was nothing I could teach him."

"May I come in?" Kadinsky said.

Edgecomb noted that the stranger's perfunctory smile did not extend to the eyes. "Yes, of course. Have you come for the weapon?"

"Yes."

"I have it in the living room," Edgecomb said, leading the way. "It's packed and ready to go. He chose a modified Czech Mauser mounted with a six-power scope. I also packed the twelve-power scope, as instructed, but it's not to his liking, and I quite agree with him."

Kadinsky made no response. In the living room on the oak table was the rifle packed in a long carrying case.

"He's been checked out on the rifle," Edgecomb said, walking to the table. "It's been thoroughly cleaned, and he sighted it in himself. That's another reason for not changing scopes. I guess that wraps things up."

"Not quite."

Edgecomb turned and froze as he caught sight of the ugly Mauser automatic in Kadinsky's hand.

"My apologies, Major, but one must tie up the loose ends."

"Bloody hell," Edgecomb said an instant before the bullet caught him in the forehead.

"We should have stayed the night in that motel," Elana said. "God only knows how late it will be when we get back to the city."

"We'll get in at two in the morning," Ritter said.

"Oh, God," Elana groaned.

They were seated in a roadside diner on the Massachusetts–Connecticut border.

"You still haven't explained to me why you insisted on making the drive back to New York tonight," Elana said, stifling a yawn.

Their waitress, a middle-aged woman whose overfed body strained the seams of her starched green uniform, came over to their table and deposited their orders of hamburgers, fries and shakes. "Anything else I can get you folks?" she asked pleasantly.

"No, thanks," Ritter said, eyeing the food mistrustfully. He was hungry, but the smell of grease in the diner's hot, steamy interior was so strong he imagined he could see grease in the droplets of moisture condensing on the window beside their table. He bit into his hamburger and discovered to his surprise that it was good, grease and all. Elana was watching him, still waiting for an explanation.

"I don't know," he said. "Nerves, I guess. I'm on edge, and I don't think I'd get any sleep in a motel."

That was part of it. When he had left Edgecomb's farm, he had felt as if an hourglass had been turned over and that time was running out. The moment was approaching when he would have to tip his hand, and from that moment on, Werewolf would stop at nothing to kill him.

But there was another reason for his unwillingness to spend the night in the motel, a reason he was less willing to admit. Elana's and his pretended intimacy had begun to grate on his nerves. When they were apart, he missed her; but when he was with her, he wanted to get away.

"Are you sure Edgecomb said nothing that could give us a clue to the identity of your — of Werewolf's target?" Elana asked.

"I told you," Ritter snapped. "He knows nothing."

"What's the matter, Erich?"

"What the hell do you think is the matter? An assassination is being planned, and I'm the man who's supposed to pull the trigger. Time is running out, and all Barlev tells me is to hang on as long as possible. He's just fiddling around, hoping everything will come out all right."

Elana reached out and touched his hand. "Don't underestimate Barlev," she said. "He promised me he'd get you clear."

Elana withdrew her hand as she saw Ritter's expression harden. She knew she had said the wrong thing, but she was not sure why. They still didn't really know each other; neither of them had let the other get too close. She looked at the tall, ruggedly handsome man across the table from her and tried to visualize him in German uniform. The mental image was blurred and had no effect on her.

Erich Ritter was no longer the stranger she had once mistrusted and half feared, nor was he the pawn Barlev had assigned her to control. Now he was just — Erich. "Don't get involved," Barlev had said, but those were just words, empty words. She felt an urge to say something to break down the last barrier between them, yet she said nothing. Discipline was a part of her life.

They finished their meal and went out to the car for the long run back to New York City. On the trip back, Elana fell asleep on Ritter's shoulder. He was tired, but wide awake. Midnight came and went as they sped south along the deserted Merritt Parkway, and Ritter had the eerie sensation of being alone in a dead world. An endless string of questions without answers threaded its way through his thoughts until one question stubbornly refused to give way to the others. It rose to the surface of his mind, swelling like a bubble, until it dominated his consciousness.

Whom was he supposed to kill?

. . . . FOURTEEN . . . .

DALLAS WELCOMES PRESIDENT KENNEDY TODAY, read the headline of the *Dallas Examiner*'s morning edition that was rolling off the presses.

Fifteen hundred miles away, Erich Ritter was awakened by the shrilling of the telephone beside his bed. He struggled free of his covers and fumbled in the darkness for the phone.

"Ritter," he said hoarsely.

"Dietrich sends this message," said an unfamiliar voice. "The time has come. He said you would understand. I have instructions to pick you up at your house in half an hour. Wear what you wish, but do not pack anything."

Before Ritter could respond, there was a click and the line went dead. He shivered, but not because he was cold; after more than a month of waiting, the summons he had dreaded had come. He swung his feet over the side of the bed and sat up. He turned on a bedside lamp and checked his watch; it was 4:45 A.M.

He picked up the phone and dialed Barlev's number. The Israeli answered in a voice husky from sleep.

"It's started," Ritter said. "A man is about to pick me up at my house, but I don't know my destination yet — and I don't know the target. Do I stick with it?"

Barlev did not respond immediately. "It's up to you."

"Terrific," Ritter said tensely. "All right, I'll call again when I know more — if I get the chance."

"Ritter, don't get backed into a corner."

"Thanks for the advice," Ritter said and hung up.

It took him less than ten minutes to shower, shave and dress. He took the automatic Edgecomb had given him from its hiding place in his bedroom and loaded the clip with copper-clad 9mm shells. He slipped the clip into the butt, switched on the safety and chambered the first round.

With its safety on, loading the Walther P-38 did not cock the hammer, and when the safety was reset to the firing position, the automatic was ready for instant use, but with its hammer still down for safety. As with a double-action revolver, the first shot could be fired by pulling the trigger, or the hammer could be cocked first for a lighter trigger pull. After the first shot, the pistol operated like any other automatic.

Ritter shoved the pistol into the holster, which already held the silencer, and attached the holster to his belt. The rig fitted snugly against the small of his back, and it was well hidden by his suit jacket. There were no telltale bulges. The gun might not be of any use to him, but he felt better wearing it.

He went downstairs to the kitchen, where he washed down a stale roll with instant coffee mixed with hot water from the tap. Then he swallowed some ready-made orange juice to rinse away the evil taste of the tepid coffee. He had just finished when the doorbell rang.

Opening the front door, he was greeted by a skinny man with a pale, pinched face. At the curb was a car with its lights on and engine running.

"Who are you?" Ritter demanded.

"'Karl Freya," the stranger said. He had a thin, reedy voice that was accustomed to whining.

"And Dietrich sent you?"

"Yes. Let's go. We don't have that much time."

"Where?"

"Idlewild. There's a round-trip ticket to Dallas waiting for you at the Braniff desk. You're booked on a seven o'clock flight. Let's go."

"Wait a minute. Will I be met in Dallas?"

"I don't know. Look, I'm just providing limousine service."

"Okay, I'll be right with you," Ritter said, turning away. He walked quickly down the hall and into his living room, intending to cut through to the phone in the kitchen. Now at least he knew where Dietrich was sending him. But Freya gave him no chance to make the call; Ritter could hear him coming into the house after him. "Okay," Ritter called, switching off the room lights. "I'm coming."

They walked into the airline terminal at six A.M. The lobby was deserted, save for a stooped old man pushing bits of debris across the floor with his broom. Freya confronted him and asked where to find the Braniff desk. The old man looked up, slowly rolled the stub of his dead cigar from one corner of his mouth to the other, and pointed.

"Come on," Freya said impatiently to Ritter. "It's this way."

Ritter tried to get rid of Freya, but the little man was afraid to violate Dietrich's orders, which were to personally see Ritter onto the plane. If Ritter missed the flight for any reason, Freya was to call an emergency number. Ritter wondered how many men Dietrich had working for him. Ritter had memorized the license number of Freya's car to pass on to Barlev, but he doubted that it would be useful. The man was just a flunky.

But a flunky could carry tales, which was the reason Ritter didn't try to call Barlev with Freya around. As Barlev had requested, Ritter would play along until the last possible moment in the hope that the assassination might be called off. As long as there was still a chance of staying inside Werewolf, he would do nothing to arouse suspicion.

Ritter joined the knot of yawning, bleary-eyed passengers waiting in front of the Braniff check-in counter, and he, too, began to yawn, partly from lack of sleep and partly from nervousness. Canned music drifted softly through the terminal building. There was little talking among the passengers, and when people spoke their voices were hushed.

Two young men with fixed smiles on their sleep-puffed faces appeared through a doorway behind the counter and began to process the waiting passengers. When it was Ritter's turn, he said, "Erich Ritter. You have a ticket waiting for me for Flight two-o-one to Dallas."

The young man behind the desk nodded, checked through a stack of tickets in a drawer and extracted one of them. "Yes, sir," he said, ruffling and stamping his way through the ticket's several layers. "Any luggage?"

"No."

"Here's your boarding pass, sir. We'll be boarding from Gate Three at six forty-five. Have a good flight."

"Thank you."

Ritter walked over to Freya and said, "You can take off now. I've got my ticket and my boarding pass. There's nothing more for you to do."

Freya shook his head stubbornly. "I'm staying. What's the gate number?"

"Three. But we don't have to go there just yet."

"We'd better. Come on."

They walked through a long, glass-walled corridor with boarding gates on both sides that extended out from the main terminal building. It was still dark out, and the airline personnel servicing the waiting jets worked under the glare of floodlights. Blue lights dotted the airfield beyond, stretching out into the darkness. On the horizon, a faint band of red signaled the approach of dawn.

When they reached Gate 3, Freya saw that only passengers were being allowed into the waiting area, and he put his hand on Ritter's arm. "I do have some final instructions for you," he said. "I was told not to give them to you until just before you boarded the plane. You are to go directly from the airport to the Adolphus Hotel in Dallas. Get there before eleven o'clock. A room has been reserved in your name. Go straight up to the room and wait there. Have you got that?"

"Adolphus Hotel. Eleven o'clock. Go straight to my room," Ritter said.

"Right."

"Are you sure that I don't have to knock three times and ask for Joe?"

"What?"

"Never mind," Ritter said and turned away. He presented his boarding pass to the girl at the counter and walked into the waiting area. Dietrich must have seen too many spy movies, he thought. In different circumstances it might have amused him.

Ritter felt the jarring thump of the landing gear being lowered, and he looked out his window at the layer of snowy, blue-shadowed clouds coming up toward them as the Boeing 707 lost altitude. He swallowed to relieve the increased pressure on his eardrums. The hours of in-flight limbo had done nothing to calm his nerves, and his palms were filmed with cold sweat.

As the aircraft dropped down through the cloud layer, it was swallowed up in a thick white mist, which suddenly parted to reveal the Texas plain below. The earth was a patchwork quilt of olive green, ocher and rust-colored squares bordered by gray, leafless trees. As the pilot banked the plane and they turned in a quarter circle to make the approach to the airfield, Ritter caught a glimpse of Dallas in the distance, a toy city isolated on the brown plain.

Their air speed dropped perceptibly, and the ground rushed up to meet them. Yellow grass and gray stretches of dirt swept by beneath the wings till suddenly they were over the runway. A moment later the 707 dropped onto the concrete strip with a bump, and the engines roared as the pilot applied reverse thrust.

"Welcome to Dallas–Fort Worth," came the cheerful voice of the stewardess over the loudspeaker. "We hope you enjoyed your flight, and we wish you a pleasant day."

"Christ," Ritter muttered under his breath.

In the terminal, Ritter went straight to the pay phone. Barlev answered the instant the call went through.

"I've just flown into Dallas," Ritter said, trying to keep the nervousness out of his voice. "This is the first chance I've had to call. I still don't know who the target is."

"Dallas?"

Barlev's voice sounded unnaturally loud.

"Yes."

"It can't be."

"What can't be?" Ritter snapped. He looked at his watch. He had less than forty minutes to reach the hotel on time.

"My God, man, don't you read the papers? President Kennedy is going to be in Dallas today — in a parade right through the middle of the city."

The shock hit Ritter like a kick in the stomach. For a moment he tried to convince himself that it was a coincidence, but it was no use. It explained Dietrich's excitement — and his extreme secretiveness. The killing of an American president would send shock waves throughout the world. There was no way to calculate the long-term effect on confidence and stability in the West.

"Ritter, are you still on the line? Ritter!"

"Can you stop it?"

"I can try, but I can't promise anything."

"Why the hell not!"

"The warning would have to come from my government to be effective immediately, and there may be complications."

"What the hell are you talking about? Just do it!"

"I'll do what I can, and you get out of Dallas now. Take the first available flight back east — to any damned city. We'll meet you there."

"No."

· 170 ·

"What? Ritter, listen . . ."

But Ritter wasn't listening. He was transfixed by a single thought that had darted into his mind and screamed for attention. Dietrich had brought him into Dallas at the last possible moment, with no time allowed for error or accident, and Dietrich was a careful man. There might be a backup man, another assassin. Ritter couldn't take the chance; he had to stay. Without a word to Barlev, he hung up.

An icy calm settled over him, and for the first time since his personal nightmare had begun with a single word on a telegram, Ritter knew clearly what he had to do. He wouldn't cut and run. Someone might die this day, but it would not be the President. He could feel the weight of the Walther automatic against his spine, and he was prepared to use it.

The Adolphus Hotel was on Main Street in the heart of Dallas's business district. The street was a narrow canyon walled by buildings of clashing architectural styles. Modern glass monoliths vied for attention with stately, old granite office buildings, with squat, red-brick warehouses sandwiched between them.

Ritter arrived at the Adolphus at 10:40. The air in the hushed, deserted lobby of the venerable hotel was hot and stuffy, and Ritter began to perspire before he reached the reception desk. The Adolphus's lobby reflected an outdated concept of elegance with its massive, graceless chandeliers and extravagantly large oil paintings, apparently selected for their size, which hung on dark, wood-paneled walls. Ritter found the sepulchral quiet in the dimly lit lobby oppressive.

"My name is Ritter. I have a reservation," he said to the desk clerk.

The man smiled perfunctorily and checked his file. "Yes, sir. For three nights, paid in advance." He noticed for the first time that Ritter had no luggage, and he cocked an eyebrow. Then he reached out to ring his bell.

"I don't need a bellboy. Just give me my key, please."

"As you wish, sir."

"Are there pay phones in the lobby?"

"Yes, sir, right around the corner."

Ritter looked at his watch. He still had enough time to make a phone call. He had little hope that it would work, but it was worth a try. He walked quickly to the bank of pay phones, hastily looked up the number he wanted in the Dallas phone directory, inserted a dime in the slot and dialed.

"Federal Bureau of Investigation," said a woman's voice; "one moment, please."

To his fury, Ritter found himself placed on hold. Thirty seconds later the woman came back on the line.

"Federal Bureau of Investigation, may I help you?"

"Please let me speak to the Special Agent in charge," Ritter said. "It's urgent."

"Who is calling, please?"

"Just put me through to the Special Agent in charge!"

"Mr. Kowalski isn't available at the moment," came the maddeningly even-tempered reply.

"Then let me speak with his assistant — second-in-command — whatever."

"One moment, please."

Ritter twisted around to check the lobby. There was still no one within earshot, but he wished the phone were inside a booth.

"Burns," said a cigarette-hoarse voice on the other end of the line. "Can I help you?"

"I hope so. I'm calling to warn you that an attempt on President Kennedy's life will be made today."

"May I have your name and the source of your information, sir?"

"No. And I can't give you any proof; nor can I give you a specific time or place. But it's going to happen."

"How?"

"Rifle fire — a sniper. You must believe me! The parade must be canceled."

"Look, it doesn't matter whether I believe you or not. The Secret Service won't call off the motorcade because of a vague, anonymous warning. Without detail, it won't wash. You'll have to give me something concrete."

Out of the corner of his eye, Ritter glimpsed a familiar figure. "Do what you can," Ritter said and hung up. Then he turned to face Dietrich.

"I wondered if you would be here," Ritter said.

"What was the call?" Dietrich demanded.

"Local weather; I wanted the air temperature. It affects the air density, and for a long shot it might make a difference. What time does the motorcade start?"

"Ah, so you put two and two together."

"Bringing me in on this morning's flight was cutting it a bit fine, wouldn't you say?"

"It couldn't be helped. There is a tricky aspect to this project that precluded a set timetable."

"I don't know what you're talking about. You must have known for weeks that Kennedy was coming to Dallas today."

Dietrich looked at his watch. "You were instructed to go directly to your room. Don't make a habit of disregarding your instructions. We'll go up there now."

Special Agent Burns held the receiver in his hand for several seconds before replacing it in its cradle. He grimaced as pain lanced through his stomach, and he pressed his palm against his distended belly. Ten years under Hoover had ruined his stomach lining.

"Problem?" asked a trim young man, who was seated across the desk from Burns.

Burns regarded him sourly. He didn't like this kid. He was too young, too fit, and too eager — and he was after Burns's job. Burns hoped Hoover would ruin the kid's stomach, too.

"That was some guy calling to warn us that Kennedy will be shot today."

"So what else is new? This town's crawling with nuts. The ones that call don't worry me."

"Yeah," Burns grunted and lit a cigarette. It tasted rotten. "The only trouble is," Burns added, almost as an afterthought, "This guy may have been on the level."

"Why?" the kid asked nonchalantly, but Burns could see the wheels in the kid's head begin to turn.

Burns blew a stream of smoke across the desk into the kid's eyes. "His voice. He was keyed up, but there was an undertone of resignation, as if he knew I wouldn't believe him. I don't think he was a crank."

"Well?"

"Well, what?" Burns growled.

"What are you going to do?"

Burns sighed and picked up the phone. "Notify the Secret Service and file a report — in other words, cover my ass. The Service won't stop the parade now — not on the basis of a crank call. Let's hope it *was* a crank." Burns looked at his watch. "We won't have to wait long to find out."

In Ritter's hotel room, piled on the bed, was a collection of photographic equipment and the rifle case Edgecomb had provided.

"That paraphernalia is for cover," Dietrich said. "No one will pay any attention to the rifle case; it looks like part of the equipment." As Ritter started for the bed, Dietrich pulled a pair of gloves from his pocket. "Put these on. You'll be leaving the rifle and equipment at the scene, so we don't want fingerprints."

Ritter slipped on the gloves and opened the rifle case. Inside was the light Mauser-action rifle he had tested, but it was mounted with a twelve-power scope.

"This is the wrong scope," Ritter snapped.

"We made the switch because the target will be stationary. We thought a head shot would be more sure with the more powerful scope. It has been sighted in precisely as the other one was."

"You thought!" Ritter said in apparent anger, playing out his role. "This scope is the wrong one for the job, stationary target or not. And why stationary? Why should the motorcade stop? What's the setup?"

Dietrich shook his head. "Not yet. This operation is so delicate it may yet fail, and you will not be given the details until it is time for action. I know you don't like it, but it's a policy that has served us well."

"How much longer, then?" Ritter demanded in genuine anger.

"I am waiting for a phone call. When I receive it, I will explain everything to your satisfaction."

Ritter expelled his breath in a hiss of frustration and turned back to the bed. He lifted the rifle from its case and inspected the weapon. He raised it to his shoulder, aimed out the hotel window and squeezed off several dry shots, getting the feel of the trigger. It was a pointless exercise, but Dietrich might expect it. Finally, he loaded the three rounds that had been included with the rifle. He slipped on the safety and replaced the rifle in its case.

"I'm set," Ritter said. "How much longer is it likely to be?"

"Soon. You must be patient."

But the time continued to drag by. Fifteen minutes . . . a half hour . . . an hour. The streets below began to fill with noontime crowds, and knots of onlookers started to collect along the curbs in anticipation of the motorcade. Dietrich checked his watch at shorter and shorter intervals as his own impatience grew and began to sour into nervousness.

When the phone rang at 12:20, both men jumped. Dietrich snatched up the receiver. "Dietrich." He nodded and then smiled. *"Gut; ausgezeichnet!"*

Dietrich hung up, pulled a sheet of paper from his inside suit-jacket pocket and spread it out on a small desk by the window. "Come," he said, motioning to Ritter.

The paper was a pencil-drawn street map of what Ritter assumed was a section of Dallas.

"This is the parade route," Dietrich said, tracing it on the map with his manicured forefinger. He seemed almost gleeful, and his hand quivered with suppressed excitement. "The motorcade will begin soon. It will run right past this hotel, but we will strike at the very end of the route — here. This is Dealey Plaza. The President's car must slow down as it enters the plaza and make a right turn, followed by an immediate, sharp turn to the left. At this point there will be ample time for a good shot at a slowly moving target — easy enough for an amateur."

"Where is my position?" Ritter said tensely.

Dietrich's finger stabbed the map at a point on the far side of the plaza. "You will be here, across the green from the motorcade, behind the wall of a concrete arbor. There is a windowlike opening in the wall through which you will have a clear field of fire. The range is somewhat over two hundred yards."

"That's crazy," Ritter said. "There must be dozens of better firing positions along the route — including this very room. You have me on the ground — exposed — and firing at a traversing target with that damned twelve-power scope."

Even as he spoke, he knew that there was something wrong. Dietrich was too careful, too thorough to choose such a poor firing position. Anyone would know better. And earlier Dietrich had said that the target would be stationary. . . .

"You will *not* be exposed," Dietrich said. "You will be completely screened from the front by the arbor wall, and no one will be behind you — or anywhere near you, for that matter. As to the target — it's not quite what you think."

A shot at a slowly moving target — easy enough for an amateur. Suddenly Ritter understood, and his stomach churned.

"Your target is not the President," Dietrich said with an infuriating half-smile. "He will be shot, but not by you. The man who will kill Kennedy is acting out of his own twisted impulses. We did little more than encourage him — and give him some tactical advice."

"But how could . . . ?"

"We are manipulators, Ritter; it is our specialty. The man knows nothing of Werewolf, but we don't want him telling about the 'friends' who encouraged him. The instant he kills the President, you are to kill him. He will fire on the motorcade from a fifth-floor window in this building here, the corner window nearest the business district. It overlooks the route, as you can see. From your position, you will have a clear shot at him, and it must be a certain kill."

"It will be," Ritter said grimly. Time was too short to rely on the FBI or the police; he couldn't be sure that they would react swiftly or surely enough. Ritter would follow through with Dietrich's plan, with one alteration. He would kill the assassin before the man could fire at Kennedy.

"What's my escape route?" Ritter said.

"Your retreat is simple. Leave the rifle behind and move straight back away from the arbor through the trees behind it. You will find yourself behind the post office — here. Go across the rear of the post office, turn left, and cut back to Houston Street — this street here. Go right on Houston and walk directly to the Hotel Scott. It's only a block farther up on Houston. I'll be waiting for you in room four ten. That's our bolt hole. We'll stay undercover there until the coast is clear. It should take you less than two minutes to reach the hotel."

"And if someone is behind that arbor when the time comes?"

"There won't be."

"But if there is?"

"Then kill him." Dietrich looked again at his watch. "It's time for you to leave. There's no need to hurry; it will only take you ten minutes to walk there from here. The motorcade will reach Dealey Plaza a little after one. Once again, your target will be in the fifth-floor corner window nearest the business district. Don't miss."

"Don't worry," Ritter said icily. "I won't."

Squinting in the bright sunlight, Ritter stared out across Dealey Plaza at the dingy red-brick building harboring the assassin. Ritter stood alone behind the semicircular concrete wall of an ornamental arbor built atop an embankment overlooking the open, grass-covered slope of the plaza's central green. The green was cut by three highways, which converged as they ran down the slope away from the city to pass beneath a railway overpass at the bottom. A scatter of people lounged on the park grass between the highways, but most of the waiting parade-watchers had positioned themselves along the motorcade route on the north side of Dealey Plaza.

The arbor hid Ritter from the eyes of people on the green, and a thick grove of pine oaks screened him from anyone looking out the post office windows behind him and to his right. Beside him on the ground were a camera tripod, two shoulder bags and the rifle case.

Ritter could see no one behind the fifth-floor window the sniper would use, but the distance was too great for him to be sure and it was still too soon to use the rifle scope. He didn't want to risk the possibility, however slight, that someone might spot the rifle before he could draw a bead on the assassin.

In the distance he could hear the gradually swelling sound of cheering and applause as the President's motorcade rolled west along Main Street, moving inexorably toward Dealey Plaza. The positions of the onlookers confirmed for Ritter what Dietrich had shown him on the map. The motorcade would enter Dealey Plaza on Main Street, turn right onto Houston and immediately left again, to follow the highway extension of Elm Street down the slope to the railway underpass. As the President's limousine turned onto Elm and headed toward the underpass, it would pass directly beneath the sniper's window.

Ritter had estimated the range to the window on the fifth floor to be just under two hundred fifty yards, and he would have little trouble with a head shot. It would have to be a head shot, for Ritter didn't want the assassin to fire reflexively when he was hit.

Ritter's hands were ice cold, and his stomach had tightened into a knot, but he knew it wouldn't affect his shooting. With the weapon in his hands, he would become rock steady.

The cheering was louder now, and Ritter estimated the motorcade to be no more than two blocks from the intersection of Main and Houston. People who had been sitting on the green got up and started moving to join the crowd lining the parade route. It was time.

Ritter knelt beside the rifle case, snapped back its catches and opened the lid. Sunlight gleamed on the rifle's polished stock. He lifted out the rifle, adjusted the sling and moved to the rectangular opening in the arbor wall. After taking one last look around him, he released the safety and eased the barrel out through the opening, which was at shoulder height. He took up the tension in the sling around his left arm, braced his arm against the edge of the opening, pulled the butt into his shoulder and put his eye to the telescopic sight.

The bricks in the wall of the building across the plaza leaped toward him in sharp relief. Wary of the scope's narrow field of view, Ritter slowly raised the cross hairs up the face of the building, floor by floor, counting them off. His finger curled around the trigger as the cross hairs moved into the center of the fifth-floor corner window. The window was closed, and the room beyond the dusty panes was dark. Ritter could detect no movement behind the window, but even if the assassin did not open it before he fired, Ritter was sure the man would be visible when he moved closer to the window for his shot.

Ritter could tell by ear alone that the motorcade had reached the corner of Main and Houston at the eastern edge of the plaza, and still there was no sign of the assassin. A breeze stirred, cooling the back of Ritter's neck, which glistened with nervous sweat. He noted the slight wind and discounted its effect on the bullet's trajectory. *Show yourself, you bastard. Show yourself!*

Applause rippled around the corner of Main and followed the President's limousine up Houston. Still there was no movement behind the window. Ritter tore his eye away from the scope for a glance at the motorcade. The President's car was slowing for its left turn onto Elm, where it would pass beneath the sniper's window. Ritter caught a flash of pink from the limousine as the First Lady waved to the crowd. He blinked and again put his eye to the scope. The cross hairs had shifted only slightly; they were still trained on thc fifth-floor window, and still there was no hint of anyone behind the glass.

Ritter could feel the time running out, measured in fractions of seconds. His mind raced. Dietrich had given him the wrong window, or the assassin had chosen another at the last minute; it was the only possible explanation. Ritter hastily traversed the scope to the left, cursing its narrow field of view. The neighboring window flashed into view — empty — and the next, also empty. Trickles of sweat ran down over Ritter's ribs. He traversed farther to the left and then swung back to the original window. Nothing, and he lost a full second of precious time.

Maybe the sniper had lost his nerve. *God, let it be that!*

Ritter gasped aloud as he heard the sharp, dry crack of a rifle shot, and in that instant he realized what had happened. He jerked the cross hairs upward, knowing, too late, where the assassin was. A second shot from the sniper rang out as the cross hairs of Ritter's scope swept upward across the image of the assassin standing in the window above the one Ritter had been watching. Ritter's rifle barked as he fired a desperate snap shot, but he knew at once that he had missed. The bullet ricocheted off the building above the window.

Even as the rifle slammed back into Ritter's shoulder, he was reaching for the bolt. His hand was a blur of motion as he snapped the bolt back, ejecting the spent cartridge, and thrust it forward again, ramming a fresh shell into the breech. But he was too late. The sniper fired a third and last time just as Ritter's sights steadied again on the sixth-floor window, and the sniper stepped back out of sight.

In Dallas Police Headquarters, a recorder monitoring the transmission from a motorcycle patrolman's radio had registered the reports of four rifle shots.

For a moment Ritter continued to stare through the telescopic sight into the empty storage room, unwilling to accept what had happened. He could hear the cries of shock and confusion in the plaza as the crowd belatedly reacted to the rifle fire. He lowered the rifle and looked out across the green at the President's limousine. Jacqueline Kennedy was crawling out onto the trunk of the open car as a Secret Service agent sprinted down the highway, trying to overtake the limousine. The President was not visible, and Ritter's fear turned to certainty. At least one of the sniper's bullets had found its mark.

A confused motorcycle patrolman, thinking the shots had come from the arbor across the green from Ritter, drove his motorcycle into the embankment, overturned, and scrambled up the embankment toward the arbor. No one looked in Ritter's direction. Ritter stepped back from the opening in the wall and knelt to replace the rifle in its case. His movements were slow and mechanical like those of an automaton.

He knew what had happened, but he couldn't feel it. Not yet. It was as if an emotional circuit breaker had been tripped inside him. His mind registered irrelevancies: the strange cry of a bird in a tree behind him, which sounded like the hiss of a photograph needle over a loudspeaker; the heat of the sun's rays on his cheek; the rumble of a jet high overhead.

He picked up the rifle case and stood up. His eye caught the glint of brass in the dirt as his feet, and he automatically stopped to retrieve the spent cartridge and slipped it into his pocket. He turned and walked through the stand of pine oaks behind the arbor, crossed the deserted loading area behind the post office and walked up the alley to Houston Street.

Confusion was spreading out from the assassination scene like ripples from a stone dropped into a pool. People were running, shouting, crying. Sirens wailed. No one noticed the tall, blond man carrying a long leather case, who walked woodenly toward the Hotel Scott with one killing on his conscience and murder in his heart.

Ritter knocked on the door of Room 410, and an instant later it was yanked open by a pale, tight-lipped Dietrich. "How could you miss!" Dietrich hissed.

Over Dietrich's shoulder, Ritter saw a pair of field glasses resting on a table beside a window facing Dealey Plaza. Dietrich had had a grandstand seat. Without a word, Ritter placed his hand on

Dietrich's chest, shoved him aside and walked past him into the room, closing the door behind him.

"*Du Hund!* How dare you lay hands on me! You are supposed to be an expert with a rifle, but you are incompetent!"

Ritter put down the rifle case and turned to face Dietrich, whose face was now flushed with anger.

"And the rifle," Dietrich shouted. "I told you to leave it at the scene. *Du Idiot!*"

Ritter stepped forward and drove his fist deep into Dietrich's solar plexus, doubling him over. Dietrich's knees folded, and he collapsed, his eyes bulging, his contorted mouth opening and closing like a fish as he vainly tried to drag air into his lungs. Ritter slipped his hand beneath his suit jacket and removed the pistol and its silencer from the holster.

"You are the idiot," he said, screwing the silencer onto the pistol barrel. "You told me to watch the fifth floor window, and you were speaking English at the time. You made a schoolboy's mistake. In *German* it is the fifth floor; in English it is the sixth."

At last Dietrich's stunned diaphragm began to respond and he was able to take his first gasping breaths. Ritter walked to the table by the window and laid the pistol beside the field glasses; he would not be needing it yet. Dietrich struggled weakly to his knees and looked dazedly up at Ritter, who was coming back toward him.

"You're crazy," Dietrich gasped. "I'll . . ."

Ritter kicked him in the face.

Dietrich's nose broke with an audible crunch, and the force of the kick spun him onto his back. Bright red blood poured from his nostrils and soaked into his mustache.

"Wha-at are you doing?" he cried shrilly.

Ritter kicked him again, hard in the ribs. When Dietrich reflexively rolled onto his side to shield his cracked ribs, Ritter kicked him viciously in the mouth. "I'm killing you," Ritter said to the gurgling, twitching heap spitting blood and teeth onto the carpet. "It's up to you how long it takes."

Dietrich mouthed a series of gagging, frenzied sounds.

"Shut up," Ritter snapped, kicking Dietrich again. "Listen to me. The pain you feel is nothing compared to what you will suffer if you don't tell me what I want to know. Are you listening?"

Dietrich groaned and nodded his head feebly.

"I want to know the name of the man who gives you orders, and I want to know where I can find him."

It was then that Dietrich realized that Ritter had not gone crazy. He looked up at Ritter, hatred supplanting his fear. The lower half of his face was a bloody, pulpy mess and one eye was swollen closed. The other eye glared defiantly at Ritter. "Traitor," Dietrich croaked, "I'll tell you nothing."

"You *will* tell me. I saw it done once — a long time ago on the Eastern Front. One of your colleagues, Dietrich, an SS officer, broke a Russian who had refused to talk. Don't make me do it, Dietrich. Tell me the name I must know, and you will die easily."

"Fuck you," Dietrich said in English.

Ritter stared for a moment at the man on the floor, and the hatred he saw in Dietrich's eyes was nothing compared to his own. He began his bloody work.

FIFTEEN

Ritter had washed Dietrich's blood from his hands, but he could still feel it, warm and sticky on his fingers. He could still smell the sour stench of Dietrich's vomit and hear the man's muffled, strangling screams. In the end, Dietrich had talked, but not without cost to Ritter's soul. In the dark recesses of Ritter's mind a private hell now existed, a hell in which a dying man's screams would forever echo.

The long-distance telephone operator told Ritter the price of his call, and he inserted the necessary coins in the pay phone slot. As he waited for the call to be put through, he looked out through the glass of the phone booth at an approaching pair of Texas Rangers. They were only making a routine sweep of the bus station's waiting room. The killer of President Kennedy was already in custody in the Dallas City Jail.

"Barlev," said the voice on the other end of the line.

"Ritter."

"My God, man, what happened? We couldn't —"

"I have the information you need," Ritter cut in. His voice was thick with weariness. "I know the name of the man who gave Dietrich his orders. Gunter Heissler. He works out of an office in Munich. Eighteen Alexanderstrasse. Werewolf may be run by a directorate, but Heissler is at the very center of the organization."

There was a pause before Barlev responded, and Ritter had the impression that the Israeli was writing the information down.

"Are you sure?" Barlev asked.

Ritter made a sound something like a laugh. "I tortured and killed the man for that information. I'm sure."

"Ritter, are you all right? What happened?"

"Just get Heissler," Ritter said and started to hang up.

Barlev must have sensed it, for he shouted, "Wait, Ritter, listen! Where is the body? We can have a clean-up squad in Dallas in a matter of hours."

"Hotel Scott, Room four ten; and clean-up is the right phrase," Ritter said, noting with detachment the edge of hysteria in his own voice.

"Are you all right?"

"I will be. I got you what you wanted, and now we're quits, you and I."

"I understand how you —"

Ritter sighed and hung up the phone. He pushed his way out of the phone booth and walked to one of the benches and sat down. His bus didn't depart for another half hour. Ritter hadn't analyzed his reasons for discarding his airline ticket and buying a seat on a bus for a twenty-four-hour ride back to New York; it had just seemed the thing to do. On the bus he would be in limbo, riding on and on over the highways with no need to act, talk, or think.

A man on one of the nearby benches turned up the volume of his transistor radio to catch the news. An announcer was giving the latest information on the accused assassin. All over the city, radios and TV sets were tuned in to the news, and Ritter had already heard the name: Oswald.

Ritter got up from his seat and moved away. He didn't want to hear the report; it was like rubbing salt into an open wound. If only he had been a heartbeat faster in shifting his sights . . . Ritter looked out one of the dusty terminal windows at the clear early evening sky. It should be raining, he thought, with thunder rumbling and lightning ripping across a black sky.

Ritter's bus pulled into New York's Port Authority Terminal at ten o'clock at night. The revving of the bus engine echoed in the dank concrete cavern of the terminal's lower level and brought Ritter out of a restless sleep. He blinked groggily and stretched his stiff muscles. He was tired, rumpled and gritty, and his tongue was raw from chain smoking.

He focused his bleary eyes with difficulty and looked out the window as the driver maneuvered the bus into its allotted parking space. A handful of people waited behind the glass doors of the arrival gate. In the center of the group stood a grizzled, barrel-chested man; it was Barlev.

"Shit," Ritter muttered and reached for his cigarettes. He waited for the entire busload of passengers to disembark before he got off.

"No luggage?" Barlev said as Ritter came through the arrival gate.

Ritter shook his head and kept walking, heading for the escalator that led to the terminal's upper level. Barlev fell into step beside him.

"How did you know?" Ritter asked, without real interest.

"Process of elimination. We covered La Guardia, Idlewild and Newark, but you didn't show. Rail service is practically non-existent, and I didn't think you'd rent a car. So, here I am."

"I'm flattered," Ritter said tonelessly, stepping onto the escalator. Barlev got on behind him.

"You said you were through," Barlev said. "All right. But we've still got to talk — to close out the books."

"Does it have to be now?"

"Yes. I can check you into a hotel, or we can go to Elana's place."

"A hotel," Ritter said.

"You look like hell."

"I'm tired."

"You'll need a change of clothes. We'll take care of that."

"Terrific."

Outside the terminal, Barlev herded Ritter into a taxi, took him to a small hotel off Sixth Avenue, checked him in and accompanied him to his room. Ritter walked directly to the bed, kicked off his shoes and dropped onto the mattress.

"Jesus," Barlev said, wrinkling his nose. "You need a shower."

"Yes, I know," Ritter said, staring at the reflection of the wallpaper behind his head in the mirror on the opposite wall. The wallpaper's design had a hypnotic effect, and he felt sleep tugging at his eyelids.

"Don't drop off on me," Barlev said sharply. "We have to talk."

Ritter grunted wearily and propped himself up against the bed's headboard. "Okay, talk."

Barlev lit one of his cheap cigars to cover the smell of Ritter's feet. "First, I have to know what happened in Dallas."

Ritter told him; it didn't take long. When Ritter finished, Barlev nodded slowly, and for a long while he was silent. Ritter very nearly fell asleep on him.

"My boys cleaned up the mess at the hotel," he said at last. "The body will never be found."

Ritter had the impression that Barlev was simply talking to keep him awake, that Barlev was preoccupied with other thoughts. Abruptly, Barlev's expression changed, and he looked at Ritter with fresh intensity.

"We've already checked out the lead you gave me on the phone, and we think you hit the jackpot. Heissler lives at the address you gave me. He owns the whole damned building — or at least his construction firm does. The building stands alone on a full square block of land that was blasted flat in the war and never rebuilt. The firm owns the land as well, and has never built anything on it but that single building, which houses the firm's offices.

"The isolation of the Heissler building makes surveillance difficult, and it has a sophisticated security system. As for Heissler himself, we drew a blank. He is a man with influence, money and no past whatsoever. I think that Heissler may be the top man in Werewolf and that his building is their headquarters. I never did buy the idea of a directorate. Nazis want a Führer, not a board of directors. Ritter, are you listening?"

"What?"

He hadn't been listening. His mind had flashed back to the bright, sunlit green of Dealey Plaza, the excited, happy crowds lining the motorcade route — the sharp crack of a rifle.

"Why didn't you people stop it?" Ritter said bitterly.

"There wasn't time," Barlev said, spreading his hands in an unaccustomed gesture of defensiveness. "I sent a signal, but someone up the line fouled up. There was a delay and a request for more information, and by then it was too late. I'm not Moses; I can't part the Red Sea. I'm just a field man. Sometimes they listen to me, sometimes not."

"Oh, Christ!" Ritter snarled.

Barlev's expression hardened. "Snap out of it, man. Stop feeling sorry for yourself. A man is dead because time ran out, but it wasn't your fault and it wasn't mine. Men die every day, and the world doesn't come to an end. But if Werewolf isn't stopped, it just might. World War Three: *that*'s what you should be worried about."

"Not me, you. I told you, Barlev, I'm through. It's your problem now. You have Heissler in your sights, so go get him — or blow the whistle on Werewolf. Call in other governments."

"And have everyone dismiss Werewolf as another example of Jewish paranoia? Or should Tel Aviv broadcast the news that it had advance warning of Kennedy's assassination? No, we'll strike at Werewolf ourselves, and we'll have to do it before they realize they've lost one of their agents."

"Strike? How?"

"We'll raid eighteen Alexanderstrasse, seize Heissler if we can, kill him if we can't. And we'll be after documents. This is still an SS operation, and the SS documented everything."

"Then do it, and leave me alone."

"We could be wrong about Heissler. It would be better if we

could be sure. A raid on West German territory is not something Tel Aviv relishes."

"I don't know what you want from me. My cover is blown."

"Not necessarily. Wait!" Barlev said, holding up his hand as Ritter started to interrupt. "Hear me out before you say no. If you refuse me, I'll still keep my end of our bargain. I promised to get you away from Werewolf if you helped us. That still stands. I've obtained flawless identity papers for you, and certain friends have arranged suitable employment for you at a bank in Chicago. You can disappear any time you want to. Say the word, and you'll be free of us and free of Werewolf. Just hear me out first."

"All right," Ritter said wearily, "I'll listen."

"I want to send you into the Heissler building just before the raid to confirm that it is Werewolf headquarters. Until you told me what happened in Dallas, I thought your cover was blown, but now I think we have a chance to keep you in the game — long enough to get you inside their headquarters."

"How?"

"You've heard that Oswald has been killed?"

"Yes." The news had swept through the bus like wildfire.

"Ruby's killing of Oswald is the key. You are the only one who knows what really happened in Dallas, and you can feed Werewolf anything you want, as long as your story fits the external facts. I want you to use the telephone number Dietrich gave you to send a message to Werewolf. Tell them that Dietrich blew the original plan and that you set Ruby up to kill Oswald in order to save the situation. When Dietrich panicked, you were forced to liquidate him."

Ritter laughed derisively. "Are you serious? What am I supposed to be, a miracle worker? How the hell could I have induced Ruby to kill Oswald? And why should I have to kill Dietrich? It's ludicrous. Heissler knew Dietrich, and he knows that I was only Dietrich's trigger man."

"Heissler *knows* nothing," Barlev said, stabbing the air with his forefinger for emphasis. "Imagine what must be going through his mind right at this moment. With no word from Dietrich, he had to sweat out the twenty-four hours Oswald was in custody, wondering what had gone wrong, worrying about what Oswald might tell the authorities. And then — bang. Oswald is snuffed out. He's not going to believe that was a coincidence. Send him a message now, and he'll call you in. He'll bring you right into his headquarters; I feel it in my bones."

Ritter shook his head. "The story is too wild. They'll never buy it."

"They *will* buy it. The alternative is to believe that Oswald's death was a lucky coincidence, and no one believes in coincidence. No one. And how can Heissler know that Dietrich didn't panic? If the SS ever had an operational weakness it was their mistrust of each other. Even if Heissler doesn't buy your story completely, he'll bring you in. That message will get you inside eighteen Alexanderstrasse, and when you go in, we'll be right there waiting. Confirm it as their headquarters, and we'll strike immediately — in broad daylight, if necessary."

Ritter's cigarette had burned itself down to his fingers. He ground it out in the ashtray beside the bed. He could feel the coils of circumstance and of his own conscience tightening around him, and he fought against them. He wanted to be free.

"I'll think about it," he said.

"Twenty-four hours. I'll wait that long, but then I'll put a raid together without you." Barlev approached the bed and stuck out his hand. "It's for you to decide. You've done enough already, and I won't hold it against you if you say no."

Ritter shook hands, and Barlev smiled crookedly. "Just one thing more. Do the world a favor and take a shower."

Wintry gusts of wind snatched at Ritter as he emerged from his hotel into a gray Manhattan dawn. He pulled up his overcoat collar against the wind and started walking toward Sixth Avenue in search of a place to have breakfast. Beer cans and scraps of paper littered the deserted sidewalks.

The first coffee shop Ritter found open was nearly empty. Through the window, he saw comatose waiters moving like zombies among the tables, and he walked on. Two blocks farther on, he found a corner breakfast shop that was filled to capacity, and he went inside. A hostess squeezed him into a seat at the end of a row of narrow tables.

A waiter with an unintelligible foreign accent took his order and returned with the food in an ominously short time. It was hard for Ritter to believe that there had been enough time to cook the eggs. He had no appetite, only a rumbling in his stomach that demanded food. He picked up his fork and listlessly began to eat.

Through the restaurant window, Ritter watched a drunk in expensive clothes steer a wobbly course toward a subway entrance across the street. Ritter's eyes followed the forlorn figure until the man staggered down the subway steps and disappeared from view. Ritter shivered slightly as he felt loneliness close in on him.

He looked at the pay phone on the wall nearby and briefly toyed with the thought of calling Elana, just to hear her voice one more time, but he discarded the notion. She was part of the chapter in his life that he meant to close. He was through with Werewolf and through with Barlev. He would call the Israeli from work and tell him to arrange his disappearance. Dallas had taken all Ritter had to give.

He signaled the waiter and asked for more coffee. He still had nearly two hours to kill before he could go to his office.

"Good morning, Mr. Ritter," said the receptionist as Ritter walked into the anteroom to the offices of Garcia Exports. She smiled as usual, and as usual the smile did not quite extend to her eyes, which were regarding him with thinly veiled curiosity. On Friday, the day he had been summoned to Dallas, he had not called in to explain his absence.

"Good morning, Miss Borg," Ritter responded, wondering what it was about her he didn't like. She was a slim blond in her forties, who did her job well enough, but Ritter had never felt at ease in her presence. He walked past her down the short passage to his office.

Moments after he had settled in behind his desk, Marianne

Becker came into the office. She looked worried. "Where were you on Friday, Mr. Ritter? Mr. Garcia called three times. I tried to reach you at home, but there was no answer. You had us worried."

"I'm sorry, but I was called away suddenly — on a personal matter."

"Is anything wrong?"

"No, everything is squared away now. Besides Garcia's calls, did I miss anything important?"

"No," his secretary said. "Of course, the President . . . How could something like that happen? It still doesn't seem possible."

"I know," Ritter said, and again the scene at Dealey Plaza flashed before him: the limousine turning to pass beneath the squat, ugly brick building, the flash of pink as the First Lady waved to the crowd.

". . . right there in broad daylight," Marianne Becker was saying.

"If you'll excuse me," Ritter said sharply, "I have work to catch up on."

His secretary flushed. "Of course. Shall I put through a call to Mr. Garcia?"

"Please do."

Flustered by Ritter's coldness, Marianne Becker left the office, closing the door softly behind her. Ritter shook his head in self-contempt and lit a cigarette. He was becoming careless of other people's feelings; he would have to get hold of himself. Five minutes later, his phone rang.

"I have Mr. Garcia on the line."

"Thanks, Marianne. Put him on."

Ritter pulled the receiver away from his ear as Garcia's angry voice burst from the phone. Ritter's unexplained absence had infuriated the South American millionaire. Ritter waited for a break in the storm and then said calmly, "You're quite right, Mr. Garcia, and I'll save you the trouble of firing me. I quit."

Before Garcia could react, Ritter hung up.

Having cast the die, Ritter pressed his intercom and asked his secretary to come in. When he told her that he had resigned, she surprised him by bursting into tears. It was a bitter moment for him, and he wished he could have explained; but there could be no explanation and no turning back. Werewolf would come after him; he had to disappear.

Ritter worked through the day, setting the firm's affairs in order as best he could to smooth the way for his successor. One by one, the members of the office staff came in to say goodbye and to wish him well. They all seemed taken aback by his sudden departure, and he realized for the first time how much his subordinates liked him.

He knew he should call Barlev to give him his final refusal, but he kept putting it off. He wondered how long Barlev would wait before contacting him. At four in the afternoon the phone rang, but it wasn't Barlev.

"Erich?"

Ritter felt his pulse quicken. One word — just the sound of her lightly-accented voice — was all it took to throw him off balance. *Barlev, you bastard. You counted on me to fall for her. That was your ace in the hole.*

"Hello, Elana."

"Erich, are you all right?"

It won't work, Barlev. I won't let you play me for a sucker.

"I'm all right."

"Why didn't you call me?"

Ritter said nothing.

"I've got to see you, Erich."

"Did Barlev tell you to call?"

"What? No. He doesn't know I'm calling you. Look, Erich, we have to talk. It's important — for me — for both of us."

Ritter felt his resolve weaken. Barlev must have put her up to this, but he wanted to believe her. He couldn't help himself, he wanted to believe.

"Please, Erich."

Ritter hesitated. He had wanted to make a clean break, and he had been determined not to see her again.

"All right. When and where?"

"Can you leave now?"

"Yes."

"Good. I'll pick you up in two minutes."

"Where are you?"

"Downstairs in the lobby of your building. See you in a minute."

The line went dead before Ritter could have second thoughts. He pushed his chair back from the desk and looked around his office for the last time. It was hard to believe he wouldn't be coming back. How long had he been with the firm? Could it really be six years? The older he got, the faster time slipped by, like sand through his fingers. A jumble of memories tumbled into his mind.

The door opened and his secretary poked her head in. "Miss Miller is here."

Ritter stood up quickly and crossed the room. "I guess it's time to say goodbye, Marianne, and I'm afraid I'm not very good at farewells. Good luck with your new boss."

She smiled up at him. "Good luck to you, as well, Mr. Ritter. You know that we all hate to see you leave."

"Thanks. Thanks very much."

Elana was waiting for him in the anteroom. She and the receptionist seemed to be studiously ignoring each other.

"Hello," Elana said with a warm smile.

"Hello," Ritter answered.

"I'm glad you decided to," Elana said lightly.

"Decided what?"

"To smile back."

Ritter glanced at the receptionist and felt his cheeks flush. It was no use trying to hide his feelings from Elana; she could read his face like a book.

"Supper at my place?" Elana asked.

"Sure, that's fine. Goodbye, Miss Borg."

The receptionist glanced up from the card file she was rearranging. "Goodbye, Mr. Ritter," she said coolly.

As they walked down the outer corridor toward the elevators, Elana slipped her arm familiarly under his. She was wearing a light tan trenchcoat and a black beret, and she looked very European — and very beautiful.

"There's no need for that," Ritter said stiffly. "It's all over; we don't have to put on an act any longer."

"That's right," Elana said softly, continuing to hold onto his arm, "we don't."

Ritter looked at her in surprise, and she smiled and shook her head. "You know, Erich, sometimes you're a little slow on the uptake."

And suddenly for Ritter the world no longer seemed a cold, forbidding place.

On the way down in the elevator, Elana said, "That woman is a strange one."

"What woman?" Ritter said. He was smiling. He couldn't seem to stop smiling.

"Your receptionist. It may have been my imagination, but when I came into the office she looked as if she recognized me. Yet I'm sure I've never seen her before. Then her eyes went blank, as if a curtain had dropped behind them. Have you ever noticed her eyes? They're so cold. Cold, gray eyes, like stones."

. . . . SIXTEEN . . . .

Kadinsky never hurried a kill. She always took the time to watch and to plan. Dressed in black from head to foot, her blond hair hidden beneath a woolen cap, she stood in the deep shadow of a narrow alley across the street from the Israeli girl's brownstone. She had been watching the residence for an hour.

Encountering the girl in the office had been a shock. It had been the first time she had seen her close up since that day at Idlewild, but she had recognized her instantly. Her shock, however, had immediately given way to anger. Dietrich had used one of his incompetent underlings to check out the girl when Ritter had begun dating her, and the fool had discovered little more than her address. It had been careless of Dietrich, and Kadinsky detested carelessness.

Ritter's association with an Israeli agent could mean only one thing: he was a traitor. Kadinsky wasted no time wondering how, or why; others could sort that out later. Security had been breached, and her standing orders were explicit. She would kill both the girl and the traitor.

Kadinsky had gone back to her own apartment to change, pick

up her equipment, and to look up the girl's address, which she had recorded in her notebook. She had tried one more time to reach Dietrich by phone, but she had not been surprised when he had not answered. Alarm bells had been ringing in her mind ever since she had heard the news from Dallas on Friday. Dietrich, she assumed, had already paid the price for his carelessness.

Kadinsky had eaten a light supper and then had taken a taxi to Grammercy Park. From what she had overheard in the office, she had expected Ritter still to be there, and soon after she had taken up her position, she had seen the shadows of two people behind the curtain screening a front window.

A cold drizzle began to fall, and Kadinsky moved close to one wall of the alley, which afforded her some protection from the rain. The black leather bag resting on the ground at her feet contained her burglar's tools and her Mauser automatic. If Ritter left the girl's apartment, she would take the girl immediately afterwards and then go after him. If he stayed the night, she would have to deal with them both at the same time.

Kadinsky looked at the radium dial of her watch. It was only 9:30 P.M. She leaned against the wall and settled down for a long wait.

Ritter arched his back and stretched contentedly. As he settled back, Elana nestled herself in the crook of his arm. They were seated on the living room floor before a fire in the small hearth, their backs against the front of the sofa. The fire's glow tinted Elana's cheeks, and tiny reflections of the flames danced and sparkled in her dark eyes.

"I thought beautiful women couldn't cook," Ritter said. "Now I know better."

"Thank you," Elana said, turning and brushing her lips against his cheek.

They had shared a quiet supper, talking about meaningless things, intentionally avoiding saying anything that might again throw up a barrier between them.

"I wish . . ." Ritter began and then fell silent.

"What do you wish?"

Ritter had been about to say that he wished these moments of happiness could last, for he didn't believe in them — at least not completely. For the past several hours, he had steadfastly suppressed his doubts, determined to snatch what happiness he could, even if it was all an illusion; but now he could wait no longer. He had to know.

"On the phone this afternoon you said that you had to talk to me — about something important to both of us."

Ritter felt Elana's body stiffen, not from his words, but from his tone of voice.

"You don't trust me, do you?" Elana said, edging away from him. "You won't let yourself trust anyone."

"Jesus Christ, should I?"

"I had hopes," Elana said. She drew up her knees, clasped her arms around her legs and stared fixedly at the fire.

"You said you had to talk to me," Ritter repeated tonelessly. He felt like a man digging his own grave.

"Barlev wants you to do one last job for us, and he asked me to help persuade you to agree. Any way I could," she said coldly, still not looking at him. "That's what you expected, isn't it?"

Ritter felt his throat constrict. So it had been an illusion, after all. The look in her eyes, the words of endearment — all an illusion conjured up by Barlev.

"Why tell me now?" he said hoarsely. "It was working. You had me on the hook."

"Go to hell," Elana said bitterly, and Ritter saw with astonishment that tears were running down her cheeks.

"Elana . . ."

"Don't say anything. You've said more than enough," she said, angrily wiping away her tears. "Yes, I wanted to talk to you, but not for the reason you think. I wanted to tell you to refuse him. I wanted to tell you that you'd done enough. But you were so damned sure that Barlev was using me — that I'd let him use me to get to you. Well, to hell with you, Erich Ritter. No, don't touch me!"

Ritter had reached out and caught her arm. "Elana, I love you."
He pulled her into his arms. She resisted, but he held her fast. "I
wanted to believe in you," he said, the words tumbling out. "God,
how I wanted to believe. But I couldn't — not completely. It just
didn't seem possible. It was something I wanted too much — like
I wanted my wife to live, like I wanted to be free of my past."

Ritter realized that Elana had stopped trying to pull away from
him. He could taste the salt in the tears on her cheeks. . . .

Much later, they lay together on the carpet, locked in each other's arms. The fire had died down to a glowing heap of embers.

"Erich?" Elana said drowsily. "Are you awake?"

Ritter stirred and laughed softly. "Very much so. I feel like a
man awakened from a long nightmare."

"Why did you say you didn't think it possible — that I should
love you?"

"I don't know. It just didn't seem possible — because of who
you are and who I was. Maybe I was worried about my age. I'm
old enough to be your father."

"Don't be ridiculous! You'd have to have married at fifteen."

"Ah, so you've been doing some calculating."

Ritter grunted as she gave him a sharp dig in the ribs.

"You've been quiet a long time," she said. "What have you been
thinking about?"

"I've been wondering where we go from here."

Elana rolled against him and pressed her lips against his chest.
"We live happily ever after," she said in a muffled voice.

"Where?" he said, stroking her hair.

"You could come to Israel. You'd be safe there, even if Barlev
doesn't manage to put an end to Werewolf."

"I already have a country. I'm an American."

Elana sighed and slowly sat up. She reached out, picked up
Ritter's shirt and slipped it on. She didn't look at him. "Where are
your cigarettes?" she asked.

"They're in my jacket pocket. I thought you were giving up
smoking."

"I'd rather smoke than cry," she said, reaching across him to get his jacket. She found cigarettes and matches and hastily lit a cigarette. She took several quick puffs and said, "We could live together in the States."

Ritter shook his head. "Sooner or later you'd regret it. You said yourself that you couldn't live as an expatriate."

Ritter saw that her eyes were blinking rapidly, and again she looked away from him. "There must be a way," she said. "There has to be."

Ritter propped himself up against the edge of the sofa and put his arm around her. "Maybe there is, and if there is, we'll find it."

Elana leaned her head on his shoulder. "Oh, Erich, why did we wait so long? Barlev will have to get you under cover soon, and Mossad will have work for me elsewhere. We have to make a decision, and now there's so little time."

Ritter kissed her gently on the eyes. "We'll make a decision," he said, "but not tonight. Tonight it's enough that we're together."

Outside the rain had stopped, but the temperature was dropping. Kadinsky cautiously moved out of the alley's shadow and checked to make sure the street was deserted. She didn't like coming out into the open before it was time, but movement had become necessary; she couldn't allow her muscles to stiffen in the cold. She walked briskly up the block and back again, the footfalls of her rubber-soled shoes soundless on the wet pavement. Never once, as she walked, did her eyes leave the doorway to Elana's residence.

A small pendulum clock on the mantelpiece above the fireplace chimed twelve. Ritter looked down at the sleeping girl beside him and kissed her on the mouth. She opened her eyes.

"Time to go to bed," he said.

"Okay," she responded drowsily.

Ritter got to one knee, scooped her up in his arms and stood up. As they passed by the single lamp that burned on a table by the door, Elana reached out and switched it off, plunging the room into darkness. Ritter carried her through the hallway and up the stairs to her bedroom on the floor above.

Kadinsky waited until two A.M. before she made her move. A police cruiser had passed down the street five minutes earlier, but now the street was completely deserted. The windows in the brownstones along the block were all dark. Kadinsky picked up her leather bag and crossed the street to the wrought-iron gate in front of Elana's brownstone. She tested the hinge and then silently eased the gate open.

She slipped through the gate and up the steps to the front door. She was exposed and clearly visible in the light from the twin lamps above the doorway, but there was no other way. She inspected the lock and nodded in satisfaction. As she had expected, it was a standard pin-and-tumbler model. She set down her bag and removed an L-shaped tension wrench and a thin, spoon-shaped lock pick.

She took a quick look up and down the street and then inserted the tension wrench in the keyhole, twisting it to exert torque on the cylinder's plug. Next she slipped the pick in along the top of the keyhole and felt for each one of the pins in turn, gently pushing them into alignment with the plug-cylinder shear line. Sixty seconds later, the plug turned smoothly under the pressure of the tension wrench, and the lock cam slid the bolt aside.

Kadinsky gently opened the door and heard the metallic slither of a chain lock. Again she checked the street to make sure it was deserted. Satisfied, she replaced the wrench and pick in her bag and took out a long loop of elastic rubber tied at one end to a strip of adhesive tape. She slipped her hand through the opening between the door and the jam, reached around the edge of the door as far as she could, and pressed the tape firmly against the inside surface of the door. Slowly she extended the rubber band until she could loop it over the knob on the end of the chain. When she released the rubber band, it snapped back, pulling the knob with it and releasing the chain latch. The chain fell against the door jam with a faint rattle, but otherwise there was no sound.

Kadinsky stood at the open door for several seconds, listening, but inside nothing stirred. She picked up her bag and slipped inside, closing the door soundlessly behind her.

Ritter awoke with a start from a dreamless sleep. He had been eighteen when his commando instructors had drilled into him the instincts for survival behind enemy lines. Night after night, they had crept into the recruits' barracks to pounce on any man who did not awaken at the slightest unusual sound. Twenty years had dulled that conditioning, but had not erased it.

Ritter blinked in the darkness and rolled irritably onto his side, not knowing what had awakened him. A cold draft of air brushed his cheek. One of the bedroom windows was open a crack, and the curtain in front of it billowed gently in response to the inrush of cold air. Ritter was about to close his eyes again when the draft was abruptly cut off and the curtain fell back into place. It did not stir again.

Ritter frowned in the darkness, annoyed that he had come fully awake and puzzled that he should be wondering about a random gust of wind. *But there was no wind outside.* The curtain continued to hang limply before the window. What had caused the draft? What had awakened him?

From the recesses of his subconscious memory came the sound of a chain's rattle — faint, yet still audible in the silent house. A door opening to the outside could have caused the draft. A door that had opened and was now closed. . . . Ritter felt goose flesh rise on his arms.

Kadinsky stood inside the front entrance, listening. She waited a full two minutes before she moved again. The house was completely silent and pitch dark. Ritter and the girl were surely asleep. Kadinsky knelt and extracted her Mauser from the leather bag. The silencer was already in place, and the automatic was loaded and cocked, with the safety on. She slipped the safety catch and started down the hallway, feeling her way toward the staircase she guessed she would find at the end of the hall. The bedrooms would be upstairs.

Kadinsky wasn't nervous — she didn't know what the feeling was like — but she disliked killing without detailed preparation, so she was even more wary than usual. At the end of the hall she made out the outline of the staircase, and she felt for the first step with the toe of her left foot. She found it, placed her foot on the step and gradually increased the pressure. The wood was old, but solid, and there was no creak as it took her weight. She felt for the second step.

Ritter lay on his side, listening. The only sound was Elana's soft breathing beside him. He thought of waking her, but he decided against it. If there was a cat burglar in the house, he didn't want to risk her making a warning sound, and if he was just letting his imagination run away with him, there was no point in alarming her.

Seconds ticked by, stretching into minutes. Still he heard no foreign sounds, and he relaxed slightly. Perhaps it was his imagination, after all. But if it wasn't. . . . Feeling slightly foolish, Ritter slipped out of bed and silently padded across the room to a position beside the open door. The bedroom air was cool, and he was naked; he began to shiver.

Kadinsky froze as a stair creaked beneath her foot, and she cursed silently. She waited, listening, and then shifted the foot closer to the wall and tried again. This time, the stair took her weight without protest, and she crept one step higher on the staircase.

Ritter heard the creak from the staircase outside the bedroom door, and he tensed. It had been a small sound, but unmistakable. Someone was in the house and coming up the stairs. Ritter started as Elana moaned softly in her sleep.

Kadinsky had reached the top of the stairs when she heard the soft moan. It had come from the room at the head of the stairs.

Kadinsky nodded to herself in the darkness. Now she at least knew where the girl was. Would Ritter be with her? He was a traitor, so she wouldn't put it past him to sleep with a Jewess. Her lip curled in disgust. She could see the doorway ahead of her from the light coming in through the bedroom windows.

A short hallway led to another room, its doorway hidden in the darkness, and Kadinsky guessed that it would be another bedroom. If Ritter was not sleeping with the girl, he would probably be there. She would have to check, because she wanted to take him before the girl.

Ritter felt, rather than heard, the intruder move past the bedroom door and down the hall to the next room. Adrenaline was pumping into his bloodstream, and his lungs demanded oxygen. He gritted his teeth with the effort of restraining his breathing. Elana stirred again, and Ritter prayed she wouldn't awaken now. He heard the faintest click from the end of the hall as the intruder opened the door to the next room, and moments later he heard the scuff of a foot on the hall carpet as the intruder returned.

It was then that Ritter stopped thinking of the intruder as a cat burglar. Without knowing why, Ritter was suddenly sure that the intruder was searching for them, and he raised his right arm, poised to strike. Though he shivered with cold, beads of sweat broke out on his forehead.

Kadinsky paused at the threshold of the door to the room where the girl was sleeping and adjusted her grip on the Mauser. She extended her index finger out along the barrel and curled her middle finger around the trigger. Now her trigger control would not be precise, but the barrel would automatically point where she pointed her index finger. Ritter was probably in the room, too, and she would not make the mistake of underestimating him. If he awoke and moved quickly, she would have to make a snap shot.

She frowned; she could hear the girl's breathing, but not Ritter's. Could he be downstairs, sleeping in the living room? As sure-footed and silent as a cat, she stepped across the threshold, her automatic pointing toward the bed. She could see the bed; the girl was alone. Knowing her silencer was effective and that she could kill the girl soundlessly, Kadinsky started to press the trigger.

The sight of the pistol coming through the doorway jolted Ritter like an electric shock; the intruder had come to kill. Ritter didn't hesitate; he attacked instantly.

His right arm swept down and the heel of his hand knifed into the intruder's wrist, but the blow came a millisecond too late; Kadinsky had already pressed the hair trigger. The Mauser fired with a muffled pop an instant before Ritter's blow snapped Kadinsky's wrist bone like a dry twig.

Kadinsky gasped, and the automatic clattered to the floor, but she struck back instantly, whirling toward Ritter and driving the outstretched fingers of her left hand straight into his face, aiming for his eyes. Ritter was as quick as she. He ducked and slammed his fist into her midsection as her pointed nails buried themselves uselessly in the flesh of his forehead. The force of Ritter's blow jackknifed her body, and she crumpled to the floor and lay still.

"Elana!" Ritter cried, slapping the wall in search of the light switch. He found it and drenched the room in yellow light from the ceiling lamp. Elana lay on her back, her dark eyes wide with shock and pain. A scarlet stain appeared on the blanket where she clasped it against her abdomen, and slowly the stain began to widen. Ritter started toward her, but a scrabbling sound behind him arrested him in midstride.

The woman he had known as Helen Borg was on her knees, reaching with her good arm for the gun on the floor. A tangle of blond hair hung across her eyes, and her lips were drawn back in a silent snarl of pain and hatred. Her left hand closed on the gun butt, but Ritter gave her no time to raise the pistol. He delivered a deliberate, vicious chopping blow to the back of her head, just above the nape of the neck. The blow was meant to kill, and Kadinsky was dead as her body hit the floor.

Ritter spun around and leaped for the telephone on the night-stand by Elana's bed. He ripped the receiver from its cradle, started to dial, cursed as he missed a digit, and began again. Elana lay quite still with her eyes closed. Her face was chalk white, and her breathing was terrifyingly shallow. The red stain on the blanket continued to widen.

"Come on, come on!" Ritter cried in frustration. At last he heard ringing on the other end of the line. A trickle of blood from the cuts on his forehead ran down the bridge of his nose, and he absently brushed it away. Barlev answered on the third ring.

"Barlev, this is Ritter. I'm in Elana's apartment. She's been shot through the stomach. She's still alive, but bleeding badly. I killed the intruder."

"Stay there. Help will be on the way."

"Hurry, for Christ's sake!" Ritter yelled into the phone, but the line was already dead.

Knowing it was probably useless, he still tried to staunch the flow of blood from Elana's wound. He dashed into the bathroom, ripped a towel from the rack, folded it into a thick pad, and raced back to the bedroom. Elana's hands were still clasped over her wound, and he was afraid of hurting her. As gently as he could, he pulled her hands apart, but he wasn't gentle enough, and her low moan of pain cut through him like a knife. Slowly he lifted her arms away from the blood-soaked blanket and drew it back to expose her abdomen. Blood pulsed from the bullet hole with every breath she took. He placed the towel over the wound, found a fresh blanket and covered her with it. There was nothing more he could do but hold her hand and wait. Her fingers were ice cold.

"Hang on, Elana," he whispered. "Hang on."

Two minutes later the phone rang, and Ritter, without releasing Elana's hand, reached out and picked up the receiver. Dr. Weiss was on the line.

"A private ambulance is on the way," Weiss said. "It should get to you in a matter of minutes. Is she still alive?"

"Yes."

"The ambulance will take her to a private clinic on the Island. I'll meet it there and operate immediately."

"Long Island! Why not a Manhattan emergency room, for God's sake? She's bleeding to death!"

"It was Barlev's decision. It's a matter of . . . discretion."

"That dirty bastard . . ."

"The medics know what to do," Weiss cut in. "They have her blood type and will give her a transfusion as soon as they arrive. They'll do all that can be done to stabilize her. Was the bullet jacketed or soft-point?"

"Just a minute," Ritter said.

He put down the phone and quickly retrieved the Mauser from where it lay beside Kadinsky's body. He checked the clip and picked up the phone again. "Full copper jacket."

"Thank God for small favors. Where is the wound, exactly?"

"About three centimeters to the left of the navel."

"Is there an exit wound?"

"I don't think so, but I can't be sure without rolling her over."

"Leave her be, and keep her warm. I'm on the way to the clinic now."

Ritter hung up and looked helplessly at Elana's still form. He was aware that he was shivering violently, but it didn't seem important. Through the window he heard the distant wail of a siren, which gradually increased in intensity, and he breathed a sigh of relief. He started to dress, and then he remembered the body. Hastily he threw on the last of his clothes and dragged Kadinsky's body out of Elana's room, down the hall and into the second bedroom. Outside, the ambulance pulled up in front of the brownstone, its siren dying in a drawn-out moan, and Ritter ran downstairs to open the front door.

But it was Barlev who came running up the front steps as Ritter opened the door, and Ritter wondered irrelevantly how many red lights the Israeli had run on his way downtown. In neighboring brownstones the lights went on in upper-story windows as people awakened by the siren got out of bed to see what was going on.

The street was bathed in the flashing red light from the ambulance's turret lamp.

"Upstairs," Ritter said as Barlev brushed past him. "Upstairs," he repeated as two white-jacketed medics, carrying a stretcher and a bulky medical bag, came running up the steps and through the door. Ritter was taken aback by their youth; they looked like teenagers. He closed the door and hurried after the medics, but halfway up the stairs to the second floor, he was stopped by Barlev coming back down.

"You'll only be in the way," Barlev said when Ritter tried to push past him. "They know what they're doing, and we have to talk." He led Ritter down the stairs and into the living room, switched on the light and closed the door.

"Where's the body?" Barlev asked.

"In the other bedroom upstairs. It was a woman — a receptionist who came to work for my firm shortly before Werewolf contacted me. She was a pro, a trained killer."

"What happened?"

"I heard a noise and woke up. The woman came after us in the dark. I jumped her, but she had time to get off one shot."

"Then you were sleeping with Elana?"

"Tonight I was."

Barlev digested the information without comment.

"And you think this woman was a Werewolf plant," he said.

"What else?"

Ritter heard the medics coming back downstairs with Elana, and he opened the door and went to the foot of the stairs.

"She's got a chance," said the medic carrying the front end of the stretcher, motioning Ritter out of the way with a toss of his head.

Ritter only caught a glimpse of Elana's pinched, chalky face as the stretcher swept by him. Two bottles, one filled with whole blood, the other with a clear liquid, hung from a rack attached to the stretcher. Thin plastic tubes ran from the bottles to needles taped to each of Elana's arms. Ritter started after her, but Barlev stopped him.

"I'm going with her," Ritter insisted.

"No."

"Go to hell!" Ritter snarled, pulling free of Barlev's grasp.

"Use your head, man. The girl was hit because we made a mistake, and we have to know what it was; we can't afford to make a second one. You can't do a damned thing to help her now anyway."

Ritter started for the door and then stopped, knowing that Barlev was right. There was nothing he could do for her now. He'd had his chance, and he'd failed — as he had in Dallas. His shoulders sagged. The adrenaline was washing out of his system, and fatigue settled over him like a shroud. He felt Barlev's hand grasp him roughly by the shoulder.

"You heard the man," Barlev said. "She has a chance. Now, come on back to the living room. We must get to the bottom of this if we can."

Outside the siren started up as the ambulance pulled away, and Ritter silently uttered a prayer for Elana's life. He didn't believe in God, but he prayed just the same. He followed Barlev into the living room and dropped into a chair.

"It doesn't make sense to me," Barlev said. "The woman must have been planted on you as a precaution in case you turned out to be unreliable after so many years. But Dietrich would never have brought you to Dallas if he hadn't trusted you, so why did the woman stay on, and, more important, what set her onto you? She might have become suspicious when Oswald was killed by Ruby instead of by you, and she might have worried when she couldn't contact Dietrich, but she wouldn't have tried to kill you on suspicion alone."

"She didn't suspect me yesterday morning," Ritter said, absently rubbing the bruise on his hand where he had struck Kadinsky.

"Why do you say that?"

"Because of the way she looked at me when I came into the office yesterday morning. I noticed it because she always kept her expression so carefully neutral. But yesterday there was curiosity and puzzlement in her eyes — only for an instant, but it was there. Now it's clear why. She must have known Dietrich's plan for Dallas, and she couldn't figure out what had happened. But there was no suspicion in her eyes. None. Something must have happened later in the day, something that tipped her off."

"Dietrich may have had a man watching his back in Dallas. If so, that man could have sent a warning about you."

"It's possible. Maybe it's the only explanation, because I did nothing yesterday that could have aroused her suspicion. As far as she and the rest of the office staff knew, I didn't really quit, I was fired; and otherwise the day was routine, right up to the time Elana came by to . . ."

Ritter broke off, and the two men looked at each other with the same thought in their minds.

"Was that the first time Elana ever came to your office?"

Ritter nodded. "And now I remember something Elana said, as we left — that Helen Borg had looked as if she had recognized her. I didn't think anything of it at the time."

"The airport!" Barlev said, angrily slamming his fist into the palm of his other hand. "That woman must have seen you intercept Elana at Idlewild. They didn't give a damn whether or not we followed Braun; they were just testing you. We're blown!"

Ritter shook his head slowly. "Not necessarily. The woman came for us immediately. She may not have sent a warning to Werewolf."

"Wishful thinking," Barlev growled.

"Think about it. If she had contacted Werewolf, wouldn't they have held off until they learned what I was up to? I think she acted automatically in response to some kind of standing order, and if she didn't take the time to consult her superiors, she probably didn't take the time to send them any message at all. I doubt that the possibility of failure even entered her head. She was a professional killer, with a professional's self-confidence."

Ritter saw the wheels begin to turn inside Barlev's head. "If you're right," Barlev mused, "we could still raid their headquarters, but we'd have to act immediately. They have two missing agents to account for now. Of course if you're wrong, we could walk right into a trap."

Ritter could see that Barlev wanted to believe that he still had a chance to raid Werewolf headquarters, and he guessed that the Israeli would go through with the raid even though the risks were greater now. Ritter waited for Barlev to ask him again to go in ahead of the raiding party, but Barlev surprised him.

"Come on," Barlev said. "Let's get out to that clinic."

The private clinic to which Elana had been taken was located in a three-story brick building at the end of a block of middle-class tenements in Queens. The clinic catered to a wealthy clientele, and its slightly seedy exterior belied the efficient, modern medical facility within. In addition to competent medical care, the clinic offered something even more important to its patients: absolute discretion. Here, a senator's wife could dry out after a bout with alcoholism, or a distraught debutante could obtain a quiet abortion.

Long ago at Barlev's request, Dr. Weiss had made standing arrangements for emergency medical treatment with the clinic and with a Manhattan ambulance service also noted for its discretion. This was the first time the facilities had been needed, for Barlev ran a safe, quiet operation in the United States.

Barlev and Ritter sat opposite each other in a small waiting room. The wide ashtray resting on a coffee table between them overflowed with their cigar and cigarette butts, and the stale air was blue with tobacco smoke. The clock on the wall told Ritter that it would soon be dawn, but it still felt like two in the morning, as if time had stood still, locking him into the darkest, loneliest part of the night.

"They've been working on her for hours," Ritter said into the silence. "How can it take so long?"

Barlev looked up from the ragged, six-month-old magazine he was reading. "Weiss is good. He'll pull her through if anyone can."

Far down the corridor a swinging door opened, and Ritter heard the approaching tread of rubber-soled shoes squeaking on the waxed linoleum floor. Both men looked toward the doorway, and a moment later Weiss appeared. He was smiling.

"It's too early to be sure," Weiss said, "but I think she'll pull through."

"Thank God," Ritter breathed. "Can we see her?"

"Not yet. I just came out to tell you that the operation was a success. We got the bullet and repaired most of the damage. I must emphasize that it's still too early to be certain, but she's young and healthy. She's got a good chance. Why don't you two go and get some rest? I'll call if there's any change in her condition."

Ritter shook his head, and Barlev said, "We'll stay."

"Suit yourselves. I've got to get back to my patient."

A few minutes after Weiss had left, Barlev stretched and ground out his cigar. "I'm going to see if I can scrounge up some coffee," he said. "Do you take yours black or white?"

"Black. I'll come with you."

"No, stay here — in case Weiss should come back."

Barlev left the waiting room, and Ritter leaned back in his chair and closed his eyes, feeling his tension drain away. She was going to be all right; he knew it. Moments later he was asleep.

Barlev made no attempt to find coffee. He went up to the next floor, down a long hall passing over the waiting room, and returned by a different staircase to the original floor. At the intersection of two corridors was a nursing station, and he walked briskly up to it.

"I'm Dr. Barlev," he said to the young nurse behind the desk. "My colleague, Dr. Weiss, just finished operating. Where can I find him?"

"Through that door and to the right, doctor. Dr. Weiss is with his patient in the room at the very end of the hall."

"Thank you."

Dr. Weiss frowned when Barlev appeared in the doorway to Elana's room, but he didn't protest; he knew from experience that it would be a waste of breath.

"She's coming out of anesthesia already," Weiss said. "It's earlier than I expected. All her vital signs are positive."

"I want to speak to her."

Weiss shrugged. "You can try, but she's still dopey. I'll give you two minutes. That's all."

Weiss knew Barlev wanted privacy, and he left the room, signaling the nurse at Elana's bedside to follow him. Barlev approached the bed. Elana lay on her back with her eyes closed, her left arm tied down so she wouldn't disturb the I.V. needle in her vein. A clear plastic tube taped to her face ran up into one nostril. Her skin was so pale it looked translucent, and if Weiss had not been so optimistic, Barlev would have thought she was dying.

It was always the young ones who got hit, he thought bitterly, and for a moment he was tempted to let it go. Ritter and she might make a life together if they were given the chance. But sentiment was not a luxury Barlev could afford.

"Elana," he said softly. "Elana," he repeated more loudly.

Her eyelids fluttered and finally opened. She looked blankly at Barlev.

"You're going to be all right, Elana. I have Weiss's word on it. You're going to be fine."

"Erich?"

"He's fine, but he couldn't be here. He had to leave — to do one last job for us."

Elana's fingers twitched spasmodically, and she shook her head.

"He wanted to do it," Barlev said firmly. "He'll be back. He sends his love."

"Erich," she said, her voice slurred and barely above a whisper. "I love . . ."

"I'll tell him."

Elana mumbled something unintelligible, and Barlev leaned closer. "What did you say? I didn't catch it."

"My amulet. Give it . . . for luck."

Barlev knew what she meant. He unwound the tape covering the bracelet on her wrist and fumbled unsuccessfully with the clasp. Finally, as gently as he could, he snapped the thin chain and slipped off the oval piece of amber.

"I'll give it to him, Elana. Now go to sleep. You need to rest."

Ritter was still asleep in his chair when Barlev returned. The Israeli stood over him for a moment, hesitating, and then reached out and woke him with a tap on the shoulder. Ritter blinked and straightened up.

"What? . . . What time is it?"

Barlev remained silent, his expression grave. Then he held out his hand, palm upward, in which Elana's amulet lay. "She wanted you to have this. For luck."

Barlev stepped back as Ritter thrust himself up out of the chair. "What do you mean, she *wanted* me to have it?" he demanded.

"She's dead, Erich. Weiss did all he could, but it wasn't enough."

"But . . . but he said . . . No, Goddamnit, no!"

Ritter spun around and slammed his fist into the wall again and again until Barlev's powerful arms seized him and pulled him away.

"Take it," Barlev said, holding out the amulet again. "She wanted you to have it. It was the last thing she said."

Ritter looked down at the amulet in Barlev's hand, blinking back the tears that blurred his vision. He picked it up and turned it over in his fingers. "But why didn't you call me?"

"There wasn't time; it happened too fast. Apparently there was a massive internal hemorrhage."

Ritter continued to stare at the amulet, and as Barlev watched, his expression slowly changed. Grief hardened into hatred; Ritter's features might have been chiseled from stone.

"You asked me to help finish off those bastards," Ritter said grimly. "Now you couldn't stop me if you wanted to. I'm going to Munich."

"I know," Barlev said. "We'll go together."

That afternoon, Ritter dialed the emergency contact number Dietrich had given him. There was a single ring, a click, and then silence. Ritter waited several seconds and then read out the message he and Barlev had composed. At the other end of the line, in a vacant Manhattan apartment, an automatic tape device recorded his clipped, toneless voice.

"This is Erich Ritter speaking. We have an emergency. Dietrich's original plan for Dallas failed because he mistakenly believed American agents had laid a trap for us. He panicked, and I was forced to eliminate him. I then set an alternate plan in motion which, as you know from news broadcasts, was successful. However, upon my return to New York, a woman, apparently one of your operatives, attempted to kill me — possibly because she believed I had betrayed Dietrich. I was forced to kill her in self-defense. I am requesting instructions."

That night, at a preset time, a twenty-watt transmitter automatically switched on in the vacant apartment, and Ritter's message was fed through a scrambler and sent out. A Werewolf operative in the West German consulate in New York recorded the coded transmission and forwarded the tape to Germany by diplomatic pouch. Two days later, Ritter received a special-delivery letter at his home on Long Island. The envelope contained an airline ticket for a Lufthansa flight to Munich and a short set of instructions.

Werewolf had taken the bait.

SEVENTEEN

A cold wind whipped sheets of rain in stinging gusts across Karlsplatz, Munich's central square. Blurred patches of yellow, green and neon red from the lighted windows and signs surrounding the square shone dully on the dark, wet cobblestones. Ritter tugged the brim of his hat firmly down on his forehead and left the shelter of a café entrance. Dodging through the stalled rush-hour traffic, he made his way across the square toward a traffic island where several streetcar lines converged.

He darted in front of an oncoming streetcar, provoking the angry trilling clang of the driver's warning bell. The streetcars were still painted blue and white, but the stubby, rattling cars he remembered had been replaced by longer, sleeker two-car trains. Much of the rebuilt city was hauntingly familiar to Ritter, but the changes clashed disturbingly with his twenty-year-old memories. He felt out of joint with time.

He stepped onto the traffic island and squeezed his way into the crowd huddled around a large newsstand. A cold trickle of water from a woman's umbrella ran down his neck, and he stepped quickly to one side. No one in his vicinity took any notice of him, but he was sure that he was being watched; Heissler would want to be sure that no one followed Ritter to Werewolf's lair.

Ritter's instructions were to take Streetcar 21 from Karlsplatz to Rosenheimerplatz, which lay on the far side of the Isar River. At Rosenheimerplatz he was to get off and walk away from the streetcar stop. Ritter assumed Werewolf would pick him up soon afterward, once it was clear he wasn't being followed.

The cold began to penetrate Ritter's lightweight coat. He hunched his shoulders and thrust his hands into his coat pockets, and the fingers of his right hand brushed against Elana's amulet. It was smooth and cold to the touch, as cold as death. *An eye for an eye; a tooth for a tooth.* The litany repeated itself over and over in his mind, like a stuck record, and he wondered in a detached, uncaring way if he was altogether sane. Inside he was numb, as if his emotions had been burned out — all save one. He could still hate.

A streetcar from Line 21 lumbered into Karlsplatz and approached the central traffic island. As it pulled up, a throng of waiting passengers surged toward the entrance doors at the rear of each car, and Ritter allowed himself to be swept along by the crowd. Twice he was jabbed in the ribs by stocky, middle-aged women who forced their way in front of him, wielding their elbows and umbrellas with practised viciousness. Ritter was among the last to squeeze his way aboard the rear platform before the door closed.

"*Achtung!* Step back, please! Step back!" called the conductor over his loudspeaker. "Step back!"

Ignoring the conductor's warning, a determined few continued to try to force their way onto the jammed platform. The conductor, seated behind a counter beside the platform, shrugged and pressed the switch that closed the doors. One young man was too slow in jumping back, and he squealed as the door closed on his neck, trapping his head inside the car. The streetcar jerked and started forward, with the unfortunate man scampering alongside, bellowing at the top of his lungs. Satisfied that he had taught the man a lesson, the conductor opened the door, and the red, pop-eyed face disappeared from view.

The door closed again, and the streetcar gathered speed. The conductor grinned and looked around at the passengers for approval. Several grinned back at him, but when the conductor looked into Ritter's empty eyes, his smile vanished and he quickly looked away.

On the outskirts of the city, Barlev sat in the dark interior of a black Mercedes sedan, staring balefully through the rain-spattered windshield in the direction of an isolated, six-story building a block away. The ultramodern, rectangular tower of concrete and glass stood alone in the middle of an open compound surrounded by a ten-foot-high steel-mesh fence. Yellow bands of light ringed the darkened building on the uppermost floor and at ground level, where the office lights were still on. An electric sign atop the tower spelled out HEISSLER HOCHBAU in large blue letters.

Barlev saw a shadowy figure detach itself from a patch of darkness near the fence, flit across the roadway and disappear into a van parked farther down the block. A moment later a burst of static from the walkie-talkie on the seat beside Barlev signaled the pressing of a transmit button. He picked up the walkie-talkie.

"All set," came a tinny voice from the transceiver.

"Acknowledged," was Barlev's terse reply. He put down the radio, but left it on, and it continued to emit a soft hiss of static.

"I didn't see him at the fence," said a slim, dapper man behind the wheel of the Mercedes. Barlev's companion had carefully trimmed graying hair and wore conservative, expensive clothes. His name was Max Baum.

"Yoel's a good boy," Barlev said. "He's cut an opening in the fence, so now we have a way in."

Yoel Arnon was the only man Barlev had brought with him from New York. Eight members of the raiding party had been sent out from Tel Aviv. The eight now waited with Arnon in the van. Two local operatives, Baum's contribution to the operation, were stationed in cars positioned to intercept any police patrol cars that might stray into the area while the raid was in progress.

"The Germans are going to raise hell, Zev," Baum said worriedly.

"Not if we get what we're after, not if we can rip open Werewolf's operation. They'll clean up after us and clamp a security lid on the whole incident."

"And if you come up empty?"

"What's the matter, Max? You didn't used to worry so much."

"I used to be younger. Age makes you think."

"You know the stakes."

"I know what you told me, Zev. I'm not sure I believe it."

"The Old Man believes it. He sent out eight of his best for this raid. I wouldn't have dragged you into this, but I needed you. This is your territory."

"You didn't have to drag me in; I wanted in. Don't pay any attention to me. I'm just on edge, that's all."

"Shit, so am I," Barlev said, shifting restlessly in his seat and running his hand over the silencer-equipped machine pistol resting in his lap.

The air in the crowded streetcar was hot and steamy, and Ritter had begun to perspire. At Marienplatz, more passengers got off than got on, diminishing the crush on the rear platform, and after the stop at Isar Tor, Ritter had more than elbow room. The streetcar trundled out through the gate of the Old City wall, heading toward the Isar. Ritter watched the brightly lit, rebuilt city slide past the streetcar windows. The last time he had seen Munich at night, there had been only the jagged outlines of gutted ruins and rubble piles against the rosy glow of fires. Now it was difficult to believe there had ever been a war.

After the streetcar discharged more passengers at the Deutsches Museum, Ritter had the rear platform to himself. The streetcar swung to the right and crossed an arched bridge over the Isar, which was invisible in the darkness below. The conductor leaned toward his microphone.

"Next stop, Rosenheimerplatz."

Barlev's raiding party would be in place now, Ritter thought. They would be awaiting his arrival. But suppose he wasn't taken to the address Dietrich had given him? Ritter shook off the thought. If things went wrong, he would just have to play it by ear.

The streetcar slowed and came to a stop. "Rosenheimerplatz," the conductor announced.

The doors opened, and Ritter stepped out into the cold, windy night. He was the only passenger to get off. The streetcar pulled away, leaving him alone on the street corner beneath the pale glare of a streetlamp. The sidewalks on both sides of the street were nearly deserted. He waited for a few moments, but no one approached him, so, obedient to his instructions, he crossed the roadway and followed a street that led uphill away from Rosenheimerplatz.

He had walked two hundred feet up the hill when headlight beams lit up the cobblestone roadway and he heard the hiss of car tires behind him. A dull green BMW sedan slowed as it came abreast of him, glided to the curb and stopped. The rear door swung open, but no dome light came on to illuminate the dark interior.

"Get in, Herr Ritter," a voice said.

Ritter climbed in, and the car shot away from the curb the instant he closed the door behind him. He looked at the man on the rear seat beside him, but the man ignored him. He was a stern-faced man, about Ritter's age, with a square forehead and a square jaw.

"Where are we going?" Ritter asked.

"It won't take long," Squarehead replied tersely.

"I always appreciate warm welcomes," Ritter said. He shifted in his seat and took out his cigarettes and lighter.

"I'd prefer you not to smoke," Squarehead said.

"Would you?" Ritter said and nodded. Then he deliberately

tapped a cigarette out of the pack and put it between his lips. He looked coldly into the man's eyes and flicked his lighter.

Barlev groaned under his breath, reached beneath his coat and massaged his left shoulder. Baum looked over at him.

"Bursitis?"

Barlev nodded. "The cold aggravates it."

"We're too old for this kind of thing, Zev."

"Speak for yourself," Barlev grunted. He hated the idea of growing old. He didn't feel old; he felt like a young man with stiff joints.

"I'm quitting," Baum said. "Next month. I'm going back to Tel Aviv to lie in the sun. You should think of retiring, too."

"Crap."

"You should think about it. It's better to bow out gracefully before . . ."

"Before what?"

"Before you start making mistakes."

There was a long, heavy silence between them. Barlev picked up a pair of field glasses and focused them on the Heissler building. Where the hell was Ritter?

"This operation . . ." Baum said, breaking the silence. "No planning, no preparation to speak of. It isn't your style."

"There wasn't time," Barlev snapped. "Stop worrying. We're not going in blind. Ritter won't give us the go-ahead unless he's sure we'll catch some fish in our net — or if he's in trouble."

"How do you know they haven't set a trap for him?"

"I don't."

Barlev stiffened as a BMW appeared in his field of view and drove up to a gate in the fence in front of the Heissler building. The driver got out, unlocked the gate, and drove the car into the compound. Then he got out again to lock the gate behind them. The car proceeded to the entrance to the Heissler building, and two men emerged from the rear of the sedan. One of them was Ritter.

"We'll know soon enough," Barlev said.

"Straight into the lion's den," Baum said. "How did you persuade him to do it?"

Barlev shrugged. "It wasn't too difficult."

As Ritter approached the glass doors at the entrance to the Heissler building, he heard the click of an electronic lock disengaging, and the doors slid open. The lobby was deserted, and he assumed that whoever had activated the door had been watching the entrance through a concealed TV camera. He walked through the entrance, closely followed by Squarehead, and the doors closed behind them. Again there was a distinct click as the lock reengaged.

The lobby was ringed by offices, and there was light behind the panes of frosted glass in the doors. Ritter heard no voices, but still he sensed that the offices were occupied. In the center of the lobby stood a circular table fifteen feet in diameter on which rested a scale model of a building complex to be built by Heissler Hochbau.

An office door opened, and a young, hulking strong-arm man lumbered toward them, the steel taps on his shoes clicking on the lobby's polished stone floor. He halted in front of Ritter and inclined his simian head in a quick little bow.

"Permit me, please," he said and quickly frisked Ritter for weapons.

The man would have found a gun, had Ritter been carrying one, but he missed the filament antenna taped to the back of Ritter's leg. It was connected to a miniature transmitter concealed in the heel of his shoe. When Ritter activated the transmitter, Barlev's raiders would hit the building. The strong-arm man stepped back and nodded to Squarehead.

"This way," Squarehead said to Ritter. "We'll take the elevator."

They entered a small passenger elevator, and Squarehead pressed the button for the sixth floor. The two men stared at each other in silence as the elevator carried them swiftly upward, Ritter's stomach felt the sudden deceleration as the elevator reached the top floor, and a moment later the door opened with a sigh.

Ritter stepped out into a miniature jungle of tropical plants and flowers which filled a spacious foyer. One wall was entirely of glass, behind which swam schools of tropical fish in green artificial light. The atmosphere in the foyer was as hot and humid as the interior of a tropical rain forest, and Ritter hastily removed his hat and unbuttoned his trenchcoat.

Squarehead led the way across the foyer to a paneled door, knocked once and opened it, admitting a rush of cool, desert-dry air. He motioned to Ritter, and Ritter stepped across the threshold into the most bizarre office he had ever seen.

The room was huge, taking up nearly the entire floor, and virtually empty. It was bathed in fluorescent light diffusing down through a translucent ceiling. Custom drapes covered with swirling pastel patterns screened the windows along the three outer walls. The thick carpet covering the extravagant floor area was a snowy expanse of pure white. The office's inside wall was decorated with a giant abstract mural in stark, clashing colors. Ten feet out from the wall stood a great oval desk, also white, with a matching white, padded-leather chair. The desk and chair were the only furniture.

The pink toad of a man seated behind the desk looked older, and he had grown even fatter.

"Good evening, Hauptsturmführer Ritter."

Twenty years had not changed SS-*Standartenführer* Werner's high-pitched, nasal voice.

"Good evening, Herr Standartenführer," Ritter said.

"The name is Heissler now. Herr Heissler."

Out of the corner of his eye Ritter noted that Squarehead had taken up a position by the door. The man's right hand never left his coat pocket, and Ritter assumed it held a pistol.

"What do you think of this?" Werner asked, gesturing at the office with a wave of his hand.

"Pretentious," Ritter said coldly, "à la Göring."

Werner's pink face flushed darkly and his pale eyes narrowed, almost disappearing into the folds of spongy flesh surrounding them, but then, abruptly, he laughed.

"You are as arrogant as the last time we met, Ritter. I remember you well. You had the finest record of any SS man we recruited. Perfect. Almost too perfect, eh?" Werner stared up at Ritter, his eyes cold and probing. "I don't trust perfection. Perhaps that is why I delayed your activation for so long."

Ritter shrugged. "We all make mistakes. I forgive you."

Again Werner laughed, a brief explosion that heaved his massive chest and rippled the flesh of his neck and jowls. Ritter wondered how many yards of silk had been required to fashion Werner's suit. Ritter stood before the desk, feet slightly spread, his hands loose at his sides, ready for anything. He wasn't nervous; he felt no tension at all, only the acid bubbling of hatred deep within him. Werewolf had a face now.

"It would appear that I did make a mistake," Werner said. "Apparently you saved the situation in Dallas. What went wrong, exactly, and how did Dietrich and Kadinsky die?"

"Kadinsky?"

"The woman you said you were forced to kill."

"I stated the facts in my message."

"I want details."

"I'll talk to the directorate, or to no one," Ritter said. "I followed Dietrich's orders without question because I had no choice, but now I intend to deal directly with the men who run the show. I've earned that right. If it hadn't been for me, Oswald would still be alive — and talking."

"I have followed the news reports from the United States quite closely. The authorities there are more than satisfied that this man Ruby killed Oswald on impulse. Do you seriously want me to believe that you engineered Oswald's death?"

"Do you seriously believe his death was a fortunate coincidence?"

"Then how did you . . . ?"

"I'll tell that to the directorate."

Werner shook his head. "I'm disappointed in you, Ritter. Dietrich believed in the existence of a directorate, as do most of our less-imaginative agents, but I assumed you would be more acute. In any successful organization there can be only one leader. I am the 'directorate'; I control Werewolf."

Werner noted Ritter's expression, and he smiled faintly. "Ah, so you are not surprised, after all. It restores my faith. I do have advisers, of course. Some are the survivors of the original Section L. We have many younger men as well, but they are theoreticians, not leaders." Werner extended his right hand and closed his sausagelike fingers into a bloated fist. "I hold the threads of Werewolf, Ritter. I and no one else. You will talk to me."

"So Heissler Hochbau is just a front."

"Not just a front. We have made it one of the largest construction firms in Europe, with controlling stock in a half-dozen subsidiary companies. The firm is our cover, and this is our base of operations. In this building is our communications center and our data bank. From here we monitor and direct a worldwide network of agents."

Werner had just given Ritter precisely what he had come to learn; the Nazi was too self-confident to be cautious. Ritter shifted his weight slightly and worked his right foot forward in his shoe until his toe rested against the button of a microswitch. With a final forward pressure he closed the switch, activating the transmitter.

"Why did you bother inventing a mythical 'directorate'?" Ritter asked, stalling for time.

"Expediency. The idea of collective leadership reduces suspicion and jealousy. It makes my task simpler."

"And your 'worldwide network of agents,' is that just a myth, as well?"

"Werewolf is a reality. The ideas of the men in Section L actually work. Slowly but surely we are eroding the stability of the East-West power balance. There will be another war, Ritter, as surely as the sun rises, and this time *we* will emerge the victors. We will . . ."

Werner caught himself, as if he suddenly realized that Ritter was pumping him, or perhaps stalling. His eyes narrowed.

"Let us pass over Dallas for the moment. You said Kadinsky tried to kill you. Why? She was no fool; she was one of our best."

"Apparently," Ritter replied coldly, "she was not quite good enough."

At that moment, alarm bells began ringing throughout the building.

There was no finesse to Barlev's raid; he took his men straight in through the front entrance. The Heissler building was isolated, and the cold, wet weather had kept pedestrians off the streets. There were no passersby to hear the splintering crash of plate glass as a sledgehammer disintegrated the entrance door, and no one but the security guards staring in shock at their closed-circuit TV screens saw the black-clad men storm into the lobby.

The guards, armed only with pistols, never had a chance. Two died as they gamely ran into the lobby, cut down by murderous automatic fire from the stubby Uzi machine pistols in the hands of the raiders. The two remaining guards, who tried to escape, were silently knifed by the men Barlev had left outside to cover the rear exit. As Barlev's men started to fan out to search the ground-floor offices, the door to the stairwell next to the elevator flew open, and the man who had searched Ritter came through, firing an automatic.

Four Uzis opened up on him at once, their muffled rattling cough drowned out by the alarm bells. Caught in the converging streams of bullets, the gunman reeled in a jerking pirouette, spraying crimson arterial blood, and crashed to the floor. His legs kicked in a final spasm, and he lay still in a widening pool of blood.

The raiders swept through the offices, flushing out three ashen-faced men in business suits and a hysterical woman. They hustled their captives into the lobby, forced them onto the floor, and tied and gagged them.

Abruptly, the lights went out throughout the building, and the alarm bells fell silent. "Power's cut," said one of the commandos needlessly. From somewhere on an upper floor came the crump of a small explosion. Flashlights snapped on, and Barlev ran to the stairwell, barking orders. Barlev, Arnon and four commandos pounded up the stairs, heading for the top floor.

Four blocks away, a young woman with impeccable German identity papers and a flawless German accent sat behind the wheel of a VW. She tensed as a police cruiser came around a corner two blocks away and headed her way on a routine patrol. She pressed the transmit button of her transceiver. "Police coming," she said.

"Divert," came Max Baum's reply.

The girl nodded grimly to herself, opened the car window and dropped the radio onto the sidewalk. She started the engine and picked up an open bottle of gin from the seat beside her. She took several quick swallows, wincing as the alcohol burned its way down her throat, and spilled the rest of the gin over the front of her coat.

She waited until the police car was only a half-block away. Then she gunned the engine, popped the clutch and sent the VW, tires squealing, careening into the path of the oncoming police car. She sideswiped the cruiser, tearing away part of its left rear fender, and raced on up the street in low gear, headlights out and engine howling.

The shocked driver of the police car cursed vividly and swung the cruiser around in a U-turn as his partner grabbed for the radio microphone. Lights flashing and klaxon blaring, they gave chase, and their radio call pulled away every other patrol car in the vicinity.

"Schmidt!" Werner cried as the alarm bells sounded, and Squarehead jerked an automatic pistol from his coat pocket and trained it on Ritter. When Ritter's eyes snapped back to Werner, he looked into the muzzle of a Beretta automatic which Werner clutched in his fat fist. Ritter had not expected Werner to react so quickly, and he had been caught flat-footed. He tried to bluff it out.

"What the hell is going on?" Ritter challenged.

"If he blinks, kill him," Werner said to Schmidt.

"I asked what's . . ."

"Shut up!" Werner barked, and he stabbed a button on his desk.

A wall panel slid aside to reveal four TV screens. Werner heaved his bulk from his chair and moved to a position where he could see the screens and still cover Ritter. The Beretta never wavered. Schmidt moved warily toward them, his automatic trained on Ritter's midsection. The center TV screen showed the swift, one-sided fire fight in the lobby. Werner gave it but a single glance.

"Who are they?" he hissed.

"How the hell do I know?" Ritter shot back. "What's going on?"

"We'll get it out of you, *mein Lieber*. Don't doubt that for a second. We'll wring you dry."

Werner stepped forward and pushed a second button on his desk, and the TV screens went black and the alarm bells ceased ringing. A moment later Ritter felt the jolt of an explosion in the soles of his feet.

"Now your friends, whoever they are, can stumble around in the dark for as long as they wish," Werner said. "Without the elevator they can't reach us, and they won't get what they came for. That detonation just wiped out our computer data bank."

"I don't know who those men are," Ritter insisted.

"Don't you?" Werner said with a mirthless smile. "Then you will suffer considerable pain for nothing. You yourself advised me against believing in coincidence."

Werner stepped back to the wall behind his desk and pressed a camouflaged switch, and a second panel slid aside, exposing the round steel door of a wall safe. Beside the safe was a small, dark square of inlaid glass. Werner pressed the fingers of his left hand against the glass, and a bar of green light appeared behind the glass and scanned across Werner's hand. The scan completed, the dials on the safe door began to turn automatically.

Without taking his eyes off Ritter, Werner opened the safe and removed a plastic spool of computer tape. Ritter didn't need to be told that it was a copy of Werewolf's principal data file.

"It's time to go," Werner said.

"Where?" Ritter said.

Werner pointed upward. "The roof. We have a helicopter up there, and Schmidt is an excellent pilot. You'll come with us, of course. You won't die just yet — not until we discover just what sort of traitor you are. You see, Ritter, it was all for nothing. Your friends won't get me, and they won't get our files; and if they don't clear out quickly, they'll be caught by the police we'll call in once we're airborne."

It was all for nothing. Elana was dead — and for nothing.

"No," Ritter gasped as an emotional dam burst within him. Hatred surged through him out of control. His limbs trembled with it, and tears of impotent rage flooded his eyes. He heard Heissler laugh.

"So, the traitor is a coward, too. I didn't expect that."

Ritter reacted instantly, playing the only card he had left. He squeezed his eyes so that tears spilled down his cheeks, and he fell to his knees stretching out his hands in supplication.

"Please," he blubbered, fluttering his hands. "Please don't hurt me. I couldn't stand it. They made me help them. I swear it. I'll tell you anything you want to know. Just don't hurt me!"

"Enough!" Werner snapped, but Ritter continued to grovel, begging for mercy in a strangled, panicky voice.

"Schmidt!" Werner yelled. "Get him on his feet."

Out of the corner of his eye, Ritter watched Schmidt bearing down on him, the man's lip curling with contempt. They still had him in a cross fire, and he could only take one of them. Werner held the smaller-caliber weapon, so Ritter would take Schmidt.

Schmidt tried to kick Ritter to his feet, but as Schmidt kicked out, Ritter suddenly pivoted toward him on one knee, and

Schmidt's foot caromed off Ritter's hip, throwing Schmidt off balance. Ritter lunged upward, knocking aside the barrel of the automatic with his left hand and chopping at Schmidt's throat with his right.

Werner fired as the heel of Ritter's hand sliced into Schmidt's windpipe, the bang of the short-barreled pistol deafening in the closed room, and Ritter felt a streak of pain burn across his back. Schmidt's eyes bulged, and he toppled backward, clutching his throat.

Ritter whirled toward Werner and launched himself into the air in a desperate leap across the desk just as Werner fired again. The bullet caught Ritter in the stomach, but his gasp of pain was smothered by Werner's squealing cry as Ritter hurtled into him, driving Werner's obscene bulk to the floor.

Werner panted with exertion and fear as he struggled to bring his pistol to bear, but Ritter's fingers closed over his wrist like bands of steel and twisted Werner's arm behind the Nazi's back. Ritter thrust against Werner's raised shoulder and rolled him onto his back, pinning his gun arm beneath his own enormous body.

Groaning with agony, Ritter reared up and raised his right hand to strike, his lips drawn back in a rictus. For a split second he looked into the terrified, rolling eyes of the toad squirming beneath him, and then he struck. The first blow caught Werner across the bridge of the nose, crushing it and splintering the paper-thin bone just below the forehead. The second blow drove the splinters into Werner's brain.

Ritter gasped and collapsed across Werner's body. Pain filled his stomach and began to spread throughout his abdomen like liquid fire. He rolled off Werner's body and lay on the floor, fighting to stay conscious. Blood — his blood — seemed to be everywhere.

From beyond the desk came a scrabbling sound and the gurgling rasp of Schmidt's tortured breathing. Ritter had crushed Schmidt's windpipe, but the man wasn't finished. Ritter reached across Werner's body and seized the spool of computer tape lying on the floor beneath the desk. He couldn't let Schmidt escape with the tape; Barlev had to have it. *Werewolf must die.*

Ritter struggled to his knees and tried to retrieve Werner's Beretta, but he no longer had the strength to shift Werner's body. Dizziness threatened to overcome him. He grabbed the desk top with fingers that were slick with blood, and with a desperate effort of will, he pulled himself to his feet. Ten feet away, Schmidt was crawling toward his gun, one hand still clutching his throat.

Ritter took a faltering step, staggered, and lurched out from behind the desk, his eyes fixed on the windows across the room. His mind recoiled from what he had to do, but there was no other way. Twenty-five feet to the window — it seemed an impossible distance. Schmidt had reached his gun. He was picking it up.

Ritter stumbled forward, propelling his rubbery legs into a staggering, weaving run across the carpeted floor, which seemed to pitch and roll like the deck of a storm-tossed ship. Twenty feet . . . fifteen . . . ten. Again there was the bang of a pistol shot, but Ritter felt no answering pain. Five feet . . . Ritter threw himself toward the window, the computer tape clutched in his right hand. His one hundred ninety pounds ripped through the gap between two drapes, hit the window, and crashed out into empty space in a shower of glass.

Ritter fell through the darkness toward the floodlit ground below. Reflexively he stretched out his arms and legs as he had been trained to do so long ago, a paratrooper on his last jump.